Acclaim for Beth Wiseman's Amish Inn Novels

A Season of Change

"A beautiful story about love, forgiveness, and finding family in an unexpected place."

—Kathleen Fuller, author of *A Double Dose of Love*

An Unlikely Match

"With multiple vibrant story lines, Wiseman's excellent tale will have readers anticipating the next. Any fan of Amish romance will love this."

—*Publishers Weekly*

"This was such a sweet story. I cheered on Evelyn and Jayce the whole way. Jayce is having issues with his difficult father, who's brought a Hollywood crew to Amish country to film a scene in a nearby cave. Evelyn has a strong, supportive family, so she feels for Jayce immediately. As they grow closer and help each other overcome fears and phobias, they know this can't last. But God, and two persnickety Amish sisters, Lizzie and Esther, have other plans. Can a Hollywood boy fall for an Amish girl and make it work? Find out. Read this delightful, heartwarming story!"

—Lenora Worth, author of *Their Amish Reunion*

"Beth Wiseman's *An Unlikely Match* will keep you turning the pages as you are pulled into this heartwarming and unpredictable Amish romance story about Evelyn and Jayce, two interesting and compelling characters. Beth doesn't disappoint keeping you guessing as to how this story will end."

—Molly Jebber, bestselling Amish inspirational historical romance author

A Picture of Love

"This is a warm story of romance and second chances with some great characters that fans of the genre will love."

—Parkersburg News & Sentinel

"Beth Wiseman's *A Picture of Love* will delight readers of Amish fiction. Naomi and Amos's romance is a heartfelt story of love, forgiveness, and second chances. This book has everything readers love about a Beth Wiseman story—an authentic portrait of the Amish community, humor, the power of grace and hope and, above all, faith in God's Word and His promises."

—Amy Clipston, bestselling author of *The Coffee Corner*

A Season of Change

Other Books by Beth Wiseman

The Amish Bookstore Novels
The Bookseller's Promise (available April 2022)

The Amish Inn Novels
A Picture of Love
An Unlikely Match
A Season of Change

The Amish Journey Novels
Hearts in Harmony
Listening to Love
A Beautiful Arrangement

The Amish Secrets Novels
Her Brother's Keeper
Love Bears All Things
Home All Along

The Land of Canaan Novels
Seek Me with All Your Heart
The Wonder of Your Love
His Love Endures Forever

The Daughters of the Promise Novels
Plain Perfect
Plain Pursuit
Plain Promise
Plain Paradise
Plain Proposal
Plain Peace

Other Novels
Need You Now
The House that Love Built
The Promise

Story Collections

An Amish Year
Amish Celebrations

Stories

A Choice to Forgive included in *An Amish Christmas*
A Change of Heart included in *An Amish Gathering*
Healing Hearts included in *An Amish Love*
A Perfect Plan included in *An Amish Wedding*
A Recipe for Hope included in *An Amish Kitchen*
Always Beautiful included in *An Amish Miracle*
Rooted in Love included in *An Amish Garden*
When Christmas Comes Again included in *An Amish Second Christmas*
In His Father's Arms included in *An Amish Cradle*
A Cup Half Full included in *An Amish Home*
The Cedar Chest included in *An Amish Heirloom*
When Love Returns included in *An Amish Homecoming*
A Reunion of Hearts included in *An Amish Reunion*
Loaves of Love included in *An Amish Christmas Bakery*

A Season of Change

An Amish Inn Novel

Beth Wiseman

ZONDERVAN

A Season of Change

Copyright © 2021 by Elizabeth Wiseman Mackey

Requests for information should be addressed to:
Zondervan, *3900 Sparks Dr. SE, Grand Rapids, Michigan 49546*

Library of Congress Cataloging-in-Publication Data
Names: Wiseman, Beth, 1962- author.
Title: A season of change : an Amish inn novel / Beth Wiseman.
Description: Grand Rapids, Michigan : Zondervan, [2021] | Series: The Amish inn novels ; book 3 | Summary: "From beloved bestselling author Beth Wiseman comes the third and final novel in the Amish Inn series-charming, sweet stories about two widowed innkeeping sisters who are determined to help their guests find love"-- Provided by publisher.
Identifiers: LCCN 2021008637 (print) | LCCN 2021008638 (ebook) | ISBN 9780310357285 (trade paper) | ISBN 9780310363194 (library edition) | ISBN 9780310357292 (ebook) | ISBN 9780310357308 (downloadable audio)
Subjects: GSAFD: Christian fiction. | Love stories.
Classification: LCC PS3623.I83 S43 2021 (print) | LCC PS3623.I83 (ebook) | DDC 813/.6--dc23
LC record available at https://lccn.loc.gov/2021008637
LC ebook record available at https://lccn.loc.gov/2021008638

Scripture quotations taken from The Holy Bible, New International Version®, NIV®. Copyright © 1973, 1978, 1984, 2011 by Biblica, Inc.® Used by permission of Zondervan. All rights reserved worldwide. www.Zondervan.com. The "NIV" and "New International Version" are trademarks registered in the United States Patent and Trademark Office by Biblica, Inc.®

Publisher's Note: This novel is a work of fiction. Names, characters, places, and incidents are either products of the author's imagination or used fictitiously. All characters are fictional, and any similarity to people living or dead is purely coincidental.

No part of this publication may be reproduced, stored in a retrieval system, or transmitted in any form or by any means—electronic, mechanical, photocopy, recording, or any other—except for brief quotations in printed reviews, without the prior permission of the publisher.

Zondervan titles may be purchased in bulk for educational, business, fundraising, or sales promotional use. For information, please email SpecialMarkets@Zondervan.com.

Printed in the United States of America

21 22 23 24 25 LSC 10 9 8 7 6 5 4 3 2 1

To my sister Laurie

Glossary

ab im kopp: crazy, off in the head
ach: oh
bruder(s): brother(s)
daadi haus: a small house built onto or near the main house for grandparents to live in
daed: dad
danki: thank you
dochder: daughter
Englisch: those who are not Amish; the English language
fraa: wife
Gott: God
gut: good
haus: house
kaffi: coffee
kapp: prayer covering worn by Amish women

Glossary

kinner: children
lieb: love
maedel: girl
mamm: mom
mei: my
mudder: mother
nee: no
Ordnung: the written and unwritten rules of the Amish; the understood behavior by which the Amish are expected to live, passed down from generation to generation. Most Amish know the rules by heart.
schweschder/schweschdere: sister
sohn: son
Wie bischt: Hello, how are you?
ya: yes

Chapter 1

Esther resisted the temptation to rub her throbbing temples as she stood in the living room listening to Rose carry on about her date this evening. Esther was excited for the young woman, but not incredibly hopeful the blind date would be a success. Esther and her sister loved to give the young people in their district a gentle nudge when it came to matters of the heart, but finding someone for Rose was proving to be a challenge.

Their employee had just recited a long list of things she'd purchased at the market, given a lengthy description of her trip there and back, along with who she saw and what they talked about, and then the girl dove right into a conversation about the weather.

"Even though it's only July, it's going to be unusually hot. At least that's what the *Englisch* man at the post office said." Rose stopped and put a finger to her chin. "I forgot to tell you that—how I stopped at the post office to get more stamps." She waved a dismissive hand. "Anyway, it's going to be very hot, not just today but this entire month. Do you think it will have cooled down by this evening when Benjamin comes to pick me up?"

Esther opened her mouth to tell Rose that the temperature was expected to drop by later this afternoon, but she didn't get a word out before Rose continued.

"I'm thinking I will wear *mei* green dress. Or maybe the maroon. But either way, I'm looking forward to meeting Benjamin." Her exuberant expression fell. "I hope it goes well."

Rose was surely recalling her past dates, and Esther wanted to offer words of encouragement, but by the time she organized her thoughts, Rose was off and running again.

"I've already roasted a chicken, prepared a salad, and cooked and seasoned the green beans for your and Lizzie's supper. It's all in the refrigerator." Rose drew in a breath. "And there are two loaves of bread on the counter. I know we don't have any guests right now, but we'll have the extra loaf if anyone books a room at the last minute."

Esther nodded repeatedly as she usually did when struggling to focus on a conversation.

"Okay then." Rose bounced up on her toes and smiled. Sometimes she reminded Esther of a young child, as opposed to the twenty-five-year-old woman she was. "I'll be upstairs if you need me."

As Rose bounded upstairs, Esther shuffled to the kitchen and sat across from Lizzie, her temples still throbbing. She propped her elbows on the kitchen table and cupped her chin in her hands.

"Things aren't going to go well this evening if Rose can't control her chatter," Esther said as she shook her head. "We've talked to her about being a better listener, but she obviously didn't hear us because she talked over us, or she chose not to hear us because she can't control herself when it comes to talking too much."

Lizzie sighed as she slouched into her chair. "The *maedel* has a *gut* heart, and she's outwardly attractive and equally as lovely on the inside. I still think the herbal doctor might have something to hush her up a bit." Lizzie scratched her cheek before folding her arms across her chest.

Esther tucked away gray strands of hair that had come loose from beneath her prayer covering. "I already told you, we aren't going to do anything to change Rose's personality. The right man will love her for exactly who she is." Esther thought back to something Lizzie had said. She glanced over her shoulder to make sure Rose hadn't come back downstairs for anything, something Esther should have done when they'd first started talking about the girl. "You mentioned that this fellow is perfect for Rose," she said in a whisper. "What makes you think that?"

"His *mamm* told me he is so shy that he barely says anything at all," Lizzie responded, lowering her voice as well. "They're new to Montgomery. They've been here less than two weeks. His mother, Catherine, said he has trouble communicating with women because of his shyness. And this will be a perfect match since Rose can carry enough conversation for both of them."

"I'm surprised Rose agreed to this supper tonight, but I'm glad she's excited about it." Esther lowered her hand and ran a finger around the edge of her glass of tea. "Our other attempts at playing matchmaker have failed miserably, and she's been here a year." She sighed. "I hope this man will work out for Rose. Sometimes I hear her crying in her room. She's twenty-five and surely longing to find the man of her dreams, someone to marry and start a family with."

Esther sipped her tea as Lizzie took a napkin and dabbed at the sweat beads dotting her forehead. Spring had rolled into summer in what seemed like the blink of an eye. July felt hotter this year, but Esther thought that every year. Maybe it was because she'd just turned seventy-four and old age was fueling her lack of tolerance to the heat.

"I have higher hopes that this fellow is going to work out." Lizzie gave a taut nod. "He barely talks, and Rose never stops talking. So, they're perfect for each other."

They continued to speak in a whisper so as not to alert Rose to their conversation from her room upstairs. Her responsibilities at The Peony Inn were to cook, help with the cleaning, and tend to the guests. Most of their visitors enjoyed listening to Rose carry on about most anything. Granted, there were some who politely excused themselves right after a meal. But the English tourists were usually fascinated to hear Rose answer their questions in lengthy detail.

Esther and Lizzie loved the girl, but Esther often had a headache after a conversation with Rose. She'd never known another person who had so much to say. Maybe they hadn't been firm enough when talking to Rose about rambling on, but neither of the sisters wanted to hurt the young woman's feelings by bringing it up again.

"We will just hope for the best," Esther said. "At least she has turned into a *gut* cook." When they'd first hired Rose, the girl couldn't cook at all.

Lizzie chuckled. "We're pretty *gut* in the kitchen, but we have Jayce to thank for some of the fancier meals Rose prepares." Their previous boarder hadn't stayed with them long—just until he was able to get a place of his own. But the young man was an amazing cook and had patiently taught Rose some of his culinary skills while he was there. Jayce married a local girl, Evelyn, in November, and Esther and Lizzie were thrilled, even though English folks rarely converted the way Jayce had. *True love.* Esther wanted that for Rose.

"At least the new fellow is Amish, and his mother said he has already been baptized," Lizzie said. "And Rose has been baptized. Now they just need to fall in love and get married."

"If that happens, we will lose our employee. And Rose is meticulous at cleaning," Esther said, smiling. "But the girl is deserving of the life she longs for, and God will provide us with someone else to help around the inn when the time comes."

Esther and Lizzie had opened their family homestead as a bed-and-breakfast late in life, following the death of both their husbands. They loved catering to others and they loved the opportunity to play matchmaker when they could. Tonight was one of those opportunities, and Esther hoped Lizzie was right, that Rose and this young man would hit it off and fall in love.

Rose tiptoed up the stairs with an ache in her chest and tears welling in her eyes. She'd come back downstairs to retrieve some hand lotion she left on the coffee table, but she'd stopped halfway down when she heard her name.

She didn't hear anything past, *The right man will love her for exactly who she is.* Then Esther and Lizzie had started to whisper, and Rose hadn't heard anything else. But she'd already heard enough. And she'd overheard the sisters talking about her more often than they were aware. Esther and Lizzie loved her, though. Their gentle conversations about talking too much had resonated deep within her, and they were right. She often struggled to be quiet. However, whether it was nerves or something else, she was going to force herself to be silent this evening. She suspected the "something else" was bothering her more than nerves, but when those thoughts surfaced, she forced them away.

As the sisters had told her before, Rose needed to be a better listener. She knew Esther and Lizzie had her best interest at heart. However, even though Rose had been hearing how she talked too much her entire life, the comments still stung. If she didn't change, she was never going to find a husband.

Maybe Lizzie was right. Perhaps there was a medication to help her not talk so much. But the thought of being drugged, natural or otherwise, didn't sit well with Rose. Wasn't Esther right? Wouldn't the right man love her the way she is? Still, after so many failed attempts to find her perfect match, Rose was going to have to change. No matter how nervous she was this evening, she was going to keep her mouth closed. Doing so would be especially hard since this was a blind date and already had awkwardness built in. But she was going to prove to herself, to this man, and to Esther and Lizzie that she could do it—unless she felt no attraction to her date. Then she wouldn't worry so much what he thought of her. But recently, two nice men she'd found quite handsome had never asked her out again.

Tonight she was going to force herself to be silent—be a better listener.

∞

Benjamin walked into the living room in the house that he and his mother shared. Once again, they lived by themselves as they had in their previous home. Benjamin's father died four years ago, and in the time since, both of his sisters had married and moved out to places too far to travel by buggy. His mother insisted that they move to Montgomery from the outskirts of Bedford for the quaint atmosphere of a smaller Amish community, also citing less upkeep on a smaller homestead. Benjamin was pretty sure her real reason was so he could meet new women. He was well aware of his shortcomings when it came to dating, and he didn't have high hopes for this evening.

"Stop looking so irritated." His mother came into the living room, stopped in front of him, and put her hands on her hips. "I'm told Rose is a lovely woman with a very high-energy personality. You might actually enjoy yourself. Lizzie said this young woman is very pretty too."

Benjamin had been out with plenty of attractive women in Bedford, and lots of them had bubbly personalities. Even though he often had things he wanted to say, he couldn't seem to find the words, nor did he want to. His fear of saying the wrong things squashed anything intelligent he hoped would come out of his mouth. No one seemed to know why he had so much trouble communicating, but he had been that way for as long as he could remember. He could still recall his grandmother concocting what she called a "potion" that would help him with his shyness. Benjamin was in second grade when he tried her magic drink, which didn't help him with his shyness. It just made him throw up.

"I told you not to set me up on any more blind dates. You did enough of that in Bedford." Benjamin's mother had good intentions, but he was still irritated at her for setting up this supper in cahoots with a lady named Lizzie.

"This woman is different," his mother said, sighing. "Please just give her a chance. Lizzie said Rose talks more than anyone she's ever known, and that will make things easier for you."

Benjamin was a grown man. He could have refused to go. But buried beneath a lengthy number of failed dates, he hadn't given up. There had to be someone out there for him, someone who didn't expect him to talk a lot. Maybe Rose, who had a lot to say, would be that person. He owed it to himself—and his mother, for her effort—to at least meet the woman.

"*Mamm*, I'm going to go." He took his straw hat from the rack by the door, and after he put it on, he turned to her. "But no more blind dates if this doesn't work out. And I mean it."

His mother smiled. "No more blind dates." Catherine King was a romantic at heart. She'd introduced one of his sisters to her husband. "But I think this might be the woman for you based on what Lizzie told me about her. And I'm told she is a *gut* cook too."

Benjamin opened the front door, then mumbled, "We'll see."

As he pulled out of the driveway, he offered up a quick prayer that maybe Rose really would be the one.

※

Rose sat on the edge of her bed and bit her bottom lip so hard it throbbed. *Do not talk, be a better listener, offer short answers to any questions.* She repeated the mantra in her mind over and over again. No matter how nervous she was or wasn't, she was going to be quiet during this meal. She'd decided that even if she felt no attraction to Benjamin King, it would be good practice to stay silent. She scurried to the window when she heard a buggy pulling onto the gravel driveway.

Before heading downstairs, she decided to have a look at the fellow and waited for him to step out of the buggy. As he got closer to the house, she gasped. Benjamin was tall with broad shoulders and a beautifully proportioned body, and as he neared, she caught a glimpse of his face under a head of dark hair. His olive skin stretched over high cheekbones, and his green eyes radiated warmth beneath his cropped brown bangs. She'd already been told that he was her age, twenty-five, and that he was a plumber.

Rose's mouth hung open. *He is the most handsome man I've ever seen.* She watched him walk up the porch steps to the front door as her heart hammered in her chest. She'd never wanted to make a good impression more than now. *Don't talk, don't talk, answer questions with short answers . . .*

By the time she got downstairs, she was breathless and had plenty to say. *So nice to meet you. I've been looking forward to our* date. *How do you like Montgomery so far? What about your job—do you like it? Where are we going to eat?*

But she bit her lip as the thoughts swirled in her mind. Esther had just opened the door when Rose stepped into the living room. Lizzie quickly made introductions, and Rose took a deep breath.

"*Wie bischt?* It's nice to meet you." She smiled, unable to help herself. When Benjamin smiled, he was even more handsome. If a person could fall for someone based on looks alone, Rose was already in love. But she was wise enough to know that a person could be lovely on the outside without being so on the inside. Still . . . she was hopeful. And was going to be very quiet the entire evening.

Esther and Lizzie watched out the window as Benjamin escorted Rose to the passenger side of the buggy and opened the door for her.

"Did you see how handsome that man is?" Lizzie pressed her face closer to the windowpane.

Esther leaned in for a better look too. "*Ya*, he's a looker for sure."

"I'm telling you"—Lizzie faced Esther, grinning—"they are perfect for each other. I have a *gut* feeling about this. He's handsome and quiet. She's beautiful and a talker."

"It takes more than that combination to make a relationship." Esther scooted away from the window and sat in one of the rocking chairs. She picked up a calendar she kept on the table next to her. "So far, we don't have any rooms booked until Saturday night."

"*Gut*. I'm tired." Lizzie sat down on the couch and closed her eyes. "And old. Besides, the *Englisch* don't rent many rooms this time of year. They need their air-conditioning."

Esther placed the calendar back on the table and dabbed at the sweat beads on her forehead, despite the cross breeze in the room. "True about the *Englisch*. And you are two years younger than me. We're not that old." Her sister wasn't just younger, she was also a tiny little thing compared to Esther, who towered over her. Unlike Lizzie, Esther had a heavyset build. She'd teased Lizzie for years that one of them must be adopted, which wasn't true. The telltale sign was surely that both of them had the same shaped eyes and mouths, even if the rest of them appeared to have come from different genes. Esther had just closed her eyes and leaned her head against the back of the rocking chair when there was a knock at the door.

Lizzie turned toward the window behind the couch, then moved quickly to the door. "It's Amos with one of the babies." She pulled the door open wide, put her hands on her hips, and huffed. "Where is the other one? You can't just bring one baby. Esther and I each need to have one." Lizzie eased Regina out of Amos's arms, nuzzling the fourteen-month-old, who smiled. Esther was quickly on her feet and beside Lizzie in no time.

"Sorry." Amos chuckled. "Eve somehow got her diaper off, and uh . . . well, Naomi has a mess on her hands. I got out as quick as I could." He handed Esther a vase he was holding in his other hand. "These got delivered to our house by mistake. The card has your name on it."

Amos and Naomi lived in the *daadi haus* on Esther and Lizzie's property, along with their twin girls. The young couple had named one of the girls Regina after Lizzie and Esther's mother. Eve was named after Amos's great-grandmother. Naomi had lived with Esther and Lizzie, working in the same capacity as Rose, until she married Amos. Even though Naomi and Amos weren't actually kin, they were family, and Esther and Lizzie enjoyed playing the role of grandmothers. Especially since they hadn't been able to have children of their own.

Esther took the vase. "Who in the world would send me flowers?" She ran through the list of possibilities. She'd donated books to the local library, but that didn't seem to warrant flowers. Last week she'd taken small quilted blankets she'd made to the hospital in Bedford, but she'd taken homemade items to the hospital for years. The staff always sent a nice thank-you card, not flowers.

Lizzie bounced Regina on her hip, cooing and carrying on the way they always did around the babies. "Open the card," Lizzie said as she pressed her nose against Regina's.

Esther placed the lovely arrangement of assorted flowers on the coffee table, then took the small envelope from the spike where it rested inside the plant. She peeled back the seal, took out the card, and read:

My dearest Esther, these flowers can't compare to your beauty, but they are an offering of my love.

Esther's jaw dropped as she put a hand to her chest. Lizzie was quickly by her side, still bouncing Regina on her hip. "Who sent the flowers?"

"I don't know," she said softly as she held the card out so that Lizzie could read it.

Her sister gasped before she looked at Esther with her eyes wide and wild. "*Ach*, I know who sent them." She carried Regina back to Amos and handed the poor child over like a sack of flour before she marched back to Esther. "Grumpy Gus! That's who sent the flowers, and I will not have that man as *mei bruder*-in-law, do you hear me?"

Esther was too taken aback to say anything.

Amos cleared his throat. "I better go back and see if Naomi survived her ordeal with Eve." Laughing softly, he turned and left. Normally Esther and Lizzie would have begged him to leave the baby for a while, but this felt more urgent.

Esther faced off with her sister. "Stop with such nonsense. Gus would not send me flowers." Their renter—commonly referred to as Grumpy Gus, mostly by Lizzie—was a man about Esther's age. He rented the third house on the property, a cottage within view of the main house.

Lizzie stepped closer to Esther and slammed her hands to her hips. "When we used to have our weekly suppers with Amos and Naomi and Jayce and Evelyn, Gus was always here, and I saw the way he looked at you." She dropped her arms to her sides, scowling as she clenched her hands into fists. "Disgusting behavior. I didn't say anything because you told me I have to be nice to him." She glared at the flowers. "But now he's openly courting you."

Esther's sister threw herself on the couch, tossed her head back against the cushion, and covered her face with both hands.

"*Ach*, Lizzie, stop being so dramatic." Esther rolled her eyes before she reread the card. "Gus would never do this. Besides, he knows where I live, so why would the flowers have ended up at the wrong house?" She shook her head as she wondered who else might have sent her flowers. In truth, Esther was probably Gus's only friend—except for their former tenant Jayce. But Gus was English, and everyone agreed the man was grumpy. Sometimes that was a mild word to explain Gus's behavior. And even though the man was nicer to Esther than to others, she still couldn't wrap her mind around the possibility that Gus would try to court her.

"The flowers were probably delivered by a florist, so that's why they ended up at Naomi and Amos's house—just a mistake the delivery person made." Lizzie uncovered her face and sighed. "Since our supper group dismantled, Gus doesn't get to see you as often." She remained slumped into the couch cushions with a sour look on her face.

"He sees me plenty." Esther couldn't stop staring at the words on the card, beautifully written, probably by a florist. It didn't look like a man's handwriting.

Lizzie rose from the couch and raised her eyebrows. "You *do* go see him a lot."

"*Ach*, Lizzie, stop it. The man doesn't have anyone to cook for him, so sometimes I take him leftovers or pie. Don't you act like we're carrying on. I am sure these flowers are not from Gus." Esther chuckled. It sounded like a nervous laugh, even to her. "That's just nonsense."

Lizzie folded her arms across her chest as she lifted her chin. "Then who would send you a bouquet with a note like that?"

Esther avoided her sister's piercing glare. "I'm sure I don't know."

Lizzie gasped as her eyes widened. "Maybe you have a stalker! It could be a person who's *ab im kopp*!"

"That's enough, Lizzie. I don't have a stalker or a crazy person sending me flowers."

Lizzie tapped a finger to her chin and paced the room before she stopped and faced Esther. "What kind of man would send flowers and not sign the card? A stalker, that's who." She began to pace again, her arms folded across her chest. "But who around here would do that?" She squeezed her eyes closed and groaned. "No. It's Gus. It has to be." She stomped off toward the downstairs bathroom. "I'm going to go take a bath and force myself to think happy thoughts about Rose and Benjamin," she growled. "Because thinking of you and Gus together makes me want to vomit." Her sister forcibly closed the door to her bedroom, then slammed the door to the bathroom Esther and Lizzie shared.

Esther flinched both times before she walked to the window and stared at the cottage where Gus lived. Even though she would never admit it to anyone, she'd caught the way Gus looked at her sometimes. And he was nicer to her than he was to most people.

She tiptoed to the door and gingerly eased the screen open, making sure it didn't slam behind her. Then she made her way down the porch steps, across the front yard, and continued the trek to the cottage. Her heart pounded in her chest as she knocked on Gus's door.

Chapter 2

Rose kept her eyes in front of her, occasionally cutting them to the side to catch a quick peek at her date. His incredible looks were enough to keep her quiet, hoping now more than ever that things might work out—although her head hurt from all the thoughts swirling around in her mind with nowhere to go. She wanted to tell him how much she had looked forward to the date, ask him where they were going to eat, how he liked his job, and all of the other questions she'd thought of when he first arrived at the inn. But she sat quietly, waiting for him to start a conversation. After he turned onto the main road, he finally spoke.

"Um . . . where would you like to eat?" He glanced at her, but not for long.

"Anywhere you would like." She bit her lip, fighting the urge to give him a complete list of restaurants in the area, then tell him what she liked and disliked about each one.

He was quiet, and the situation was already awkward. They hadn't been gone ten minutes. *Why isn't he looking at me? Does he find me attractive?* Those were questions she never would have spoken aloud, of course, even if she hadn't made a vow of silence. But the thoughts were at the forefront of her mind.

"I'm new here. I don't really know where to go. *Mei mamm* always cooks." He still didn't turn her way.

So Benjamin lived with his mother. She wanted to ask him why since she knew he was her age. How had he not found the right woman? He wasn't a widow because he was clean-shaven. Did he also have some underlying personality flaw that kept him from finding his perfect match? Rose knew what hers was. Even though her head was about to explode with information that needed to be released, she took a deep breath and chose her words carefully.

"Gasthof Village isn't too far. It's a buffet." Rose forced a smile, longing to tell him that the restaurant and gift shop largely attracted tourists, but that they had very good food. She wanted to tell him about the offerings, what her favorites were, and what to stay away from. Rose had a favorite dessert there—the banana pudding. The restaurant didn't have a lot of ambience, but there was a lot to choose from. But she bit her lip so hard she hoped it didn't bleed as she folded her hands in her lap, clinging tightly to her small black purse.

"*Ya*, okay." He finally looked at her and smiled a little. "How, uh, do I get there?"

Rose gave him directions. Then she sat there and wondered if this was going to be worth it.

Esther knocked on Gus's door, and he opened it right away, as if he'd been standing on the other side of the entryway to the small cottage.

"I don't see any pie." Gus's gray hair was pulled back in a ponytail, the way it always was, and his jowls bounced like water balloons when he spoke. His gray beard was unkempt, as usual, and he rested his arms across his enlarged belly as he scowled.

Esther opened her mouth to say something, then realized she hadn't really planned out her question, or how she would handle Gus's response.

"Woman, I'm in the middle of eating supper." He quickly held up his palms. "Stop. Before you tear into me about calling you 'woman,' I'll just go ahead and say I'm sorry now. So what do you want, *Esther*? My delicious meal, which came out of a box by the way, is getting cold."

She chuckled, mostly to herself. They'd made huge strides over the past year. There was a time when Gus never would have apologized about anything. Now, though, Esther occasionally saw a glimpse of the man Gus might have been at one time, someone kinder and not so rude. But the moments were so fleeting that she felt silly for even being here. There was no way the man was capable of sending her flowers. "Never mind," she finally said as she turned to leave.

"Well, there must have been some reason you came over," he called after her.

Esther stopped slowly, turned around, and sighed. The only

way she would get Lizzie off her back was to confirm that Gus didn't send the floral arrangement.

"I received a gift today." She waited for any kind of reaction. When there wasn't one, she continued. "Someone sent me flowers, along with a card that wasn't signed. I was just wondering . . . uh . . . if it was you?"

His face turned red as he shifted his weight from one foot to the other. He looked a bit flustered, which caused a spike in Esther's blood pressure. *Surely he didn't do it.* "Esther . . ." he said before he sighed. She held her breath and braced herself for whatever response was coming. "Do I look like the type of man who sends flowers to a woman?" He raised an eyebrow as his face returned to its normal color. She'd mistaken flustered for disgruntled. She was interrupting his meal.

Esther chuckled, louder this time as her pulse returned to normal. "*Nee*, you don't. But I don't know many unmarried men, and I needed to confirm that you didn't send the flowers. Lizzie is back at the *haus* about to have a heart attack because she thinks you sent the bouquet. I told her she was being ridiculous. Equally as ridiculous, she even mentioned that I might have a stalker."

She waited for him to laugh along with her, but he just stared at her with his mouth hanging open for a few seconds. "Why does she think you have a stalker?" He spoke in his usual discontented voice as he scratched his scruffy beard.

Esther reached into her apron pocket and pulled out the card. She handed it to him. "This doesn't sound like it came from someone in my quilting group." She smirked, yet was still flattered by the flowers and card. She could feel herself blushing.

He frowned as he read the card, then pushed it back at her. "If your crazy sister thinks you have a stalker, then go home and lock your doors." He waved a dismissive hand. "I'm going in to finish my supper." Gus closed the door in her face in his typical fashion.

At least now she could go home and tell Lizzie that Gus definitely did not send her flowers.

But as she crossed the field that separated the three houses like a baseball diamond without a home plate, she allowed herself a few minutes to consider what Lizzie said. Could she have a stalker? Gus didn't seem to rule out the idea either, suggesting they lock the doors.

By the time she was back at the house, her ponderings had gone full circle, and she had to laugh. *I do* not *have a stalker. I have a secret admirer.*

When she walked in the door, Lizzie was standing in the middle of the living room with her arms across her chest and tapping a bare foot against the wood floor. "You just couldn't wait to get over there to thank that baboon for the flowers, could you?"

"*Ach*, hush, Lizzie." Esther eyed the beautiful arrangement still on the coffee table before she faced off with her sister. "I can assure you that Gus did not send me the flowers. As a matter of fact"—she chortled—"he actually said to lock our doors if you think we might have a stalker."

She waited for Lizzie to laugh, too, but her sister's mouth took on an unpleasant twist. "I hate to agree with Gus about *anything*, but maybe we *should* lock the doors." She tapped a finger to her chin.

Esther was having a hard time processing the fact that no one seemed to see the gesture as a secret admirer. "Lizzie, I'm well aware that I'm old and a somewhat large woman, but why can't you—or even Gus—consider that it might be someone who feels fondly about me?"

Lizzie dropped her arms to her sides as she shifted her dentures around in her mouth—something she did when she was in heavy thought. It had taken a long time for Lizzie to adjust to her false teeth, but these days the movement was more like a nervous tic.

"First of all, you're not a large woman. You're just big-boned." Lizzie smiled as she locked eyes with Esther. "And you're the best person I know. Secondly, you're only as old as you feel."

Esther sighed as she sat down on the couch. "I feel a hundred today."

"That's because of the heat," Lizzie said as she sat down beside her. "Any man would be blessed to win your affections, but Esther—" She paused, frowning. "How many men do we know who are widowers who might send flowers? It's not even really our way to do that, for men to send flowers." Lizzie went back to tapping her chin. "Hmm . . . let's think about who else might have sent those." She nodded to the vase. "Then Monday, we'll head out and try to confirm our suspicions. But for now, we lock the doors at night."

"I think you are overreacting, and I'm surprised Gus mentioned locking the doors."

Lizzie groaned as she leaned her head against the back of the couch and squeezed her eyes closed. "Please quit mentioning that man's name and insinuating we think alike. I'm a nice, genteel type of person. He's a grumpy, mean old man."

Esther covered her mouth to hide the humor she found in her sister's statement. Lizzie was her sister, her best friend, and Esther loved her with all her heart. But "genteel" was not a word to describe Lizzie.

"Can we please just change the subject?" Esther looked over her shoulder as the sun began its final descent. "I wonder how Rose's date is going."

Lizzie's eyes lit up. "It's July. We could have a wedding planned by November." With her head still resting on the back of the couch, she turned to Esther and smiled.

"This is their first date. Maybe we should wait to hear from Rose before we plan out her life." Esther loved weddings. As she closed her eyes to rest, she said a quick prayer that the evening was going well for Rose.

Benjamin was on the worst date of his life. Rose was the most beautiful woman he'd ever laid eyes on. She was tall and slender with gorgeous brown eyes and brown hair. She had straight white teeth and a beautiful smile—when she allowed herself to show any emotion. But the woman had no personality at all. She barely talked, and when she did, her answers were one word or a short sentence. His mother and her friend had made a huge mistake with this matchmaking effort. This was not his definition of high energy, and it was a struggle to get her to speak at all. It was especially challenging for Benjamin since he was not used to instigating conversation, nor did he enjoy it.

"The food is *gut*." Benjamin was glad to be at the dessert stage of the date. The sooner it was over, the better.

Rose was on her third dessert. She'd had a slice of pecan pie, two cookies, and went back for banana pudding. Normally, Benjamin would be happy to see one of his dates eating so heartily. Most of them nervously picked at their food without eating much at all. Rose might not be a talker, but she had no problem eating in front of him. He wanted to ask her how she stayed so thin eating like that. Or maybe she was nervous, but showing it in a different way than his other dates.

Benjamin tried to be patient as she finished her pudding. Despite the situation, he struggled not to grin. It was cute the way she ate so much, obviously not worried about what he thought. He liked that. It was the only thing he liked about her so far, if you didn't count how outwardly gorgeous she was. Benjamin could look at her all day long and never tire of it, but he was already drained mentally. Just once, he wished he could meet a woman who could carry a conversation, had something meaningful to say, and had the ability to give Benjamin something to ponder. It was selfish. There shouldn't be a need for a woman to delve into Benjamin's psyche to get him to open up.

He asked for the check as soon as she'd taken her last bite of pudding.

"The meal was *gut*. *Danki*." She smiled, and Benjamin smiled back at her. He wanted to tell her how beautiful she was. It was forward, and he wouldn't do it, but he briefly considered it. But no need to hint that there might be another date forthcoming. There wouldn't be. He was ready to get Rose Petersheim home.

This was the best date Rose had ever been on. Benjamin was handsome and polite, and Rose couldn't have handled herself any better. She'd talked when he asked a question, kept her answers brief, and had not questioned him about anything. It was exhausting, but she suspected that as time went on, she'd get more comfortable with her new way of getting to know a person. *Be a better listener.* She heard Esther's words in her head. The only problem was that Benjamin had very little to say, but Rose suspected he might be nervous. Maybe he would talk more on their next date. Rose was sure there would be a next date.

Even though it was a quiet ride back to the inn—and Rose felt like she might explode from not talking—she couldn't help but wonder if he would hug her good night, or maybe even kiss her on the cheek. She'd caught him staring at her several times. He looked at her mouth a lot so perhaps he longed to kiss her. That would be inappropriate on a first date, and she suspected Benjamin was enough of a gentleman not to be so forward. Although, a part of Rose wished he would pull her into his arms and kiss her passionately. Would the kiss be tender and light as a summer breeze, his lips warm and sweet on hers? Or would his mouth linger in harmony with hers as if a prelude for the future?

She tried to force the thoughts aside. It had been a long time since a man kissed her, and each time it had represented goodbye. Maybe she shouldn't hope for the kiss.

Her thoughts were all over the place. And no matter what happened at the end of the date, she couldn't wait to tell Esther and Lizzie how well it had gone. They would understand her excitement and be happy for her. Over time, she'd try to contain herself a bit more around Esther and Lizzie, but not tonight. She was going to burst if she didn't get to air the things on her mind. For now, she continued to wonder how the date would end, her mind whirling with possibilities.

"Here we are." Benjamin pulled back on the reins, bringing the horse and buggy to a stop at the inn.

Rose fought the wave of apprehension that swept through her. It was thrilling and frightening at the same time. She couldn't recall feeling this nervous at the end of other dates.

He turned to her, smiled a little, then got out of the buggy and walked around to open her door. Rose briefly tried to analyze his expression. Had a vaguely sensual light passed between them in that brief couple of seconds? Or was it just a glimmer of hope on Rose's end?

They stayed side by side across the yard and up the porch steps. He was tall. Rose liked that.

Her heart pounded as he stared into her eyes, but not before his gaze landed on her lips and stayed there for much too long. *He is going to kiss me*. She shouldn't let him, but the thrill outweighed the impropriety.

"*Danki* for supper." She fought the urge to lift up on her toes as excitement bubbled to the surface. She also staved off telling him about everything she'd enjoyed about the night—how the banana pudding wasn't as good as her own, how his horse was beautiful, how she had recently learned to knit, and every other thought that was swimming aimlessly around in her mind. Still, it was all overshadowed by the kiss that was coming.

When Benjamin King's lips met with hers, it was pure magic. For a man who had little to say, his kiss was like beautiful poetry he'd written just for her. Rose felt like they were truly speaking to each other for the first time. She was sure she'd never fit so perfectly with a man before. She wished this heady sensation could last forever, but he slowly drew away. As they gazed into each other's eyes, it seemed there was more to be said through the one way they had learned to communicate. He must have felt it, too, since he kissed her again, with twice the tenderness and passion as before.

She'd broken her own rule—no kissing on the first date. But she couldn't come up with a single regret. *Benjamin is the one*.

He stared at her for a while before he whispered, "Goodbye, Rose."

She searched for any hint of regret in his voice and couldn't find it. Rose wanted to say "See you soon," but instead softly said, "Goodbye, and *danki* again for supper."

He nodded before turning and walking to his buggy. As he backed up the horse, she waved from the porch, eager to tell Lizzie and Esther that they had succeeded in finding her someone special. She wondered if the sisters had seen the kisses through the window.

Rose opened the door, took in a deep breath, and was happy to find Esther and Lizzie in the living room near the window.

Benjamin wasn't feeling very good about himself. It was a horrible thing to do, to lead a woman on like that by kissing her so passionately, and on a first date no less. It would be their last date, but Benjamin had taken advantage of a situation. He'd prayed Rose would open her mouth to talk, but lips did more than form words, and Benjamin hadn't been able to take his eyes from her mouth all night. He was incredibly attracted to the woman, and even though he wouldn't be going out with her again, he'd had a strong desire to kiss her. He hadn't been able to harness it, and before he had time to think about it, his lips had met hers, and the world seemed to stop spinning for a moment. The stars shone a little brighter, and Benjamin could have sworn he'd found his life mate through two long and passionate kisses. He drifted on a cloud all the way home as he thought about the intense connection he'd felt with her in his arms. How could that be?

After a while, he forced himself to recall the rest of the evening. Goodbye had meant just that. They'd likely see each other at worship service and around town, but Benjamin wouldn't be asking her out again.

By the time he got home, anger had crept into his emotions. He was mad at himself for kissing her. Not only was it inappropriate, but now it was all he could think about. And he didn't want to think about Rose, someone so completely not right for him.

His mother was on the couch, but she quickly jumped up when he walked into the living room shaking his head.

"Uh-oh. You're home early." She flinched. "I'm guessing the date didn't go well?"

Benjamin sighed, took off his hat, and placed it on the rack by the door. "I don't know what you and your friend Lizzie were thinking."

"Lizzie said she's very pretty and pleasantly chatty." His mother was in her robe with her hair pinned up on her head as she blinked in bewilderment.

"*Ach*, she's pretty." Benjamin paused as he recalled the kisses. "Actually, she is gorgeous—one of the prettiest women I've ever met." He narrowed his eyebrows at his mother. "But bubbly or chatty? Uh, *nee*. She barely spoke, and when she did, it was one-word answers or short sentences. There were a lot of long periods of awkward silence." He gave her a stern look. "No more blind dates. Period."

His mother tucked her chin. Benjamin kissed her on the cheek. "I *lieb* you, *Mamm*, but dating is exhausting for me. I had high hopes for this woman, too, especially when I saw her. But she's not for me. So no more fix-ups."

"*Ya*, okay."

His mother sounded so defeated, and Benjamin wished it had worked out, even if just for his mom's sake. But as he trudged up the stairs and couldn't shake the feel of Rose's lips against his, he realized that he wished it had worked out also.

Chapter 3

Esther's heart warmed as she listened to Rose give details about her date. Even though Esther was surprised that there was kissing involved, she was thrilled everything had gone so well for Rose.

"I probably shouldn't have told you about the kisses. Since you were near the window, I assumed you might have seen what happened." Rose beamed as she spoke. "I know it was inappropriate to allow that, but just the fact that he wanted to kiss me..." She bounced up on her toes like a young girl. "I'm sure he'll ask me out again." She drew in a deep breath, the way she often did before she went on to another subject. "I ate three desserts at supper. Pecan pie, cookies, and banana pudding, which wasn't near as *gut* as what Jayce taught me to make."

It was nice to see Rose so happy and optimistic about this new man she'd met. Esther was happier than ever that Jayce had taken the time to teach Rose some special cooking techniques while he'd stayed with them.

"He's a very handsome fellow, and I'm so glad the date went well." Esther placed a hand over her mouth as she yawned. It wasn't very late, but she agreed with Lizzie. The heat took a toll on them, a little more with every passing year.

Esther glanced at Lizzie since she hadn't said anything. Her sister's eyes and expression screamed, *I told you so*. And for once, Esther had to agree. Lizzie might have actually chosen the perfect person for Rose.

"I'm off to bed." Rose kissed Lizzie on the cheek, then Esther. "*Danki* so much for thinking Benjamin would be a *gut* match for me. I feel so hopeful." With a bounce in her step, Rose dashed up the stairs.

After she was gone, Lizzie blew on her fingernails, rubbed them against her chest, and smiled broadly. "I told you so. I knew this man would be perfect for Rose. When his mother told me he was shy with women and found conversations difficult, I was sure Rose was his gal."

"It's nice to see her so happy." Esther yawned again as she stood up. "I'm torn about whether to have a slice of pie or go straight to bed." She reached into her pocket and took out the card, reading it again. Then she chuckled. "Perhaps I need to watch *mei* figure now that I have an admirer."

Lizzie rose from the couch and shuffled to the front door. She locked it, then turned to Esther. "There is everything to *lieb* about you, but we still can't rule out the fact that a man we don't know sent you flowers, and that's a bit creepy." Lizzie scrunched her face up until every wrinkle seemed to connect with the others.

Esther frowned. "Since when do you use words such as *creepy*?" She tried again to understand why Gus and Lizzie couldn't accept the possibility that a nice man in their community might have taken a fancy to Esther. It was the most excitement Esther had experienced in years. Maybe decades, all the way back to when her husband began courting her. "There is no reason for anyone to stalk us, so the gesture isn't *creepy*."

"Just the same, we're locking the doors." Lizzie pointed a crooked finger at Esther. "And tomorrow, we are going to do some investigating around town to see if we can figure out who your stalker"—she rolled her eyes—"I mean, admirer is."

Esther shook her head and walked toward her bedroom. "We don't have a stalker," she said one more time before she closed the door behind her.

Rose ran a brush through her hair following her bath. Once she was tucked into bed, she had time to revisit her thoughts about the date. It took everything she had not to focus on the kisses, assuredly an indicator of more dates to come.

When she began to pick apart the evening, she couldn't overlook the fact that they hadn't really talked. There had been nothing more than polite comments throughout the evening. Maybe she should have spoken more, at least a little bit. Why didn't he have more to say? She didn't know anything about him, and vice versa.

Perhaps she would ease her way into more conversation—slowly. Rose didn't think she could live the rest of her life with all her thoughts bundled inside her mind like trapped prisoners struggling to escape. But she could live the rest of her life kissing Benjamin.

She laid her head back and positioned her battery-operated fan to blow on her face, mingling with the breeze coming through the screen. She sighed. Physical attraction wasn't enough to make a relationship. Even Rose couldn't settle for that. But for tonight, she was going to dream of the possibilities.

Esther woke up suddenly when she heard a noise coming from the front porch. After she glanced at her clock, she eased out of bed and tiptoed to Lizzie's room. Her heart pounded in her chest as she put her hand on the doorknob. Could Lizzie have been right? Could someone with bad intentions have sent the flowers and note?

"Lizzie, wake up." Esther made her way over to the bed and put a hand on her sister's shoulder, gently shaking her. "Wake up."

Lizzie bolted upright and knocked heads with Esther. After both women rubbed their foreheads, Esther clicked on the flashlight she'd grabbed from her nightstand and shone it on the floor.

"I heard a noise coming from the porch." Esther flinched, wondering if Lizzie's forehead ached as much as hers. "It's probably a raccoon or some other critter, but . . ." She had to admit that all the talk about a stalker was making her nervous.

"I knew it." Lizzie reached for her teeth but knocked them on the floor. She waved a hand in the air and didn't look for her dentures. "I don't need *mei* teeth. It's not like I'm going to bite the intruder." She took something else from under her bed.

Esther felt like a giant as she cowered behind her tiny sister. Passiveness and nonviolence were what they'd been taught and believed. But Esther would let Lizzie guide the way since she'd been known to break both those rules. Mostly she'd kicked Gus in the shin from time to time, but Lizzie had also chased a solicitor with a baseball bat she kept under her bed. The same bat she was holding now.

They both looked out the living room window but didn't see anything. Lizzie slowly unlocked and opened the front door, then she bolted onto the porch with the bat in a ready position, jumping up and down and almost growling.

Esther gasped when she saw movement at the far end of the porch, but surely any intruder would be scared silly of Lizzie's wild behavior.

In the darkness, Esther could see the form of a person sitting on the edge of the porch, someone so startled they actually fell off the porch and into the yard.

Lizzie ran in that direction with her bat, and Esther followed, shining the flashlight.

When Esther saw who it was, her pulse began to slow down. But Lizzie held the bat as if she might actually strike Gus.

Their renter hoisted himself up, then blocked himself with one arm across his face. "Esther, get that flashlight out of my eyes, and tell your crazy sister that if she hits me with that bat,

I'm going to string her up in a tree upside down and leave her there."

Esther took the bat from Lizzie as she lowered the flashlight to her feet. "Gus, what are you *doing* out here?"

Lizzie hissed like an angry cat. "It's *you*. You wrote the letter because you love Esther, and now you're stalking her. You're both—the note writer and the stalker!"

Esther didn't think either scenario was true, but she did want to know why Gus was sitting on their porch. "Lizzie, hush now." She turned to Gus, his face barely visible in the darkness. "Gus, is something wrong?"

He pointed to Lizzie. "Yeah, her. She's the something wrong. Acting all crazy. I'm lucky I didn't break any bones." He cleared his throat and turned back to Esther. "I thought I saw someone walking around in your front yard, so I came over to investigate."

Gus stayed up late at night, sometimes until the early morning hours. She'd awoken several times to go to the bathroom or get a late-night snack and there was a faint glow coming from Gus's cottage.

"Are you sure you saw someone?" Esther's chest tightened.

"No!" Gus bellowed. "I'm not sure. But I thought I better come have a look, so I've just been sitting here awhile."

"So you didn't see anyone?" Esther was surprised Lizzie had calmed down and wasn't speaking.

"I don't know what I saw, if anything." Gus pushed back gray hair from his face. It was rare to see him without his ponytail. He looked older with his scraggly hair tossed in every direction. Gus was seventy-six, a couple of years older than Esther. Right now he was catching his breath and struggling to breathe.

"Gus, are you all right?" Esther inched toward him where he was standing below them in the grass.

"Do I look all right, Esther?" Gus attempted to tuck in his red checkered shirt unsuccessfully, then blew more hair from his face. Esther shone the flashlight closer to him, careful not to aim it in his eyes. He had grass in his hair.

"I come over here to offer my services, to make sure you and Rose were okay, then she"—he pointed to Lizzie, who was scowling at him, pinching her thin lips together, minus her teeth—"she comes jumping and screaming out of the house like a wild banshee!"

Lizzie took a step closer to Gus, and Esther put an arm in front of her, blocking her.

"I don't need this." Gus brushed grass from his shirt, unaware it was in his hair.

Esther felt a knot building in her throat. All this talk about an intruder or stalker was starting to scare her. Did Gus really see someone? "You scared us, Gus." Esther heard the shakiness in her voice. "All this talk about a stalker, and then I heard movement on the porch and woke up Lizzie." She glanced at her sister, who had held her expression so long that Esther wondered if Lizzie was even breathing. "We're sorry we startled you and caused you to fall."

"*Ya*, some protector you are," Lizzie said as she inched closer to him.

Gus tucked his hair behind his ears as he glared at Lizzie. "I really don't care if a pack of wolves comes to carry you off, crazy lady. But I figure Esther and Rose Petal don't deserve no harm."

"Rose. Remember, Gus. We don't call her Rose Petal." Esther took a deep breath, then let it out slowly. She was glad Rose couldn't hear them. The girl had confided in Esther that she could hear Lizzie's snoring from her upstairs bedroom, so she wore earplugs.

"Why don't you come inside, and I'll get you a slice of pie," Esther said.

"I don't want any pie." He started across the yard, and Esther thought he was limping. It was the first time he'd ever turned down pie. "You and wild thing go back to bed. Don't worry about me. I won't be coming back to check on things."

"*Gut!*" Lizzie spat as she snatched the bat back and left to return to the house. "Come on, Esther," she said softly as she opened the door.

Esther followed. Lizzie didn't sound like herself. She sounded . . . scared.

The next morning, Esther and Lizzie agreed not to say anything to Rose about what happened. Even the possibility that Gus had seen someone would surely be unsettling for her. No need to have another person worrying. Esther was thinking more and more that her note hadn't come from an admirer.

After church, they spent Sunday resting. Esther loved to worship the Lord, but it had been a hot day for church. By Monday, they still didn't have any guests booked at the inn, so it was a good day to follow up with Lizzie's suggestion—to take a ride through town to see if they could figure out who sent the flowers. Esther didn't have high hopes, but their first stop would be the local florist.

"Rose, Lizzie and I are going into town to run some errands." Esther wiped her mouth with her napkin. She hadn't eaten much breakfast, but enough for Rose to know she appreciated the meal. Her stomach was jittery. "Is there anything you need while we're out?" Esther held her breath and waited for a long response, potentially full of all kinds of conversation that had nothing to do with the subject at hand.

Rose shook her head. "*Nee*, I don't need anything, but *danki* for asking. Do you think you'll be gone long? I'm going to mop the floors, and they'll need time to dry." Her voice held a rasp of excitement. She was probably still floating on a romantic cloud, hoping to hear from Benjamin soon. "It shouldn't take long with this heat," she went on. "Then I plan to read because I'm sure I'll be hot from chores. I hope that's okay. I work best when I take breaks in between. And if it's not too hot, then I'll—"

"Hon, you schedule your day however you see fit." After interrupting Rose, Lizzie stood up and looked at Esther. "Are you ready?" She raised an eyebrow.

"*Ya, ya*. I'm ready." Esther eased herself up, her knees putting up some opposition.

"Have a wonderful time, but be sure to stay hydrated. It's hot out there." Rose smiled as she turned to face them, holding a stack of breakfast dishes. "You can always stop to get lemonade, or—"

"We'll be fine," Lizzie said loudly over her shoulder as she made her way to the living room.

"Don't worry," Esther said to Rose before she rushed to catch up with Lizzie.

Once they were in the yard, Lizzie climbed into the driver's side of the buggy. Esther winced. Lizzie drove too fast, but Esther stayed quiet and eased onto the other side of the seat. They'd debated whether or not to take the spring buggy, but they decided the covered buggy would keep the sun off of them. In their younger days, their choice would have been different.

Esther recalled the rides she and Joe used to take in the topless spring buggy when they were first courting, and even well into their forties. Even on a hot summer day, the warm wind slapping against their faces and the feel of the sunshine beaming down on them was rejuvenating. As they got older, they guarded themselves from the sun after Joe had his first skin cancer.

Esther bounced when one of the buggy wheels hit a pothole in the road. "Lizzie, that hole has been there for a very long time. But you always seem to hit it."

Lizzie was silent. Esther hadn't meant to start an argument, but it was unusual for her sister to remain quiet and not fire back some kind of retort.

"I know who sent you the flowers." Lizzie shifted her teeth back and forth, then picked up speed. "*Ya*, I know who your, uh, admirer is."

"Who?" Esther kept her eyes on Lizzie as her stomach swirled with anticipation. If it was someone they knew, it likely wasn't a stalker. Esther disliked that word more and more. *Stalker.*

"It's that man who sells homemade birdhouses in front of his *haus*." The lines of concentration deepened across Lizzie's forehead as she pressed her lips together. "I just can't think of his name."

Esther laughed. "You don't know what you're talking about. His name is Johnny Hostetler, and I'm sure that man hasn't taken a fancy to me." Esther felt twenty years younger just hearing herself reject the idea.

"He was sweet on you last time we were there." Lizzie gave a taut nod of her head, obviously deciding she had solved the mystery.

Ether shook her head, grinning. "The only thing that man was sweet on was the fact that I bought six birdhouses." She cut her eyes at Lizzie. "For obvious reasons, Johnny wouldn't be interested in me." *I can't believe anyone would be.*

Lizzie shot Esther a look of disgust. "Shame on you. Looks shouldn't matter. He's a nice fellow. And he lost Suzanne almost a year ago."

"He's barely five feet tall. I'm an Amazon compared to him." She held up a palm toward her sister. "And *ya*, I know looks shouldn't matter. But if he was interested in anyone, it would be you."

"Why? Because I'm more size appropriate?"

They were quiet, then Esther burst out laughing. "This is all so silly. Let's just go to the florist and ask who sent the flowers."

Lizzie giggled. "I feel like a teenager. I remember when Reuben picked a bunch of wildflowers and brought them to me on our first real date." She was quiet for a few seconds. "That seems like a lifetime ago."

Esther thought back to more youthful times too. "*Ya*, most men don't bring flowers, but Joe gave me flowers once. I was mad at him about something." She put a finger to her chin. "We were rarely cross with each other, and I don't remember what we'd had words about. But I remember the red roses he gave me that evening."

Lizzie eased the buggy into the small flower shop parking lot, then pulled back on the reins until they'd stopped completely. Turning to Esther, she said, "As long as the flower sender isn't a stalker, it's kind of exciting, isn't it?"

Esther grinned. "Maybe a little." They sat there quietly again. "But, Lizzie, I'm a seventy-four-year-old woman. This is just nonsense. Who in the world would want to be romantically involved with someone *mei* age?"

Lizzie hopped out of the buggy, but stuck her face in the window before Esther had moved. "A seventy-something man. That's who." Then she smiled wide, flashing her dentures, but not before giving them a little shuffle in her mouth. "Now let's go ask Sarah Mae who your admirer is."

Esther stepped out of the buggy with a quickening pulse. She appreciated Lizzie referring to the person as an admirer instead of that other word. But now that they were here, Esther was nervous to find out who wrote the note and sent the flowers.

Chapter 4

SARAH MAE WAS BUSY PUTTING TOGETHER AN ARRANGEMENT of red roses, and it took Esther back to her earlier thoughts about Joe, which brought forth a smile.

"Esther and Lizzie." Sarah Mae set down a pair of scissors she'd been using to cut ribbon. "*Wie bischt*. In the market for flowers? You two usually have beautiful flower beds in full bloom this time of year."

Sarah Mae was a tiny woman, like Lizzie, and also in her seventies. She'd owned the small flower shop for as long as Esther could remember.

"Someone sent Esther flowers," Lizzie said in a whisper, even though there wasn't anyone else in the shop. "With a love note attached. We want you to tell us who sent the flowers." Lizzie set her small black purse on the counter and put her palms on the glass top. "We won't tell that you told," she said, still whispering.

Sarah Mae's mouth fell open, and Esther could feel herself blushing. But she was as curious as Lizzie, probably more so, to find out who the person was.

"A love note?" Sarah Mae finally asked as she glanced back and forth between Esther and Lizzie.

"Do you have the note with you?" Lizzie turned to Esther and raised both eyebrows.

Esther was tempted to say no, but she slowly took the card from her purse, a black bag almost identical to Lizzie's. She could feel the heat radiating from her face as she passed it to Sarah Mae.

"*Ach*, oh my." Sarah Mae handed the card back without saying anything else.

Lizzie leaned forward a little. "Well?"

Sarah Mae couldn't seem to lose the astonished expression on her face. Esther was sure her own face was burning an even brighter shade of red.

"I don't know." Sarah Mae pushed a small card about the same size as the love note toward Lizzie. "I handwrite my notes in print, like this one." She tapped her card that read, *To Hannah*, Lieb, *John*. "The card you have is in cursive writing, and it's all *Englisch*. *Mei Englisch* has never been *gut* when I'm writing. I write mostly in *Deutsch* for our people. If an outsider orders flowers, they usually have to spell out some of the words." She pointed to the card in Esther's hand. "That's a fancy card with fancy *Englisch*."

Lizzie gasped, turned to Esther, and locked eyes with her. But she quickly turned back to Sarah Mae. "*Danki*, Sarah Mae. See you Sunday at worship." Then she latched on to Esther's arm and practically dragged her out of the shop.

Once they were outside, Esther shook loose of her sister's grip. "We should have thought this out. Sarah Mae will tell people." Esther's purse slipped from her wrist to the crook of her elbow as she covered her face in shame.

"Esther, look at me."

When Esther uncovered her face, Lizzie glared at her. "We didn't pick up on that important clue." Lizzie stomped a foot before she started toward the buggy. As she untethered the horse, she shook her head.

Esther held a hand to her forehead to block the sun. "What are you talking about?"

"The note. Not one word is in Pennsylvania *Deutsch*. Whoever sent the flowers is *Englisch*. And the sender went to a fancy florist in the city, and that's who wrote the note." Lizzie shook her head, stepped into the buggy, and slammed the door. "It's Gus."

"It's *not* Gus." Esther rolled her eyes, but Lizzie was right about the perfect English.

Lizzie clicked her tongue and backed up the buggy. "It's not one of our people. So let's make a list of all the *Englisch* men you know who are widowers." She glowered. "Or it could be a married man, or a divorced man."

Esther was too shaken to think about outsiders she knew. The word *stalker* was back in her mind. "Let's just go home. I don't know many *Englisch* men. And by noon, it's going to be too hot for us to be out."

Lizzie sighed. "I guess you're right. We can think on it at home."

By the time they returned to the inn, Lizzie was yawning, and

Esther was hungry since she hadn't eaten much that morning. But they both kicked off their shoes at the door and went directly to the couch. Esther put her socked feet up on the coffee table, and Lizzie did the same. Both stayed quiet for a while. Lizzie had her chin cupped with one hand and her other arm folded across her stomach, obviously in serious contemplation.

Esther's stomach growled, but she was enjoying the fan blowing in her face for the moment. She made a mental note to buy more batteries next time they went to town for supplies. The grandfather clock in the dining room rang eleven times, but then only the quiet buzz of the fans sounded in the house.

"It's too quiet when Rose is gone." Lizzie lowered her hand and yawned again.

Esther chuckled. "We complain about Rose's chatter all the time, but you're right. It's too quiet without her here, especially when we don't have any guests."

"After she and Benjamin fall in *lieb* and Rose moves out, we better hope for more overnight guests, even in the summer." Lizzie laid her head back against the couch cushion, then turned to Esther. "Where is she anyway?"

Esther pushed through a yawn, trying to decide which sounded better, lunch or a nap. "She said something yesterday about possibly visiting Big Roy and Katie Marie today since we don't have anyone staying at the inn."

"I wonder if she will tell them about her date with Benjamin." Lizzie crossed one ankle over the other.

"I'm sure she will tell anyone who listens," Esther said, then grinned. "It was nice to see her so happy."

"I wonder if her whole family talks a lot." Lizzie scratched her cheek, yawning again. "She's got a bunch of *bruders* and *schweschdere*. I asked her not long after she got here why she left Ohio. She actually got quiet and just shrugged."

"I remember you telling me that." Esther lowered her feet to the floor, deciding food and a nap were in order soon. "But I see her putting letters to her family in the mailbox a couple of times a week, and there are always letters coming back to her from Ohio." Esther stood up and stretched her arms over her head. "I need a sandwich and a nap."

Lizzie slowly lifted herself from the couch. "I'll skip the sandwich. I'm going straight to the nap."

Esther made herself a ham sandwich and sat down at the kitchen table to eat, pondering what English man might have sent her flowers. She didn't really know many single men who weren't Amish. It didn't matter in the big scheme of things. At her age, Esther wasn't in the market for a romantic relationship, and she'd never love anyone the way she loved Joe.

Then she stopped chewing and straightened. She did know two English men who were unattached. One of them she saw every day, and the other one she saw once a week.

She put her sandwich down. "Hmm . . ."

∞

Benjamin was dripping in sweat when he walked into the living room. Even with all the fans blowing, he wasn't sure it was any cooler in the house.

"I'm in the kitchen!" his mother hollered, which was necessary above the noise from the fans.

He went straight to the refrigerator and took out the iced tea.

"After you cool off, can you check how much propane is left?" His mother sighed. "I've gone through every entry in your checkbook twice and compared it to your bank statement. I'm still two cents off."

Benjamin filled his glass with ice, then tea. After he'd gulped down over half of it, he said, "*Mamm*, don't worry about two cents."

"It bothers me," she said as she scratched her head.

"It doesn't bother me." He set his glass on the counter, thinking he might need a refill. "Any jobs today?"

"Two messages were on the answering machine. I wrote down the names and phone numbers. They're in your office."

It wasn't really an office. It was a converted mudroom. But it worked for now. "*Danki*." He headed that way, retrieved the messages, then went to the barn to return the calls, disappointed that both were minor repairs. He'd lost most of his regular customers when they moved from Bedford, but the move had seemed important to his mother. And they weren't hurting for money. Benjamin had a hefty savings account he'd been building since he started his own business three years ago.

"Both jobs are scheduled for tomorrow," he said when he walked back into the kitchen. He refilled his glass with tea. "I'll be upstairs for a while."

His mother had her head buried in his checkbook. "*Ya*, okay."

Upstairs, he threw himself on the bed, arms spread wide, and closed his eyes. It was even hotter upstairs. But he'd insisted his mother take the only downstairs bedroom. August was going to be brutal. He hoped he would pick up some English business so he could work in the air-conditioning. Benjamin needed to advertise more. As he tried to think of different strategies, he kept seeing Rose's face and recalled the soft fullness of her lips against his.

I'm such a cad. He'd allowed his physical desire to dominate over what was right. He should have never kissed her. Now he would have to face her at worship service. He wondered what she was thinking. Did she enjoy the kisses as much as he did? Why had she allowed it? Was she as attracted to him as he was to her?

Why did any of it matter? Their personalities were not a good fit. Benjamin worried he'd end up living with his mother forever. He could afford to purchase a home of his own, but he feared loneliness would consume him. His mother had already found a quilting group, volunteered at the food pantry in a neighboring town, and established herself within the community, all in only a couple of weeks. Benjamin ate, slept, and worked.

He wished things could have turned out differently with Rose.

∞

When Rose returned from visiting her only relatives in Montgomery, she went straight to the barn to check for messages. She hadn't even asked Benjamin if he had a cell phone. Rose didn't, but he probably did for his work. He hadn't asked her for a phone number. She would have given him the number at the inn. But it was only Monday. Maybe he didn't want to appear too anxious. Just recalling the kisses they shared caused her stomach to swirl with anticipation. She'd see him at worship if she didn't hear from him before Sunday. But that seemed unlikely based on the way their date had gone.

When she exited the barn, the mailman was just putting mail in the box. He always delivered the mail between two and two thirty. Rose headed toward him and waved. "*Wie bischt*, Mr. Holden." She paused. "I mean, hello."

Their mailman should have retired years ago. Rose had asked him about it once, and he'd said that with his wife deceased, he'd go crazy without seeing people. Harvey Holden was one of the nicest English men Rose had ever met. He always had a kind word, wished her a good day, and listened to her talk about whatever was on her mind. Certainly, Mr. Holden would be polite and listen to all the thoughts rattling around in her mind today, but he would also be good practice for her. *Don't ramble*, she reminded herself as she took a deep breath and reached inside the box for the mail.

Mr. Holden drove a small blue pickup truck, and he always wore one of several baseball caps.

"How are you today, Rose?" He had a crooked smile and enough wrinkles to resemble a road map, but his blue eyes were filled with kindness.

"I'm *gut*." She bit her bottom lip, longing to tell him about her lengthy visit with Big Roy and Katie Marie. Mr. Holden surely knew them and would be interested in all the happenings going on in their life. They were going to be grandparents for the sixth time, and they were also planning a vacation to Florida soon.

Maybe Mr. Holden knows those things already. Either way, she gave a quick wave and said, "Have a *gut* day."

As she neared the house and Mr. Holden drove away, she saw Esther and Lizzie with their noses almost pressed against the windowpane. They both jumped back when they saw her.

"What are you two doing?" Rose put her hands on her hips, grinning.

Both women stiffened. "Nothing, dear," Esther said before she cleared her throat. "Any mail for us?"

Lizzie didn't move or speak. Rose was sure she'd interrupted something. "It looks like junk mail." She handed over two flyers and decided to practice on Esther and Lizzie, even though she could be herself around them. All this not talking was bottling up like a fizzy soda about to burst. But she drew in a breath and blew it out slowly. "I'm going to do a little dusting upstairs."

"Okay." Lizzie grabbed Esther by the sleeve of her dress and dragged her toward Lizzie's bedroom. "I need to have a chat with Esther."

Esther looked over her shoulder and smiled, but it didn't look like a real smile. Rose wasn't sure what was going on, but she had definitely interrupted something important.

∞

"It's him," Lizzie said right after she had closed the bedroom door. "Harvey Holden. I don't know why we didn't think of him earlier. He's about our age, *Englisch*, and a widower. He's your admirer." She nudged Esther. "I knew I'd figure it out."

Esther sat on Lizzie's bed. "I actually thought about him earlier. But, Lizzie, the mailman—of all people—knows where we live. He wouldn't have left the flowers at Amos and Naomi's *haus*."

Still standing, Lizzie's lips puckered with annoyance. "He just did that to throw us off. Or a fancy florist delivered the flowers to the wrong address, like I said was possible before."

Esther rolled her eyes. "It isn't Harvey." She thought about the other person who might be a contender.

"*Ach*, it might be. We'll call him suspect number one." Lizzie tugged on her ear, sighing. "He was right under our noses, and we didn't even think about him."

Esther grunted. "Suspect number one? This isn't a murder investigation, Lizzie."

Her sister sat down on the bed. They'd both had a decent nap, and the much-needed rest had felt good. "I-I did think of someone else," she said meekly.

Lizzie gasped as her eyes rounded. "Who?"

"I'm sure it isn't who sent the flowers, but . . ."

Lizzie bolted to a standing position. "Who?"

Esther swallowed hard before clearing her throat. "Maybe Edgar."

Lizzie gasped again as she held up two fingers. "Suspect number two!"

"*Ach*, quit calling them suspects." Esther sighed, but she was becoming more and more intrigued about who might have taken a fancy to her. Edgar Thompson was their yardman, and he came every Thursday.

"He's in the running for sure." Lizzie paced the bedroom, cupping her chin with one hand. "Age appropriate and also a widower."

"Someone's here." Esther looked over her shoulder out the bedroom window. She waited until their visitor stepped out of the buggy. "It's Jayce."

Lizzie stopped pacing and they went into the living room. Lizzie rushed ahead, pushing open the screen door. "I am still getting used to seeing you in Amish clothes and with the short hair." Lizzie grinned. "Even after all this time."

"It's a look that works for you, Jayce." Esther hugged the boy, recalling the time he'd spent with them. Of all the folks she'd known to convert to their ways—and there weren't very many—Jayce had been the most shocking of all. He was a levelheaded young man who had fallen in love with Evelyn Schrock. But Jayce came from a world filled with movie stars, fancy cars, and extravagant houses—luxuries Esther couldn't even imagine. Jayce's father made movies in Los Angeles. But giving Jayce and Evelyn a little push toward romance had been the right thing to do. Jayce had adapted naturally, and he and Evelyn were happy and expecting their first child.

"We're always happy to see you." Lizzie's smiled faded. "Is everything all right?"

"*Ya, ya.*" Jayce scratched his cheek just above his short beard. "Do you remember when I was staying here, one of you made a stew? I said it was the best stew I've ever had, but I never got the recipe. Can I get that for Evelyn to make?"

"I made that, and Rose makes it sometimes now. Let me go see if I have it written down." Esther went to the kitchen, thumbed through her little tin filled with recipes, then returned to the living room. She handed the small recipe card to Jayce. "You can keep it. I know it by heart, and if Rose doesn't, I can write it down for her."

"Thanks," Jayce said. "I mean *danki*."

Esther smiled. "Not to worry. Your Pennsylvania *Deutsch* continues to get better and better."

"Guess what?" Lizzie sidled up to Jayce and looked up at him, speaking in a whisper. "Esther has a secret admirer."

Esther rolled her eyes. "Lizzie..." The entire town was going to know, and Esther didn't want to be the center of attention, especially over something like this.

"Really?" Jayce raised a curious eyebrow as he glanced at Esther. "And who might that be?"

Lizzie grunted, scowling. "Did you not hear me say *secret* admirer?"

Esther's face was fire hot, she was sure. "It's all quite silly really," she said, keeping her eyes from meeting with Jayce's.

"Someone sent Esther flowers and a mushy love note." Lizzie folded her arms across her chest as she continued to look up at Jayce. "And we've got two suspects."

Esther hung her head and shook it. When she looked up, Jayce was grinning ear to ear. "You can forget about your suspects. I know exactly who your secret admirer is."

Esther met his amused expression in less than a second and waited, her heart pounding against her chest.

Jayce pointed over his shoulder. "It's Gus."

Esther shook her head. "*Nee*, it's not. That's what Lizzie thought, too, but I asked him about it."

Jayce chuckled. "I don't care what he said. He practically told me as much one time." He paused, scratching his cheek again. "Well, maybe he didn't exactly come out and say it, but I could tell. Trust me, it's Gus." He spoke the last part of his statement with such confidence, Esther's stomach roiled.

Lizzie stomped her foot. "I told you so. I told you so. I told you so. Just bury me now."

Esther recalled Gus's response. *Esther, do I look like the type of man who sends flowers to a woman?* "I just don't think so," Esther said, barely above a whisper.

"By the way, where is the old guy?" Jayce grinned. "You know I like to stop by and give him a hard time. But I didn't see his truck yesterday, and it's not there now."

It was an odd friendship between Gus and Jayce, but for some reason Gus tolerated Jayce the same way he did Esther.

"Gone forever, I hope." Lizzie lifted her chin as she pressed her lips into a thin line.

Esther thought about what they'd done yesterday, which was a bunch of nothing. "I don't recall seeing his truck yesterday either. Or today. Hmm . . ." Gus ran to town for supplies, but she couldn't think of a time when he had stayed away from home overnight.

"*Wie bischt*, Jayce." Rose's bare feet descended the stairs, and she joined them in the living room.

"Hey, Rose. I'm helping these lovely ladies figure out who Esther's secret admirer is. It was pretty easy." He waved before he turned to leave. "*Danki* for the recipe, Esther."

After he was gone, Esther and Lizzie looked at Rose. Her

mouth was agape, so Lizzie quickly told her about the flowers and card. The girl was going to have a lot to say about this. Esther braced herself.

Rose sighed. "It's Gus, isn't it?"

Lizzie clenched her fists at her sides and groaned before she headed toward the kitchen. "I think I feel a cough coming on."

"You stay out of that cough syrup, Lizzie." Esther spoke with authority, knowing Lizzie would do what she wanted. The honey and lemon concoction—with a touch of rum—was reserved for illness. Well, it was supposed to be.

Esther locked eyes with Rose, waiting for her to elaborate in detail, but Rose just shook her head. "Esther . . ." Rose eyed her with sympathy. "I think it *is* Gus."

Chapter 5

By Thursday, Rose had fallen into a slump. She took care of her household duties but mostly stayed in her room. If Benjamin had wanted to see her, he would have called or visited by now. She lay back on her bed, her legs dangling over the side, and fought the urge to cry.

She could talk to Naomi or Evelyn, but there had already been enough discussion about poor Rose's love life. Maybe it was time for her to go back to Ohio. She'd had plenty of reasons to leave her hometown, with no plans to return. But perhaps living there was still a better alternative than staying in a place with a limited number of available men. Even though the move to Montgomery hadn't been solely to find a husband, a new location had given her hope at the possibility. She refused to be a burden by moving in with one of her siblings. Her only choice would be to move back in with her mother. She cringed when she thought about it.

There were three knocks on the door. "Can I come in?"

Rose sat up and took a deep breath. "*Ya*, Lizzie, come in."

Lizzie peeked her head in, then eased open the door and walked to the middle of the room. "What's going on with you?"

Rose had tried to appear upbeat around Esther and Lizzie, but it was getting harder and harder. "Nothing."

Lizzie stomped across the room and sat down on the bed, twisting to face Rose. "That's it? Nothing? Hon, I *lieb* you, but you always have more to say than that. Now, tell me what has you so upset?"

Rose fought the sentences scrambling around in her mind, and she couldn't hold back anymore. "I haven't heard from Benjamin. If he was interested in me, he would have made contact. And I feel horrible that I let him kiss me, but I could tell he wanted to, and I wanted him to, and I'm sure I shouldn't have told you and Esther. I'm hoping Benjamin didn't tell anyone. Could it be that I'm just not pretty enough? I know that shouldn't matter, but my failure to find someone to love me makes me think there's something unattractive about me. I even thought about going back to Ohio. Sometimes I miss *mei* family, but . . ." She paused, lost in recollections for a few seconds. "I really don't want to do that. And I think of you and Esther as family. I don't understand why"—she pressed her lips closed and held her breath before blowing it out slowly—"I talk too much."

Lizzie shrugged. "And I shuffle *mei* teeth around, and sometimes I spit them out. I know I snore." She rolled her eyes. "Esther reminds me of it. And I have no tolerance for people who ask dumb questions, and I react to our guests in ways I shouldn't sometimes. I'm terrified of those wicked cats running around outside. And sometimes I envision ways to poison Gus, which I wouldn't do, but the thought entertains me when I'm bored." She put a hand on Rose's knee. "*Mei maedel*, we all have quirky things, and when the right person comes along, you'll know it. As for talking a lot"—Lizzie shrugged again—"you just have a lot of things going on in your mind all at once."

Rose was tempted to tell Lizzie that she'd overheard her and Esther talking about how chatty she was, not to mention the times they'd sat her down to discuss it in a gentle manner. But Rose knew they loved her, and she didn't want them to feel badly. "I'm working on being a better listener. I really am interested in other people, how they feel, their wants and needs, but it's as if all my thoughts come out of *mei* mouth before I get the sentences organized."

"I know you must miss your family, but I'll be selfishly hoping you don't decide to go back to Ohio." Lizzie patted her leg before she eased her hand away. "The Lord always has a plan, and He has a plan for you." She stood up and sighed. "We have guests coming tomorrow around noon, just so you know. Three *Englisch* women from Texas. I'm betting they won't last past the first night in this heat."

Rose nodded. "I'll have everything ready."

After Lizzie left, Rose took her keepsake box from underneath the bed. Then she thumbed through the contents, the way she had been doing recently. It wasn't a healthy ritual. Some things were better left behind and not recalled daily. And as she thought more about it, she was sure she could never go back home.

Esther lowered the gardening magazine she was reading when she heard Lizzie coming down the stairs.

As Lizzie hit the landing, she shook her head and said, "I really thought Benjamin was the man for Rose. She's upset because she hasn't heard from him."

"Just because one of them is an introvert and the other an extrovert, that doesn't mean it's a perfect match." Even though it was the truth, Esther still felt for the girl.

Lizzie sat in one of the rocking chairs, crossed one leg over the other, and kicked it into motion. "Well, there was definitely an attraction or he wouldn't have kissed her."

"Maybe that's all it was, just a physical attraction they both acted on." Esther looked over her shoulder and out the window toward Gus's cottage.

"Stop worrying about that grump." Lizzie slipped on a pair of gold reading glasses and picked up her Bible. Ironic since her serious dislike of Gus didn't line up with the Lord's teachings.

"He's never been gone this long since he's rented the cottage." Esther didn't want Gus's romantic affections—which she still found hard to believe—but she cared about the man.

"If it makes you feel any better, I talked to Naomi this morning. Gus is alive and well . . . somewhere."

"How do you know that?" Esther closed the magazine and put it in her lap.

"Gus called Naomi Tuesday and said he might not be home for a few days. He asked her to leave food and water out on his porch for the cats. I think Naomi and Gus share custody of those wretched creatures, but they are mostly at Gus's *haus*." Lizzie shivered as she squeezed her eyes shut. "He is probably training them to attack me in *mei* sleep."

Esther shook her head. "They are just cats, and I am relieved to hear that Gus is all right." She paused, tipped her head to one side. "I wonder where he is."

Lizzie scrunched up her face and squeezed her eyes closed again. "Esther, if you get romantically involved with Gus, just throw me in a grave and cover me with dirt."

"*Ach*, stop it. There hasn't been and never will be anything romantic with me and Gus." Sighing, she shook her head again. "Such nonsense. But I am concerned."

"I'm sure he's fine." Lizzie spoke with less venom, almost in a comforting way. Sometimes Esther wasn't convinced her sister despised Gus as much as she let on. But their sparring had become a way of life, more a battle of wits sometimes. "Maybe he went to visit his *dochder*," Lizzie added.

"*Nee*. They haven't seen each other since she came to that little mini movie preview Jayce's father held. His *dochder*—Heather—accepted Gus's money he received for his part in the show, then to my knowledge, Gus never heard from her again."

Esther had thought that was a horrible thing to do, attending just to get money from her father. But Gus said she deserved it, that he hadn't been a good father. It didn't sound like Heather was a good woman, but it wasn't Esther's place to pass judgment.

"Did you let Rose know we have guests tomorrow?" Esther was looking forward to visitors. Rose had been unusually quiet.

"*Ya.* And even though she's sad, she was talkative."

Esther was glad to hear that. Somewhere along the line, she had gotten used to Rose's chatter. Even though it contributed to her headaches sometimes, her silence was worse. The ticking clock on the mantel seemed to reverberate off the walls when all was still and quiet. Esther hadn't realized how much she missed the girl's vivacious ways.

They were quiet for a while, then Esther stood up. "I'm going to the barn to call the Bedford and Bloomington hospitals." She peered at Lizzie. "And I don't want to hear one word about it. I do consider Gus a friend, despite what others might feel."

To Esther's surprise, Lizzie stayed quiet, and Esther left the room and went to the barn. Bedford was a small hospital, whereas Bloomington was larger. She decided to call Bedford first and was surprised when the woman who answered the phone confirmed that there was a Gus Owens who was admitted Sunday. Four days ago. But the woman wouldn't give Esther any information about Gus's condition or say what he was being hospitalized for. After she hung up, she called for a driver. Bedford was too far to go by buggy—forty miles. Doable if absolutely necessary, but not in this heat.

"I'll go with you," Lizzie said after Esther came back in the house and told her sister she'd be leaving soon.

Esther slipped into her loafers by the door. "Why? You can't stand the man." She faced Lizzie, who was getting up from the rocking chair. "What if he hurt himself when he fell off our porch Saturday night? If he went to the hospital Sunday, that could be why." Esther put a hand to her chest. "I hope this isn't our fault."

"Gus does what Gus wants. You know that. We didn't ask him to sit vigil on the porch watching for stalkers. Dense old man." Lizzie shrugged. "Besides, I know how much you hate hospitals and anything to do with medical stuff."

Her sister was right, and Esther didn't relish the idea of going inside any hospital, but she had to know if Gus was all right. "Can you go let Rose know we're leaving? My knees scream every time I have to go up those stairs."

Lizzie bolted up to the second story with the energy of a teenager, and when she returned, they went out on the porch to wait for the driver.

By the time they reached the hospital, Esther had concocted plenty of reasons Gus could be a patient. Cancer, heart problems, an injury from falling off the porch, or a possible fall inside the cottage. Whatever it was, he had been well enough to drive himself, and that was a good sign.

Lizzie followed Esther to the entrance of the hospital, but Esther's feet didn't want to take the final few steps inside. "I dislike the smell of hospitals. And there is so much sickness, and—"

Her sister looped an arm through hers and eased Esther over the threshold when the automated doors opened. "It's also a place where babies are born and new life begins. Envision all those mommies with new *kinner* and the *lieb* they are feeling toward those precious gifts."

Esther forced her feet to move and went inside, trying to do as Lizzie said, which was nearly impossible with the smells of the medical facility assaulting her senses.

After she was told what room Gus was in and that he was

allowed visitors, Esther padded down the long hallway until she got to room 221. Lizzie chose to stay in the waiting room, which was probably a good idea. No reason to upset Gus since he was sick.

Esther stood outside the door and wondered if Gus would be hooked up to all kinds of tubes and monitors. Would he be fighting pain? Would he be happy to see her, or angry that she'd come? Then she heard soft laughter and pushed the door open.

"Esther." Gus's mouth fell open as his jowls hung low. His gray hair was in the usual ponytail, but he'd actually trimmed his beard. "What are you doing here?"

There weren't any tubes or monitors. Just Gus lying in bed wearing a hospital gown and covered to his waist with white linens. He had apparently been watching television, and there was a food tray stacked with empty plates on the bedside table.

He finally closed his mouth and narrowed his eyebrows into a frown. "What are you doing here?" he asked again.

Esther stayed right inside the doorway, her purse dangling from one arm near her elbow. "I noticed that you had not been home in days, so I called this hospital to see if you were a patient. Why didn't you tell me you were ill?" She took a step closer. "What's wrong with you?"

He motioned with his hand for her to come closer, and he continued to do so until she was right next to his bed.

"I hurt my back when I fell off your porch." He spoke in a whisper, as opposed to the thunderous voice she was used to.

Esther gasped and pressed trembling fingers to her mouth. "I knew it. I was afraid this was our fault."

"I'm fine," he said, speaking even softer.

Unsure why he was whispering, she looked over her shoulder. She'd left the door cracked. As she looked back at Gus, it was obvious by his position in the bed that he hadn't broken his back. "How bad are your injuries?" A knot was building in her throat.

"I said I'm fine," he whispered again. Then he scowled and used a remote control to lower the volume on the television. "I only *told* the doctors I hurt my back. I had to endure a few tests, but I needed a vacation. It's hotter than a furnace in that cottage. I don't remember it ever being this hot in July." He smiled broadly. "And in here, I get all my meals brought to me in this air-conditioned room and unlimited desserts." He paused, frowning. "They ain't anywhere near as good as your pies, but I can watch as much television as I want."

Esther was fuming on the inside, tempted to bop him with her purse. It was a good thing Lizzie hadn't come into the room because her sister would have certainly done so.

"Goodbye, Gus." Esther spun on her heel and left the room, even though Gus called out to her twice. By the time she reached the waiting room, her blood was boiling.

"You're red as a beet." Lizzie stood and skipped to catch up to Esther, who was already marching to the elevator. "How sick is he?"

"He's *not* sick." Inside the elevator, she reached into her purse and took out the cell phone they used for emergencies and times like this.

"What do you mean he isn't sick? What's he doing in the hospital?"

After the elevator door opened, Esther stomped across the lobby, rushed out the entrance, and sat on a bench outside the building, her knee throbbing. Lizzie sat down beside her.

"Are you going to tell me what's going on?" Lizzie adjusted her dentures, scowling.

"Gus is faking his condition so he can be in the air-conditioning and have free food." She gritted her teeth. "It just makes me so angry. What if another patient needed that room? He's taking time away from other patients when the nurses have to tend to him."

"Finally." Her sister threw her hands in the air. "You're starting to see the real man."

"Hush, Lizzie." Esther called the driver to pick them up, then said, "I know exactly how Gus is, always have. But he has been doing better lately, and there is kindness inside of him, even though he keeps it hidden most of the time. I'm just very disappointed in him right now."

Esther rubbed her knee as Lizzie shuffled her dentures around again.

"Edgar will probably be mowing the yard when we get home." Lizzie nudged Esther. "Maybe take him some iced tea and see how he acts. That would be a nice distraction from this mess with Gus."

Esther took a tissue from her apron pocket and dabbed at the sweat beads on her forehead. "I don't know about a distraction. And I know I mentioned Edgar, but I don't think he sent the flowers either." She blew out a breath of frustration. "I'm done speculating. We are on a wild goose chase." She turned to Lizzie.

"I'm an old woman. It shouldn't even matter." Even though it did. But flattery was still colliding with a small dose of fear, and she didn't want to think about it anymore. She was also surprised at how angry she was at Gus. It was a low thing to do, even for him. It was abuse of a system put in place to help those in need. What Gus needed was one of Lizzie's swift kicks in the shin.

"So you just want to quit trying to figure out who the person is?" Lizzie eyed her skeptically.

Esther raised her chin as she clutched her purse with both hands. "*Ya*, that's right."

Lizzie hung her head, shaking it, before she looked back at Esther. "I'd be haunted for the rest of *mei* life. I might still be, even though the flowers were sent to you."

"Well, I'm not going to let it bother me or take up one more second of *mei* time." She pointed to a blue van. "There's our driver."

They were quiet in the car, and by the time they got home, Esther couldn't stop yawning. She wasn't sure when she became so dependent on naps, but they were now more of a need than a luxury. Sure enough, Edgar was mowing.

"I'm not taking him tea. I'm not going to talk to him," she said with her head held high as she marched across the yard.

"I'll talk to him." Lizzie did an about-face, but Esther quickly latched on to her sister's apron strings and pulled her to a halt.

"You will do no such thing. I expect you to respect *mei* feelings about this."

Lizzie rolled her lip into a pout as she got in step with Esther. "Gus has put you in a foul mood. It's just like him to take away our fun."

"This isn't just about Gus." Esther held on to the handrail as she struggled up the steps, Lizzie rushing past her, like always. In truth, it was mostly about Gus. She thought she'd been making progress with him, especially over the past year. It bothered her more than she would have expected, that he had sunk so low as to have a vacation at the hospital. And if he were really as worried about a stalker as he'd made out to be, he wouldn't have scheduled his *vacation* right now.

It was going to be a long while before Gus Owens received another slice of pie from Esther. Or even a visit.

Chapter 6

Rose was in the kitchen preparing breakfast when Esther walked into the room Friday morning. The poor woman had huge bags underneath her eyes and looked a bit pale.

"Are you okay?" Rose carried three plates to the table and began setting them out.

Esther pulled out a chair and sat. Normally the elder sister was dressed first thing, complete with prayer covering and shoes. This morning, she was in her robe, barefoot, and with only a scarf covering the bun on her head.

"If someone truly has taken a fancy to me, why keep it a secret?" Esther put her elbows on the table and rubbed her temples. "I was awake half the night wondering who would do such a thing. I told myself that I was going to quit worrying about this, but the thoughts invaded *mei* sleep just the same."

Rose turned off the propane under the eggs, poured Esther a cup of coffee, and placed it in front of her.

"*Danki*, dear."

"I think that whoever the person is, he must be very shy. Or maybe he is afraid you won't feel the same way toward him. That can make a person nervous, worrying if someone will reciprocate feelings." She briefly thought about Benjamin. "And I'm sure this man will show himself soon, in his own good time. You shouldn't worry. *Ach*, I mean, I'm sure you are, but maybe try not to." She clamped her mouth closed, even though she had much more to say. But telling Esther that the whole thing was a little unsettling would only upset her more.

"Lizzie didn't lose any sleep." Esther stopped rubbing her temples and took a sip of coffee. "I can still hear her snoring in my mind." She shook her head. "I don't know how anyone that tiny can produce so much noise."

"Earplugs," Rose said with a taut nod of her head. "I have several more pairs, and I'm happy to give you some. They come in different sizes, but they basically all work the same way. And—"

"*Nee*, I don't need them." Esther went back to rubbing her temples. Rose was pretty sure she was talking too much again. "I normally go right to sleep so Lizzie's snoring in the next room usually doesn't bother me." Sighing, she leaned back in her chair. "I'm also upset about Gus."

"Because you think he sent the flowers? I told you that I think he did. He looks at you sometimes like he's lovesick." She shivered, unable to picture sweet Esther with Grumpy Gus. "You might have to be firm with him to get him to admit it. You—"

"I'm upset with Gus about using a hospital for a vacation destination." Esther stared into her coffee as she ran her hand around the rim. Rose had heard about Gus's little vacation. "It's so deceitful, and he's taking nurses and doctors away from real patients."

"I don't know why you're so surprised," Lizzie said, yawning as she came into the kitchen with her arms stretched above her head. "He's an awful man." She poured herself a cup of coffee, then sat down across from Esther. "But I'll admit, such a stunt is low, even for Gus."

Rose wasn't a fan of Gus's, but she felt the need to defend him a little. "He's very *gut* to his cats and has been from the beginning. Even though he was upset when Whiskers had a litter, he worried over all the kittens, almost like a parent. Remember how I helped him with the kitties at first? And they mostly stay near him, inside the cottage or on the porch." She paused when Lizzie scowled. "So he can't be all bad."

"No one is *all* bad," Lizzie said softly. Esther's eyes widened in surprise and so did Rose's. "If he was *all* bad, then he wouldn't be able to see the goodness in Esther. Surely he knew you were upset when you left his hospital room."

"*Ach*, he knew." Esther took a sip of coffee. "And no pie for that man. Not for a long time."

Lizzie snickered. "Serves him right."

Rose didn't want to make things worse, but this was one time she couldn't stifle her words. "I strongly believe Gus sent those flowers because he doesn't know how to confront you about his feelings, Esther."

"Well, taking a fake vacation in a hospital didn't earn him any points." She lowered her head and ran her finger around the rim of her coffee cup.

Rose and Lizzie locked eyes. Was Esther admitting that Gus had romantic intentions toward her? And why was she allowing herself to get so upset with him?

Esther was sure they were wrong about the flowers. Even though it was somewhat disturbing to receive the anonymous gift, she was equally as upset about what Gus had done. The man was brash, had no manners, and was often very rude. But his deceitfulness had gotten under Esther's skin.

"I know you both think Gus sent the flowers, but I'm sure he did not." Esther's head was splitting. "This whole thing is upsetting to me. I don't want to discuss it any further." She slid her chair back, then shuffled to her room, closing the door behind her. Rarely did her feathers get ruffled, but she was about to take flight. Anger bubbled up inside her, and she was tempted to go back to the hospital to tell them how Gus was taking advantage of the staff there. But there were other ways to let the man know she was upset with him. No more pie or leftovers was just for starters.

Why am I so upset about this? Maybe it was because she'd seen such progress with him over the past year or so. It felt like work undone. Or, as Lizzie said, it was low, even for Gus.

Esther lay on the bed and clasped her hands atop her stomach, which was grumbling for food. But instead of going back to the kitchen to eat, she closed her eyes and prayed for sleep.

It was nearing three o'clock when the three ladies from Texas knocked at the front door. Rose brushed the flour from her black apron and went to greet the women. Esther had been napping on and off all day, and Lizzie had gone to the Bargain Center for a few things they were out of.

As Rose opened the screen door and introduced herself, she noticed that Gus's truck was back in the driveway.

Each of the women had a small suitcase on rollers, and they appeared to be about Esther and Lizzie's age, in their seventies.

"If you'll leave your suitcases just inside the door, I'll get them to your rooms. I've set out some appetizers and melon punch in the dining room if you'd like to follow me." Rose motioned with her hand. "There's a nice cross breeze also."

"I've never had melon punch." The tallest of the women, dressed in long white shorts, a red T-shirt, and white sandals, smiled. She didn't appear to be sweating as much as the two smaller women, who were both dressed similarly but with different colored shirts.

"It's very refreshing." Rose had made the punch the night before, then about an hour ago, she poured it into a watermelon she'd sliced in half. She'd thought about her mother the entire time she prepared it. How many times had she watched her mom dice and deseed the watermelon and add pineapple juice and lemonade to a large bowl? Once everything was mashed and there was mostly juice left, her mother would pour it into a watermelon half and add small chunks of whatever fruit she had on hand. Rose had added a few diced strawberries. Her heart was suddenly back in Ohio. She corresponded with her mother regularly because it was the right thing to do, even though certain subjects were taboo. It felt good to recall memories about the punch, but unwanted thoughts always fought for space in her recollections.

Rose had three battery-operated fans in the dining room, and as the grandfather clock chimed three times, the women commented on what a lovely piece of furniture it was.

"It's over a hundred years old," Rose said as she poured each woman a glass of punch. She waved a hand near the table. "Please enjoy, and I'll cart your bags upstairs, with your permission."

"Thank you," they said in unison, and Rose heard them chatting among themselves as she took each suitcase to the second floor. She was grateful they were small and not very heavy. Some folks had enormous luggage. The younger ones and those with husbands carried their own bags, but Rose always offered to be of assistance if their guests were older.

When she placed the last of the suitcases in each room, she went across the hall to her own room and looked out the window. Edgar had mowed the yard the day before, and Rose breathed in the aroma of freshly cut grass. She'd been trying to put Benjamin out of her mind, but she would likely see him at worship service on Sunday. Would he speak to her? Perhaps he would avoid her? What had begun as hurt had slowly morphed into anger. What kind of man kisses a woman then never calls? It was easy enough to toss blame back on herself. *I shouldn't have let him kiss me.* She was lost in thought and regret when she saw Gus emerge from the cottage. Two black cats scurried up the porch steps, and Gus scooped them into his arms, nuzzling both kitties with his face.

If a person didn't know Gus, you'd think he was just a kind old man—especially at moments like this. He set the cats down, filled their bowls with food, and went back inside the cottage.

Rose needed to return to the guests downstairs. Esther was just walking out of her bedroom when Rose stepped onto the landing. She was fully dressed, complete with her prayer covering.

"I didn't mean to sleep so much today. I hear guests in the dining room. Is everything all right?" Esther pulled a tissue from her apron pocket and dabbed at the sweat on her forehead. She seemed to sweat more than Rose or Lizzie. Maybe because Esther was a larger woman. Or possibly because she'd been worrying a lot.

Rose nodded. "*Ya*, they are enjoying appetizers and melon punch." She paused, biting her lip, careful not to ramble. "Gus is home."

Esther stiffened as her lips thinned with anger. "I hope he enjoyed his vacation."

Rose cringed at Esther's hostile tone. It was unlike her. "I saw him on the porch loving on his kitties a few minutes ago."

"It is a *gut* thing he has those cats because there will be no more treats or leftovers from me."

Rose couldn't help but feel a little sorry for him. Esther and Jayce were Gus's only friends. But since Jayce had a wife and baby on the way, as well as a job, he wasn't able to stop by as often anymore. "Lizzie went to the Bargain Center to get flour and yeast. She should be back soon, unless she's shopping. You know how she does, just browsing for things that we don't really need but she gets anyway. But I guess it makes her happy, and—" She forced herself to stop, biting her lip, which was surely swollen by now.

"You've handled everything today, Rose. Go take some time for yourself. I'll chat with our guests." Esther rubbed Rose's arm before she started toward the dining room.

Time to herself would only make her think of Benjamin. She trudged up the stairs anyway.

∞

Benjamin got home about four, and his mother had the table set. Without even looking, he knew chicken and dumplings would be served for supper. It was an aroma he recognized right away—the smell of chicken simmering with carrots, celery, and dumplings. His mother had been making his favorites all week long. More and more, he thought about getting his own place, but in addition to suffering from loneliness, he might starve.

"Did you finish your last job for the week?" His mother placed a freshly baked loaf of bread on the table.

"*Ya*, nothing scheduled for tomorrow." He hung his hat on the rack and sat at the kitchen table. His mother put out jams, jelly, and chowchow, then carried the pot of chicken and dumplings to the table. After she sat down, they lowered their heads in prayer.

"I know you haven't been to worship service since we arrived, but I think it's important for you to go Sunday," his mother said after they'd prayed. She reached for a slice of bread.

"I am." Benjamin had felt badly about skipping the service, but even though mingling with people he didn't know was unappealing, he wasn't doing right by God if he used that as an excuse not to worship. He wondered if Rose would be there. The kisses they shared still lingered in his mind.

His mother shuffled her food around on her plate, twisting her mouth from side to side as she kept her head down. "Benny, maybe you should give that woman, Rose, another chance."

Benjamin set his fork down and waited for his mother to look at him. "*Nee.*"

"But you said she was beautiful, and"—she shrugged—"one date isn't really enough to get to know a person."

"*Mamm.*" He glared at her. "I don't need you to worry about *mei* love life, or lack thereof. Rose is beautiful . . . but the woman doesn't talk at all. And since I struggle with that, too, we are not a *gut* match." Again, the kisses flashed through his mind. "Do you want me to move out? Is that why you're so anxious for me to find a *fraa*?"

His mother's jaw dropped as she brought a hand to her chest. "*Nee*, of course I don't want you to move out. I mean, I want you to find someone to share your life with, but you don't interfere with *mei* life, *sohn*. I'd miss you if you left, but I pray that you'll find that special someone."

Benjamin had just about decided that wasn't going to happen.

Esther bid their three guests farewell Saturday morning. As was often the case during the summer, they chose not to spend a second night. They tried to pay for the night anyway, but as always,

Esther said she appreciated the offer but that payment for the unused night wasn't necessary. The English were just too dependent on their air-conditioning. She doubted they'd have many guests the remainder of the month and through August.

Rose was upstairs, already starting to clean the rooms the ladies had stayed in. Lizzie was putting an apple pie in the oven when Esther came into the kitchen.

"I hope Gus can smell that pie baking all the way from his cottage." Esther sat down at the table and picked up a chocolate chip cookie from a platter, taking a big bite.

Lizzie closed the oven, turned to face Esther, and folded her arms across her chest. "It's about time you saw how detestable that man is."

Esther swallowed and reached for another cookie. "He'd been making positive strides toward being kinder. He can truly be a *gut* person when he wants to be, but I'm having a hard time getting past this deceitful hospital vacation."

Lizzie wiped her mouth with her apron, and Esther was about to say something just to release some anger. She took a big breath instead, and after she'd slowly released it, she ate the second cookie. When she was done, she looked at Lizzie, who was scowling.

"What are you looking at me like that for?" Esther hoped she wasn't going to bring up the flowers again.

Her sister continued to scowl. "I think you care more about Gus than you let on." She paused, raising her chin a little. "That's what I think."

Esther sighed. "Of course I care about the man. Why do you

think I've strongly encouraged him to change some of his ways? But you and Rose need to stop saying the flowers are from Gus. We have a friendship that barely hangs on by a thread. And that's all."

Lizzie tapped a finger to her chin. "Hmm . . . I seem to recall Jayce saying Gus likes you more than as just a friend."

"Rubbish. And I'm tired of all this talk." Esther reached for another cookie, but pulled her hand back. Her middle was growing. Partly from lack of exercise and no more extra trips upstairs or other strenuous activity. But it might not hurt to ease off sweets a little. Maybe if she lost a little weight, her knees wouldn't give her such grief.

"Then I guess it's back to suspects one and two, Harvey or Edgar." Lizzie raised an eyebrow. "Don't you want to at least ask them if they sent the flowers?"

Esther recalled how awkward it was to question Gus about the delivery. "*Nee*, I don't." She lifted herself up and went outside to get some fresh air.

As she stood on the porch, she pondered even more about the lovely arrangement and wished no one had sent her flowers. At first, it was rather exciting to think someone might have taken an interest in her, especially at her age. But Esther had no interest in a romantic relationship, and she really did not think her suitor was Harvey, Edgar, or Gus. Her excitement had turned to a sense of dread. The gift made no sense.

She trekked across the yard toward Naomi and Amos's house to see Regina and Eve. There was nothing two precious toddlers couldn't cure, and that included Esther's foul mood.

She glanced to her right. Gus was sitting in his chair on the porch with two cats in his lap. He was looking down and didn't seem to notice her walking across the stretch between the three houses. Esther recalled what Rose had said about his fondness of the animals. If only he could treat humans as well as he treated those cats.

Chapter 7

Benjamin reminded himself that he was at the Troyers' house to worship the Lord, not to worry about how Rose would react to seeing him, assuming she was somewhere in the crowd. The Troyers had a large older home that had panels separating some of the rooms. Even with the panels removed and the expanded space, there were still people standing in the back of both sides of the room. The setup was similar to what it had been in Bedford—women on one side, men on the other side facing the ladies, and the bishop and elders were in the middle. And instead of just wooden benches, more comfortable chairs had also been placed toward the back of the room for older women and those expecting a child.

When he finally saw Rose, his heart skipped an unexpected beat. *She's so beautiful*. Her eyes met briefly with his, but she quickly looked away. Her chin looked a little higher, too, after she saw him. Benjamin couldn't blame her.

He spent most of the three-hour service sneaking glances at

her and trying to decide if he should apologize about the kisses. Twice he'd caught her looking at him. She was almost dangerous to be around. He worried the temptation to kiss her again would always be there.

When the service was over, he wound his way through the crowd until he found her. His words felt stuck in his throat, and he prayed he could convey how badly he felt for taking advantage of her. But every time he got close to her, she rushed off in another direction. With every step he took trying to catch up to her, he realized he must have really hurt her feelings. He felt like a jerk.

He was about to give up trying when he saw her go onto the porch. By the time he caught up to her, she was chatting with two other women. Benjamin took a deep breath and approached the trio.

"*Wie bischt.*" He glanced at each woman, his eyes landing back on the prettiest one in the group. "Can I talk to you for a minute?"

"Um, *ya*." She excused herself and walked alongside him until they were far enough out in the yard to have some privacy.

She folded her arms across her chest, lifted her chin, and smiled. Benjamin didn't think it was a real smile.

"Uh, I think I owe you an apology." He wanted to get this over with. It was difficult enough being in this large crowd. This situation caused his chest to tighten. "I shouldn't have kissed you, and—"

"I shouldn't have let you. So, no apology necessary." After another fake smile, she spun on her heels and marched back toward the house.

Benjamin tried to identify what he was feeling as he watched her storm away. In addition to being a jerk, he also felt . . . regret.

Esther shook her head, then glanced at Lizzie, who was standing beside her near the window. "That didn't look like it went well," Esther said, followed by a heavy sigh.

"I was so sure those two would hit it off." Lizzie shuffled her teeth around.

"Quit doing that with your dentures." Esther rolled her eyes.

"It helps me think."

"*Wie bischt*, Lizzie."

A woman Esther had never met spoke to Esther's sister, then introduced herself as Catherine King, Benjamin's mother.

After polite greetings were exchanged, Lizzie said, "I thought for sure that your *sohn* and our Rose would be a good fit."

"I met Rose earlier." Catherine lifted an eyebrow. "You were right. She is absolutely gorgeous." She paused as she tilted her head to one side. "But you said she was bubbly and talked a lot."

Lizzie chuckled lightly. "We *lieb* that *maedel*, but that might be an understatement."

Catherine frowned. "Benjamin said she barely talked at all, that she only answered in short sentences or one-word answers. He said it was very awkward."

Esther and Lizzie exchanged glances. "Perhaps we aren't talking about the same woman," Esther said. She had noticed Rose not being quite as talkative lately, but she still exploded with feelings via narrative when she needed to.

"That's her, right?" Catherine casually tipped her head in the direction where Rose was talking with Naomi and Evelyn.

"*Ya*," Esther and Lizzie answered at the same time.

"Hmm, well, I'm sorry it didn't work out." Catherine waved to someone across the room. "Please excuse me. Esther, it was nice to meet you."

Esther and Lizzie were left with their mouths hanging open after she walked away.

Once they'd recovered from the shock, Lizzie went to help clean up in the kitchen. Esther glanced around the room, sure that people were staring at her today, and she wondered how many people Sarah Mae had told about her flower inquiry. What must people think about a woman her age receiving flowers from a man? And most likely an English man. Sighing again, she shuffled to the kitchen to do her part.

Rose wondered if she'd done the right thing. Maybe she should have listened to what else Benjamin had to say. She'd left in her own buggy right after the meal. It had been hard to fight tears when she saw Benjamin, and Montgomery wasn't a big city. She wanted to keep her dignity intact and hoped Benjamin hadn't told anyone about the kissing. Rose wished she hadn't told Esther and Lizzie and that she'd downplayed the date. Even though Benjamin had been quiet, she'd been interested in getting to know him. He humiliated her by not bothering to call or visit. It was too late for an apology.

It's never too late for an apology, she reminded herself.

By the time she got home, she'd cried so much that all she wanted to do was lie down.

Esther had convinced Lizzie to let her drive the buggy home from worship service. They left not long after Rose since they were worried about her. And confused.

"That girl must have forced herself silent, thinking Benjamin wouldn't want to hear her talking too much," Esther said as she pulled the buggy into the driveway.

Lizzie groaned. "Of all the times to choose to be quiet. We've got to get those two together again."

"I wonder what was said out in the yard. It was a short conversation, and Rose didn't look happy when she walked away." Esther pulled back on the reins and brought the horse to a stop.

"*Ach*, well, Benjamin did kiss her and then not call or stop by." Lizzie stepped out of the buggy. "Maybe he asked her out again and Rose's pride held her back."

Pride was to be avoided, but Esther suspected that might be the case. "I think we should talk to her."

"I agree."

They found Rose in the kitchen when they went inside, and it was obvious she'd been crying. Her cheeks were red and her eyes slightly swollen.

"We saw you talking to Benjamin." Lizzie adjusted her teeth. "How did that go?"

Esther wished her sister would have eased into the conversation, but that wasn't Lizzie's way.

"He apologized for kissing me." Rose folded her arms across her chest. "I told him it was fine and walked away."

Lizzie squinted her eyes as she faced off with Rose, also folding her arms across her chest. "His mother said that you barely said a word during the date. If that's true, you weren't being yourself."

Rose held her stance. "*Ach*, apparently being myself hasn't worked out well." She paused as tears formed in the corners of her eyes. "I hear you two talking, more than you know." She glanced at Esther before turning back to Lizzie. "You both think I talk too much. I thought if I was quiet and tried to listen more that Benjamin might like me."

Lizzie slapped a hand to her forehead and sighed. "That was one date when you should have been entirely yourself."

Esther cleared her throat, hoping to defuse the situation that seemed to be developing. "Rose . . ." Her stomach churned knowing the girl had overheard them probably too many times. "Everyone is different and unique, and—"

"I've heard you, Esther." Rose's glare ping-ponged back and forth between Esther and Lizzie. "Both of you. I talk too much. I tend to ramble on about things, even though I don't really mean to, and there's a reason for it, I think, but—" She stopped abruptly.

Esther glanced at Lizzie before turning back to Rose. She couldn't imagine what could make a person have a tendency to talk a lot, but Rose remained silent.

"What's the reason?" Lizzie asked as she leaned back against the counter, her expression softening as she lowered her arms to her sides.

Rose hung her head and a tear spilled onto the wood floor.

"It doesn't matter," Esther said as she went to Rose and pulled her into a hug. Then she eased the girl away. "Look at me, Rose." She gently lifted her chin. "You are special because of who you are. God created you exactly the way you were meant to be. He would want you to be yourself in every situation." She paused to offer a sympathetic smile. "Hon, we *lieb* you. Surely you know that. But we're old, so sometimes we can't keep up with your thoughts as fast as you are able to voice them. However, we've been wrong to encourage you to be anyone but who you are. And for that, we're very sorry."

"When I was younger, I thought maybe my relationships didn't work out because I couldn't cook. Or, that's what I told myself. I think I've always known that I talk too much." Rose paused, and when her lip began to tremble, along with the tears streaming down her face, Esther thought her heart might break. "It's probably too late. I'm twenty-five. Benjamin is probably wondering what's wrong with me—the reason I'm not married yet. I forced myself to be quiet and politely answer only when spoken to. It wasn't that I didn't want to get to know him. I did. But for once, I thought I'd let the man lead the way in a conversation. And"—she shrugged—"I'm doing it again, rambling."

Lizzie walked to where Esther and Rose were standing on the other side of the kitchen. She gently eased Esther out of the way and wrapped her arms around Rose. After the hug, Lizzie reached up and wiped away Rose's tears with her thumbs and smiled. "Hon, Esther is right. You are beautiful inside and out, and just because Esther and I can't always keep up with you, that doesn't mean you should change. I think you might have met your future husband. He just doesn't know it yet."

Rose shook her head. "I don't know how you can say that. He never called or asked me out."

"Because he didn't go out with Rose Petersheim," Lizzie said. "He just went out with someone who looks like her. And he kissed you because he's attracted to you. Once he gets to know the real you, he will love you. I'm sure of it."

Rose shook her head. "*Nee*. I'm tired. I'm tired of trying. People have been fixing me up since I was old enough to date." Rose was seemingly lost in thought as her eyes drifted somewhere past them. "As soon as *mei* father would allow me to date, that is."

"I don't think you should necessarily give up on Benjamin." Esther felt it was time to interject, although Lizzie had handled things better than Esther would have thought. "Rose, Benjamin is shy. Very shy, according to his *mudder*. He was looking forward to going out with someone bubbly and vivacious, like you. A person who would carry the conversation. And you are both such pretty people." Esther smiled. "I suppose *handsome* is the correct word for Benjamin."

Rose shrugged. "Then I guess I blew it. I'm going to go lie down if there isn't anything you need me to do right now."

Lizzie stomped one of her bare feet. "*Nee, nee, nee*. You can't give up that easy."

"Let the child go, Lizzie." Esther brushed back hair that was matted to the tears on Rose's face. "You go rest. We can talk later."

"I just don't think there is anything else to say about Benjamin or any other man."

Esther and Lizzie watched Rose go upstairs. When they heard

her bedroom door close and were sure she was out of earshot, Lizzie said, "There has got to be a way to get those two together."

"After seeing each other every week at worship service, maybe they will choose to give it another go." Esther sat on a kitchen chair and stretched her legs forward. It was her left knee that gave her the most trouble.

"Shy or not, someone is going to latch on to that handsome Benjamin. I saw the young single ladies eyeing him at worship service. We don't have time to wait around." Lizzie rubbed her chin. "He's a plumber, right?"

"I believe so." Esther yawned. It was nearing that time of day.

Lizzie stomped across the kitchen and pulled the basement door open. She grabbed the flashlight they kept on a hook inside the door. "Be right back."

Esther stared at the plate of cookies on the table and forced herself not to reach for one. The apple pie Lizzie made was next to the platter of cookies. She hoped Gus got his fill of pie at the hospital since she wouldn't be taking him any.

Lizzie came back up the basement stairs and closed the door with one hand, clutching a wrench in the other.

"What are you doing?" Esther forced herself to stand up when Lizzie headed for the stairs that led to the second floor. "Lizzie?"

Her sister turned around and put a finger over her lips, an indication for Esther to be quiet, then Lizzie tiptoed upstairs. Esther didn't have a good feeling about whatever Lizzie was up to.

There was a loud bang upstairs, and Lizzie bolted down the stairs faster than Esther had ever seen the woman move. Her eyes were wild. "Oops. Overkill." She yanked the basement door open and took the flashlight from her pocket. After she'd illuminated the stairs, she rushed down. Esther heard the wrench hit the concrete floor.

Is that water running upstairs?

Rose came into the kitchen, breathless. "There's water pouring out of the pipe underneath the sink upstairs."

"Where's the main water shutoff, Esther?" Lizzie yelled from the basement.

Esther eyed the steps leading down to the basement. She'd get down them okay, but coming back up would be difficult. "On the right, behind the hot-water heater!"

Lizzie, what have you done?

"What happened?" Rose was still trying to catch her breath.

Lizzie came from the basement, breathing hard. "Rose, hon. I'm sorry to ask this, but can you get some towels and see what you can do about the puddles in the bathroom? I was trying to fix that leaky sink and made the situation worse."

Rose and Esther looked at each other, equally confused. "I use that bathroom daily, and I've never noticed the sink leaking," Rose said.

"Hurry, child. I'm sure a lot of water spilled out of that pipe before I was able to turn off the main valve." Lizzie gave Rose a gentle push. "I'm worn out from running down to the basement and back. And Esther's knees aren't going to make it up the stairs."

"*Ya*, of course. Right away." Rose hurried to the stairs and took them two at a time.

Lizzie shuffled her teeth around, then smiled. "We're going to need a plumber."

Benjamin had rushed to The Peony Inn after a frantic call from one of the widows—Lizzie, he thought she said.

But now that he was here, he took his time tethering his horse. He recalled the older woman saying she'd turned off the main water to the house, so that took away the sense of urgency. He would be forced to face Rose unless she purposely stayed out of sight.

Esther and Lizzie were on the couch when he tapped lightly on the screen door.

"Come in."

Benjamin cautiously stepped over the threshold. Lizzie had a wet rag across her forehead and her head leaned back against the couch cushion. Both women had their bare feet propped up on the coffee table.

"*Danki* for coming so quickly." Lizzie moaned as she lifted her head. "I'm afraid all the rushing around to turn off the water left me a little light-headed. The problem is in the upstairs bathroom. Esther's knees won't make it up there." She pointed to the staircase. "Last room at the end of the hall."

Benjamin nodded as his chest tightened. *Will Rose be upstairs?*

He trudged up the stairs, and when he reached the hallway, all he could see were two bare feet sticking out of the bathroom. Rose was on her hands and knees, and the rest of her body was blocked by the partially open door.

"Oh my. This is a lot of water. I can't imagine what caused this pipe to come apart like this. I'm doing the best I can to get this water up. I heard a loud bang, but I was changing clothes at the time. I spilled pickle juice on *mei* dress earlier when I was carting out a platter of pickles and olives before the meal. I've smelled like a pickle ever since."

Benjamin was at the entrance to the bathroom, grinning.

"I've already used a dozen towels trying to keep the water from reaching the wood floor in the hallway. I think I'm going to need more towels. Oh dear, this looks bad. I'm fairly certain that water in the hallway could cause the wood to buckle. It wouldn't be *gut*."

This was more than the woman had spoken throughout their entire date. He was about to open his mouth to speak so she knew it was him standing in the hallway, but she started talking again before he had a chance.

"I know this is the last thing you needed, Lizzie."

She must have assumed it was Lizzie since Esther had trouble getting upstairs.

"But as you know, my day wasn't very *gut* either. Seeing Benjamin rattled me. But I've decided not to shed one more tear over him. Handsome or not, he shouldn't have kissed me if he had no intention of seeing me again outside of worship service."

Benjamin's breath seized in his chest. He wished he could do an about-face and hurry downstairs, especially if he'd made her cry.

"So I just want you to know that the crying is over. But I do think we're going to need a plumber. Just be sure it's anyone besides Benjamin King."

She stood up and pushed the door open wider. Rose's prayer covering was tilted to one side of her head, and she was holding an armful of wet towels, which she haphazardly tossed in the bathtub. When she turned to face him, her big brown eyes widened and her mouth fell open. Stains of scarlet filled her cheeks as her bottom lip began to quiver.

Benjamin was smiling. He couldn't help it. *But please don't cry.* Their eyes stayed locked for several long seconds.

"How long have you been standing there?" She slammed her hands to her hips as she blew loose strands of dark hair away from her face.

"Long enough." He raised an eyebrow, unsure if the continued reddening of her face was due to embarrassment or anger.

"It isn't *gut* manners to let a person ramble on without announcing your presence. You should have made yourself known the moment you got here, and"—her hostile glare and gritted teeth confirmed she was angry—"why are you smiling? Do you think this is funny?"

Benjamin tried to break from the smile, but she was even more beautiful when she was mad. And when she was talking. Even though she was furious with him.

He set down his workbox, then lifted one shoulder and slowly lowered it. "*Ach. ya.* It is kind of funny."

Her nostrils flared as she took a step closer to him. Benjamin tried to stop homing in on her lips as she pointed a finger at him. "Since you never called me or stopped to visit, there is no reason why I should bottle *mei* feelings with you. It was very wrong for you to kiss me. It was even more inappropriate for me to allow such a thing. But when something like that happens, it is common courtesy to at least pay a social call." She slapped her hands to her sides. "That's just having *gut* manners. You don't get to kiss a person the way you kissed me—twice—and simply say you're sorry." She held up a palm. "But you did apologize, and I never formally accepted, so I'm telling you now that I accept your apology. And that's all there is to it." She shrugged. "We needn't have any more discussion on the subject."

Why did Benjamin feel there was more discussion coming?

She stepped closer again, close enough he could have kissed her, and there was nothing he wanted more. "Can you please wipe that smug grin from your face?"

Benjamin forced his mouth closed and clamped his lips together.

"I am going to go have a word with Esther and Lizzie." She inched around him, careful not to brush against him, and she looked at him as if his touch would burn her. She was halfway down the hall when she glanced over her shoulder and caught him gaping at her. "The problem is that way." Stretching out her arm, she pointed toward the bathroom.

Benjamin smiled again as she stomped down the stairs and out of sight. He'd never been so entranced with a woman in his life. This wasn't the same person he went out with last weekend. This woman ignited his senses. She wasn't just beautiful. She was feisty, outspoken, and filled with emotions that seemed to scatter in every direction like pieces of a puzzle that hadn't been put together yet.

He'd never wanted to get to know a person more than he wanted to know Rose Petersheim. Now that the real woman had shown up.

Chapter 8

Lizzie had her eyes covered with her hands when she heard Rose coming down the stairs. "We're in trouble," she muttered.

Esther couldn't argue. They'd heard every word spoken. "How were we to know she would say all those things? It sounded like she didn't even know he was there and listening." She gulped when Rose entered the living room with her hands fisted at her sides and her lips thinned with anger. Rose had a tendency to cry. But not right now. She was clearly livid. "Oh dear," Esther said cringing.

Lizzie barely uncovered her eyes, but covered them again when she caught a glimpse of Rose's fury. "Uh-oh," she said in a muffled voice.

Esther flinched. "I'm afraid we heard everything. It sounded as if you didn't know he was listening."

"I am humiliated more than I have ever been in *mei* life. Well, except for . . ." She paused, that faraway look in her eyes again. "Never mind. Let's just consider this the most embarrassed I have ever been. What kind of person lets someone ramble on like that without announcing their presence?"

Lizzie still had her face covered as she sunk into the couch cushions. Esther eased her legs from the coffee table and sat taller. "We're sorry."

Rose threw her head back so hard her prayer covering fell on the floor. She picked it up right away, but when she put it back on her head, it was lopsided. "I told you not to call Benjamin," she said with her hands clenched at her sides again.

Esther pointed to Lizzie and mouthed, "She did it."

Lizzie slammed her hands to her lap, then turned to Esther. "I saw that."

Esther shrugged. "It's the truth." Although Esther hadn't done anything to discourage Lizzie from making the call. She stifled a yawn. They'd missed their afternoon nap due to their matchmaking effort.

Rose drew in a big breath as she tapped one foot nervously. "*Ach*, well, it doesn't really matter what Benjamin thinks of me. I think he's made his feelings clear since our date." She raised her chin as she held her position. Esther felt sorry for her. With her red face, flared nostrils, tilted prayer covering, and continued toe tapping, she looked a bit out of control.

There was a loud noise, followed by a fairly loud "ow" from upstairs.

Rose threw her hands up in the air. "That's great. I suppose I will have to go check on our inefficient plumber who has clearly bumped his noggin or something." She spun around and marched up the stairs.

Lizzie uncovered her face. "Do you think he did that on purpose?" she asked in a whisper.

"I don't know." Esther grinned. "But Rose didn't waste any time going upstairs."

"See, I did a *gut* thing." Lizzie smiled like a Cheshire cat.

"It was a bit extreme. You could have flooded the *haus*."

"I only flooded the upstairs bathroom a tiny bit," Lizzie said in a whisper.

They held their breath as they strained to hear what was happening on the second floor.

Rose's heart thumped wildly as she went up the stairs. Somehow she had to regain a fragment of her dignity. Benjamin hadn't said much during her rant. Not surprising since Esther said he was shy. But his smile told her he was laughing on the inside.

When she got to the end of the hall, the bathroom door was open. It was one of two bathrooms, the smaller one that Rose used most often. There was a claw-foot tub, double sink with cabinets underneath, and a commode. Benjamin was lying on his back in an awkward position with his head inside the cabinet. Rose glanced around at some of the items he'd had to move to gain access to the plumbing. Mostly cleaning supplies, along with some extra bars of lavender soap.

"We heard you say 'ow' from downstairs. Are you all right?" She stood right outside the bathroom.

"I bumped *mei* head." He had a tool in his hand and was twisting something around the pipe. "I'm okay." He groaned as he shifted his position. "I don't know how this pipe came loose. There's a dent in it, almost like something hit it."

"Or *someone*," Rose mumbled.

"Ow!"

Rose stepped back as he slithered from beneath the sink with a hand on his head and stood up. As much as she wanted him to be on his way, she was a little concerned that he was bleeding on the left side of his forehead. She gave him a clean hand towel that had been hanging on the rack just inside the door. He reached to take the towel. Rose gasped when she saw how much blood there was on his hand.

Instinctively, she moved closer and took the rag from him. "Let me have a look." She flinched as she eased the towel from his forehead, but quickly put it back and held it there. "I don't think you need stitches, but at the least you need a butterfly bandage. And it needs to be cleaned up. I think I better apply some antibacterial ointment too. It looks like a hole in your head. What did you hit? Oh, I bet I know. I cut *mei* hand on a protruding nail in that cabinet one time. I was reorganizing everything, and I bumped against it. Of course, I didn't full-on smash *mei* head into it, so it wasn't nearly as bad. Hold this." She took his hand and pressed it against the towel on the side of his head. He had large hands, slightly rough from his work, she assumed. Rose was tall, but he still towered over her. After she'd observed his broad shoulders and beautiful green eyes for way too long, she edged around him and found a bandage and ointment. She also wet a clean washrag as best she could. With the water still turned off, only a small amount of water dribbled from the faucet.

"Um . . . you don't have to do that," he said when she removed the bloody towel and began to blot his forehead with the damp rag.

She looked up and locked eyes with him, piercing the short distance between them. Neither one of them spoke at first as she continued to hold the rag against his head. They were close enough to kiss. Was he recalling the end of their date like she was?

"Would you rather do it yourself?" She heard the slightly venomous tone in her voice.

"*Nee*." He grinned.

"Why do you grin and smile so much?" Rose wrinkled her forehead as she shook her head.

"I usually don't."

"Well, I'm glad I amuse you." She took his hand and put it atop the moist rag while she opened the ointment and took the backing off the bandage. Then she brushed his hand away and dabbed ointment on the injury.

He pulled away a little. "You're not very gentle."

"*Ach*. Sorry." Now she was the one grinning. She placed the bandage on his head and stepped back. "I think you'll live."

"*Danki*." He touched the spot.

"Don't touch it. You'll irritate it. Clean it again and change the bandage tonight." She folded her arms across her chest. "Are you done?" She nodded to the open cabinet.

"*Ya.*"

She waited. He didn't make a move to gather his supplies.

"Why are you staring at me?" She let out a heavy sigh.

His eyes darkened with an emotion Rose couldn't identify. "I'm sorry if I made you cry," he said softly. "I-I just don't date very well. I mean, I'm not very *gut* at it, I guess."

Rose's hands found their way to her hips again. "I talk too much. I'm trying to be a better listener. Our date was torturous because I thought if I didn't talk so much that maybe you'd like me." She threw her arms in the air, then put them back on her hips. "I don't date very well either. I have a lot on my mind, and I tend to dominate just about every conversation I'm involved in. It no longer matters what you think of me because *mei* dignity got up and hightailed it the moment I turned around and saw you had heard everything I said." She paused, glaring at him. "Do I think you're handsome? *Ya*, I do. But that doesn't justify allowing you to kiss me. Look where that got me." She grunted and heard how unladylike it sounded. "And then I'm told you're shy and that I should have talked more, and—"

"*Ya*, you should have." He grinned. "I like listening to you. It's cute . . . I mean, the way you're so honest and . . . and able to share your feelings so freely."

Rose felt the warmth crawling up the back of her neck to her ears and then filling her cheeks. She might have been angry before—mostly with herself—for not turning around to see who was behind her, but at the moment, she was speechless.

Benjamin waited for her to say something, but her face kept turning redder and redder. It was as if all the roadblocks between them had been kicked over. Now he knew she was attracted to him also. He was especially attracted to this new whirlwind tornado of a woman who said exactly what was on her mind—something he needed to do more of.

"Do you want to have supper with me Wednesday?" He waited for the familiar tightening in his chest to come, for his palms to feel clammy. But instead there was a fluttering in his stomach, an anticipation that she would say yes.

"Why?" She blinked her eyes a few times.

"What do you mean, why?" He swallowed hard and took a deep breath.

They were still standing close to each other, but Benjamin focused on her eyes, even though her lips had a strong hold on him.

"Neither of us enjoyed the last date."

Ouch. He wasn't sure if she was just saying that or if she really had as miserable a time as he had. She'd acted like she was enjoying herself, even though she was brutally quiet the entire evening.

He was tempted to just let it go, but this woman intrigued him.

While he was trying to figure out how to respond, she said, "I'm sorry if that sounds harsh. I had high hopes that we would go out again. I was proud of myself for controlling my jabbering." She rolled her eyes. "But I'm not going on another date where I have to be painfully quiet the entire time."

"I don't want you to be. I want you to be yourself."

She laughed. "*Ach*, well, you've certainly seen the real me today."

"I like what I see." He heard the seductiveness in his voice and quickly cleared his throat, surprised he'd verbalized the thought. "I'd like to try again."

She stared at him for several seconds. "*Ya*, okay. We can try again." She held up a finger. "But there will be no more kissing unless it's warranted and means something more than physical attraction. And we will be completely honest with each other." She scowled. "Not just kiss and run."

He couldn't stop grinning. She scowled more. "Sorry," he said. "I've heard of kiss and tell, but not kiss and run." He was surprised how easily conversation came with her, but she amused him.

After they'd settled on a time, she began to tell him in detail about how to tend to his wound. He found himself hanging on her every word.

∞

Esther and Lizzie were thrilled to hear that Rose was going out with Benjamin on Wednesday night, even though Rose wasn't cheerfully optimistic like she'd been after their first date.

"I'm not sure if he's taking me out because he feels bad that he made me cry. Or maybe he feels guilty. Or—"

"He's taking you out because he saw the real you today." Lizzie spit her teeth in her hand. "Stupid teeth."

"Go back to the dentist if your dentures are giving you trouble again." Esther straightened some magazines on the coffee table just as the clock in the dining room chimed six times. Yawning, she was planning on going to bed extra early tonight.

Heavy footsteps coming up the porch steps caught their attention.

"Oh no." Lizzie groaned. "I'm going to *mei* room."

"Go to your room," Gus said through the screen door. He eased it open and stuck just his head over the threshold.

"Um . . . I'll be in my room if you need anything." Rose spun around and hurried up the stairs.

Esther sat down on the couch and crossed one leg over the other. "Well, you can sure clear out a room."

Gus was normally red in the face, almost always unhappy about something, but he looked a little pale this evening.

"Esther, I haven't had any pie since I've been home from the hospital." He shook his head. "And I sense that you're mad at me."

She let out an unladylike grunt. "And what in the world gave you that impression?"

Gus looped his thumbs beneath his suspenders. Amish men all wore suspenders. Non-Amish Gus wore them to keep his pants up. "You're toying with me, and that ain't like you, Esther. You rushed out of the hospital and didn't even let me explain."

"*Ach*, I'd heard enough. You faked an injury to have food and air-conditioning." Esther was ready for this day to be over. "I heard you laughing and enjoying yourself, and you told me yourself why you were there."

He hung his head, and when he looked back at her, there was a sadness in his eyes that Esther had never seen. She waved an arm toward the kitchen. "Fine. If you want pie, go get it yourself."

Slightly moaning, she lifted herself from the couch. "Gus, this has been a long day. I'm ready for *mei* bath and to go to bed."

Shaking his head, he said, "I don't see how you people go to bed when it's still daylight outside."

"Because we get up when it's still dark outside." She covered a full yawn with her hand.

"I don't want you mad at me." His expression was sober, as if her opinion of him actually mattered.

Esther put a hand to her forehead. She wasn't completely ready to let him off the hook, but he looked so pitiful, it was hard not to feel a tiny bit sorry for him. "Help yourself to some pie, Gus. I'm going to bed."

She didn't wait for a response, but as soon as she closed her bedroom door, she heard the screen and front door close. Then Gus rattled the knob to make sure it was locked. It was the first time he hadn't taken her up on a slice of pie in all the years she'd known him.

She walked to her bedroom window and watched him walk back to the cottage with his head hung. Gus Owens was truly sorry for upsetting her. He might not be sorry about deceiving the hospital staff, but there was a level of remorse. Maybe he was still progress in the making. *Slow progress.*

Chapter 9

Wednesday morning, Esther looked out the kitchen window as soon as the sun came up. Gus's truck hadn't been parked outside the cottage since Monday. She saw him leave in the early afternoon that day, and she'd checked often to see if he'd returned. And he hadn't.

"I think your boyfriend took another vacation." Lizzie cackled as she stirred the eggs. "He sure has figured out how to play the *Englisch* system."

Esther wasn't up for a confrontation with Lizzie. "Where is Rose?" She poured herself a cup of coffee and sat down.

"Down at the chicken coop collecting eggs." Lizzie looked over her shoulder. "I think she's excited about her date tonight, but she's not saying much about it. *Ach*, well, she is . . . talking plenty. Just not too much about her and Benjamin."

"Poor *maedel* was so embarrassed about everything. But that young man asked her out. No matter Rose's embarrassment, I think Benjamin got a glimpse of the real Rose and liked what he saw." Esther blew on her coffee, took a sip, then snuck a peek out the kitchen window when Lizzie wasn't looking. She was sure Gus was soaking up more air-conditioning and free food at the hospital. Perhaps she'd been wrong about him being remorseful. *What ailment did he lie about this time?*

The front-door screen closed behind Rose as she came into the living room. When she walked into the kitchen, her face was flushed. "It's already so hot outside, and it's barely daybreak." She set the basket of eggs on the counter. "Seventeen today. Lizzie, do you want me to take over?"

"*Nee*, I've got it, hon. Just sit." Lizzie nodded to the kitchen table, which already had platters of biscuits and bacon laid out.

Rose served herself some coffee and sat across from Esther. "I saw Naomi outside, so I walked over to chat. She said Gus called her again on Monday. She doesn't keep her mobile phone on, but he left a message asking her to tend to the cats again. I wonder if he is back in the hospital. Why is he doing that? We've all suffered through tough summers. Even in Ohio, the summers were hot. Maybe he likes being waited on, having his food served to him." She shrugged. "I don't know. It just feels wrong."

"It *is* wrong." Esther scowled as she shook her head. "And I've got a *gut* mind to go to the hospital and let them know Gus is not being truthful."

"You'd think they would see through his shenanigans." Rose frowned. "I wonder what he's claiming is wrong with him this time?"

"He's overweight, lives on pie, and doesn't take care of himself." Esther sighed. "He probably uses high blood pressure, elevated blood sugar levels, or something else to get himself a room. But there would have to be some lying involved because they don't just admit you to the hospital for those things." She shook her head. "Or maybe he claims none of those things, and he's just a *gut* liar." Esther heard herself, and she sounded like Lizzie. But her blood boiled when she pictured Gus bellowing at overworked nurses.

Lizzie set the bowl of eggs on the table, then put her hands on her hips. "This really bothers you, doesn't it?" When Esther didn't respond, her sister finally sat down, shaking her head.

"Let us pray." Esther lowered her head and hoped Lizzie would stay away from any more talk about Gus.

After they prayed, she decided to guide the conversation in another direction. "Rose, do you know where Benjamin is taking you this evening?"

"*Nee*, I don't. Last time he asked me to suggest a place, and as you know, we went to Gasthof Village. If he asks me again, maybe I should suggest Stoll's. They have tables that look out onto the lake. It's also a buffet, but a very *gut* one. Or maybe I should suggest pizza. I'm not sure." She sighed. "Maybe where we eat isn't important."

"I think Stoll's is a lovely idea." Esther had eaten there a few times over the years. "Every time I've been, the food was *gut*. And it might be a little romantic overlooking the lake." She winked at Rose, who smiled.

"I'm trying not to get *mei* hopes up too much."

Esther suspected that wasn't true. She silently prayed that it would be a good night for Rose and Benjamin. Then she asked God to rid her of the bitterness in her heart about Gus. But her thoughts trailed back to Lizzie's comment—*This really bothers you, doesn't it?* Of course it bothered her. Her work in progress had taken several steps backward. *That's all there is to it.* She drew in a big breath and repeated the affirmation in her mind over and over again. *That's all there is to it . . . that's all there is to it.*

Benjamin came into the living room nicely dressed and ready to pick up Rose.

"Look how handsome you look." His mother gleamed. "I'm so glad you decided to give Rose a second chance."

He shook his head. "Your expression looks exactly the same as when I graduated from eighth grade."

She shrugged as she moved toward him, then gave him an unexpected hug. "*Ach*, a little pride slips into all our emotions from time to time. I was proud of you when you finished your schooling, and I'm proud of you for taking this next step with Rose."

He eased out of the embrace, knowing his mother already had him married off to this woman. "Let's just see how it goes." Then he decided to throw her a bone. "I don't know who I went out with the first time. It wasn't the same woman I met in the bathroom while I repaired the plumbing at The Peony Inn. Rose was animated, lively, talkative, vivacious, and I could have listened to her talk all night long." He grinned on the inside as he recalled some of the things she said.

His mother pressed her palms together. "She's the one. I just know it."

Benjamin kissed her on the forehead. "Like I said, we'll see how it goes."

On the ride to pick up Rose, images of her multifaceted personality swirled around in his mind. There was the painfully quiet woman he took to supper. The angry woman who had raised her chin and stomped away from him after worship service. Then there was the one who snatched his attention with her wit, outspoken personality, and wildly dramatic gestures. That's who he was picking up tonight. For the first time in as long as he could remember, he was looking forward to a date.

When he pulled into The Peony Inn driveway, Rose was standing on the porch. The two older ladies were sitting in rocking chairs.

Benjamin loosely tethered the horse and made his way across the yard. Now that he was here, his stomach roiled with nervous anticipation, and his voice threatened to take a hike. He silently prayed he wouldn't freeze up around her.

He tipped his hat at the three women and met Rose at the top of the porch steps. "*Wie-wie bischt*." Adrenaline flowed through him like a raging river, and now that he had hope that things might work out between them, he began to worry about saying the wrong things. He'd gone from writing her off completely to being a cowardly mess. And that is not how he wanted to present himself to this woman.

Benjamin locked eyes with Rose, so beautiful and smiling from ear to ear, and it was infectious. He smiled back at her as she said, "Ready?"

"*Ya, ya.*"

"You two have a wonderful time." Esther raised a hand and gave a quick wave. The other lady—Lizzie—did the same.

As soon as Benjamin was seated and had hold of the reins, Rose gave him a sideways glance, grinning. He backed up the buggy, wondering what was on her mind. And more importantly, was she going to tell him?

"I have five *bruders*, all older than me. Every single one of them used to race buggies. I don't know if that is popular here, but there was a place in Ohio that was perfect for it. It was a dirt road out behind an abandoned farmhouse. I used to cheer for *mei bruders* from the sidelines, along with *mei* two *schweschdere*."

Benjamin wasn't sure where she was going with this, but he didn't care. She was full of energy, talking with her hands, and he found himself smiling along with her as he got on the main road, with no idea where to go.

"*Mei schweschdere* are older than me too." She waved a hand in the air and giggled. "I don't even know why that matters." Abruptly, all the animation stopped and she was quiet and turned to him.

Was she waiting for him to respond? All he could do was look at her mouth, so he faced forward.

Sighing, she said, "It took all of that for me to say that . . . that *mei bruders* taught us girls how to race the buggies too. *Daed* was furious when he found out. He said it wasn't ladylike for women to buggy race." She was quiet for a few moments before she cut her eyes in his direction. Benjamin didn't think she could look any more seductive if she tried. She narrowed her eyes at him, her mouth turning up only a little on one side as a wisp of dark hair blew across her face. Benjamin had chosen the topless buggy for this evening.

"I like to go fast." She broke into a big smile. "There is nothing freer than flying down the road in a buggy, the wind in your face."

"Um . . . are you saying you want me to pick up the pace?" He looked ahead of him. "On this road?" It was two lanes with side roads off-shooting everywhere.

"Take the next right." She obviously wasn't hungry. At least not for food. Rose Petersheim was craving some adventure. He was happy to do as she instructed, and he took the next right.

"Better hold on to your *kapp*."

She pressed her hand down on top of her prayer covering and nodded. "Ready."

Benjamin flicked the reins repeatedly until his horse was at a hard and steady run. This was a first for him. He had driven his buggy at full capacity before, but not at the request of a woman.

"I hope that's not all you've got." She laughed and shook her head.

Benjamin couldn't stop smiling as he pushed the horse harder. Rose's laughter was contagious as she kept her hand on her prayer covering.

It was a crazy way to start the evening. And Benjamin loved it.

Rose had decided to be herself since Benjamin seemed to prefer the real Rose. If things didn't progress past this date, then it wasn't meant to be. It would be another heartbreak, but since Benjamin had still wanted to go out with her after hearing everything she said in the bathroom, it felt worth the risk.

She hadn't gone this fast in a buggy in years. It was exhilarating and a fun way to loosen things up right from the beginning. As she held her prayer covering in place, she was taken back to a time in her life when things were good—most of the time—when all her siblings still lived at home. They all suffered the same treatment—in varying degrees—from their father, but there was a secret code to protect each other and not speak about it.

When the horse became visibly tired, Benjamin slowed the pace.

"That felt wonderful." She thought she probably looked a mess and began stuffing loose strands of hair beneath her prayer covering. "I love feeling the wind in my face like that." She closed her eyes and breathed in the warm air, the smell of freshly cut hay, and someone barbecuing far in the distance. When she turned to Benjamin, he smiled.

"Would you like me to suggest somewhere to eat?" She folded her hands in her lap.

"*Ya.*"

So far he was, indeed, a man of few words. Shy, as she'd been told. Rose wasn't going to push him to be anyone different than who he was, and she'd given a lot of thought as to how to find out more about him. Slowly, she'd decided.

"Stoll's is a restaurant with a lake view. It's also a buffet like

Gasthof Village, but the food is very *gut*. The banana pudding is some of the best I've had. I like desserts. I probably eat too much sugar. They have a lot to choose from—both entrée items and desserts. They also have a small gift shop. It's popular with the tourists, but the locals eat there frequently too. Or we could eat pizza. I'm fine with anything. You choose."

He still had a half smile on his face that hadn't gone away. She didn't recall seeing that expression on their last date. It was no wonder. They had both been miserable.

"Stoll's sounds nice." He held the expression.

"*Ya*, okay. *Gut*. You can take the next right to get back on the main road, and it will be on the left. You can see it from the highway."

He nodded. Rose was quiet for a few moments, pondering what it must be like to be shy. Why was he? She wondered if he had suffered some sort of abuse. In the back of her mind, Rose always wondered if her childhood had caused her to be more outspoken than most people. Her brothers and sisters all had husbands and families. Her father had died not long before Rose made the decision to move to Indiana. She communicated with all of her family, even her mother. But maintaining a one-on-one relationship with just her and her mother in the house had become too difficult. They might not speak about certain things, but her mother had witnessed everything that took place in that house and had done nothing about it. But in Amish families, the man was the head of the household. Perhaps her mother was under his thumb as much as the rest of them.

She tossed the thoughts from her mind. Maybe Benjamin's

shyness was just who he was and it didn't stem from his childhood. Either way, she wanted to keep things upbeat, and she wanted him to feel relaxed. Diving into anything too heavy might not be the way to go.

As they pulled into the restaurant parking lot, she pointed to where the hitching posts were, then she laughed. "You know, the more I think about it, the more sure I am that bathroom wasn't leaking. I think Lizzie did something to the pipe so she could call you to come fix it." She covered her face and shook her head. "Then you heard all of my ramblings."

He eased the horse to a stop, then turned her way. "It looked like someone bashed the pipe with a crowbar or something similar." He grinned.

"The things those women do." Rose smiled back at him. "They love to play matchmaker."

His expression stilled as he gazed into her eyes. "And I'm happy that they did."

Rose's heart flipped in her chest. She had high hopes for this evening. And she planned to be herself. Benjamin would either like her for who she was, or not. There was only so much Esther and Lizzie could do. Now it was time to see if their efforts had been worth it. Rose felt hopeful.

Esther emerged from her bedroom, marched to the mantel, and clutched the vase filled with flowers. She might wonder for the rest of her life who sent the gift and note, but she didn't need a reminder on the mantel right now. And on the off chance the arrangement was from Gus, she definitely didn't want the flowers in the house.

After she dumped the somewhat wilted blooms in the garbage outside, she went back to the living room toting the empty vase.

Lizzie was on the couch reading. She stared at Esther with questioning eyes, and Esther raised her chin, waiting for her sister to say something that was going to start an argument. Esther was in the mood to give her one.

But her sister closed the book, took off her reading glasses, then slid her feet up on the coffee table and shrugged. "Well, the flowers were looking pretty sad anyway. Probably time for them to go." She shuffled her dentures from side to side. "I guess we're done investigating who your secret admirer is. Although I'm not sure what you're more upset about—that Gus disappointed you with his deceitful hospital antics, or that we never figured out who sent the flowers."

Esther set the empty vase on the floor, then sat beside Lizzie and eased her bare feet up on the coffee table. "I'm not upset about either one. I'm putting both issues out of *mei* mind. Gus is a grown man, and if he wants to pretend he's sick just to get air-conditioning and food, he has to live with that. As for the flowers and note, either someone will come forward, or it will just remain an unsolved mystery. I can't control either one of those things." Anxious to change the subject, she said, "I hope things are going well for Rose and Benjamin."

Lizzie nodded to the clock on the mantel. "I'm thinking it

must be. They've already been gone twice as long as their last date."

Esther smiled, happy to have something else to focus on. "Benjamin seemed nervous, but did you catch the way he looked at Rose?"

Lizzie slapped a hand to her knee. "Best thing I ever did, busting that pipe." She nudged Esther as she chuckled.

"I'm not entirely sure it's the best thing you've ever done, but God intervened, and Benjamin heard enough of Rose's comments to be intrigued." Esther leaned her head back against the back of the couch. She wasn't sure if she could stay awake until Rose got home.

"Has she ever talked to you much about her past?" Lizzie asked. "Every time I bring it up, she wiggles out of an answer."

"*Ya*, she's the same way with me. All we really know is that she has a lot of siblings." Esther looked at Lizzie. "I don't suppose it really matters. She's a lovely person."

They were quiet for a while, with the only sounds being those of the faint tick of the clock on the mantel and the hum of the fans.

Lizzie yawned. "It's too quiet. I think we're insashable."

Esther scowled as she fought not to yawn also. "That's not a word, *insashable*."

"See, this is why you should read books more." Lizzie rolled her eyes. "It means we're never satisfied. We moan and groan when there is too much noise, and we whine when it's too quiet."

Esther grinned. "I think the word you're looking for is *insatiable*."

"*Ya*, that's it." Lizzie sighed. "I've been wishing the date would go well. Now I'm wishing Rose would get home so I can go to bed." After she yawned, she said, "I guess we don't have to wait up for her. She's a grown woman." Smiling, she turned to Esther. "But a good nighttime story about their date would be nice."

"Remember when *Mamm* used to wait up for us like this when we went on dates?" Esther couldn't recall a time their mother hadn't stayed up to make sure she and Lizzie arrived home safely—and on time. When they were late, they were assigned extra chores the next day.

"*Ya*, I remember. And just like Naomi, Rose feels like a daughter or granddaughter."

Esther nodded, then she closed her eyes and, thinking back to earlier, asked God to forgive her lies. She *was* angry with Gus, and she would wonder, probably forever, who gave her the arrangement of flowers.

Benjamin was on the best date of his life, which was bizarrely ironic since his worst date had been with this same woman. He could watch and listen to her forever. Most of what she said was somehow meaningful. The fact that she didn't always put topics in the right order or slow down enough for him to completely catch up was just part of her quirky, yet adorable personality.

"So, some of my favorite things are"—she grinned—"to go fast, obviously. I've never been on an airplane, but even though they go fast, it wouldn't be the same as feeling the wind in your face. Cars aren't allowed, and motorcycles are out as well. But, do you know what is at the top of my list?" She took a deep breath. "I'd like to ride in a boat, the kind that goes really fast. Or at least faster than the small bass boats *mei bruders* had for fishing. Have you ever been in a fast boat?"

Benjamin shook his head. "*Nee*, I haven't. But I'd like to. Maybe we'll do that one day." He pictured being in a speedboat with Rose, but in his vision, her hair was long and blowing in the wind. She had her eyes closed as the wind nipped at her cheeks and, of course, she was smiling. This was the happiest woman he'd ever met. Most of the time. Every now and then she seemed to retreat somewhere. She'd become quiet and seemingly lost in thought. But it never lasted.

"I would *lieb* that." She took a bite of banana pudding. Like their last date, she was having her third dessert. Benjamin had kept up with her this time, eating multiple desserts, not anxious to leave.

She eyed the plate he'd used for his main meal, frowning.

"Did the carrots do something wrong?" he asked. That was the only thing left on his plate, a couple of carrots.

She grimaced even more. "I don't like carrots. At all. I had to eat them when I was growing up, and I did, but I despised them. When I turned sixteen, *mei mamm* quit making me eat them." Her eyebrows knitted into a frown as she seemed to be staring somewhere over his shoulder again. Then she was back, smiling. "Are there any foods you don't like?"

Benjamin finished chewing a bite of apple pie. "Hmm . . ." He strummed his fingers on the table. "I can only think of one thing. Bananas." He nodded at her bowl of banana pudding. "I can't get past the texture, and I don't like the taste."

She gasped as she brought a hand to her chest. "I *lieb* bananas."

"I've noticed." He grinned, something he'd been doing a lot of. Her exuberance was intoxicating, like a teenager who had just been set free out in the world, discovering it all for the first time. "The rest of *mei* family loves bananas, and *mei mamm* makes banana pudding all the time. As much as you *lieb* it, did your *mudder* make it a lot?"

Her expression fell a little. "*Nee*," she said softly.

They'd covered a lot of territory this evening. But there was one thing Benjamin picked up on. Rose's mood shifted at the mention of her family. He knew she'd been here for over a year, but he wasn't sure why she left her family in Ohio. It seemed like a huge step, to leave your loved ones and move so far away, and to do it alone. Benjamin's family might not be a buggy ride away anymore, but Bedford was less than an hour drive by car. His mother planned to visit his siblings weekly, and Benjamin thought he would see them at least every couple of weeks.

Instead of beating around the bush, the way he had been all night, he decided to be more direct. "It must be hard to be so far away from your family. Was there a reason you chose to move to Montgomery?"

She cast her eyes down, and Benjamin immediately wished he hadn't brought up the subject. The Rose he had been slowly getting to know this evening was gone, replaced by a woman with a trembling bottom lip, who reached for the string on her prayer covering, twisting it around her finger.

Maybe she didn't choose to leave at all? Perhaps she'd had a falling out with members of her family?

Without looking up, she blinked her eyes a few times. "Um . . . *mei bruders* and *schweschdere* had all married and moved out. It was just me and *mei mamm*." She looked up and seemed to force a smile as she let go of the string on her prayer covering.

It wasn't really an answer. Benjamin wasn't sure what to say. He was afraid if he ever moved out, his mother would be lonely. Rose had left her mother alone, which made him think more than ever that they'd had some sort of disagreement. Family could be a touchy subject, so he decided not to push her about hers, but waited, giving her time to elaborate if she wanted to.

"I have family here," she finally said after taking a deep breath. "Cousins. Big Roy and Katie Marie Kaufman. I don't know if you've met them yet."

Benjamin shook his head. "*Nee*, I haven't."

"They really didn't have room for me, so when the opportunity to work for Esther and Lizzie came up, I jumped on it. I have *mei* own room, and the sisters are like family to me now."

She still hadn't answered his question, so he waited again.

"I've had a lovely time this evening." Her smile returned, and Benjamin decided not bring up her family again unless she did.

"*Ya*, I have too." He was tempted to tell her it was the best date he'd ever had, but that might be too much too soon.

She tapped a finger to her chin. "Something unusual happened yesterday."

Benjamin raised an eyebrow when she smiled, glad to see her exuberance slowly returning. "What's that?"

"Chickens usually lay one egg per day. Sometimes they will skip a day, but that doesn't happen very often. But this morning . . ." A grin spread across her face. "One of the chickens laid two eggs. I gathered the eggs yesterday morning, the way I always do, and when I went back this morning, Millie—that's the name of the chicken"—she giggled and waved a hand in the air—"I named them all, which Lizzie said wasn't necessary since we'd probably eat them some day." She briefly cringed. "Anyway, Millie had two eggs this morning, meaning she laid a second one yesterday. That's very uncommon."

Benjamin couldn't shed the smile on his face. "Is that so?"

She nodded with the enthusiasm of a child, and Benjamin listened with true interest as she began to tell him things he didn't know about chickens. He even asked questions and told her a few things she didn't know about horses. She had a way of drawing him out of the shell he'd been living in, and there was a level of comfort he'd never known before. He wished the evening didn't have to end, but the check had been on the table for almost a half hour.

After Benjamin paid for the meal and they were on the road again, they talked all the way back to the inn. He couldn't remember having this much conversation with anyone outside his family. She had a way of steering him into conversation with a natural precision. Nothing felt forced or awkward.

When they pulled into The Peony Inn, Benjamin's chest tightened. He wanted to kiss her good night, but he recalled their conversation about holding off on anything physical for now.

Benjamin got down from the buggy and came around to meet Rose and walk her to the bottom of her front porch steps.

"*Danki* again for a lovely evening." She folded her hands in front of her and smiled.

Benjamin wasn't about to tell this woman goodbye again. "Do you want to spend the day with me on Saturday?" He forced his eyes to lock with hers so he wouldn't keep focusing on her lips.

"I'd like that."

He gently touched her arms, then leaned down and kissed her on the forehead, wanting her to know that he sincerely liked her, but still respecting the boundaries they'd set.

Grinning, he said, "I'll see you Saturday."

Chapter 10

Esther walked into the kitchen fully dressed Thursday morning. Lizzie was still in her robe and sipping coffee at the table while Rose flipped pancakes.

"*Wie bischt*," Esther said as she stifled a yawn and sat down across from Lizzie. She'd had another night without enough sleep. "Rose, I'm so sorry Lizzie and I fell asleep before you returned from your date. But it must have gone well since you were out for a *gut* while."

Rose spun around, and the young woman was glowing. "*Ya*, I think it went very well." She leaned up on her toes. "I was just telling Lizzie that we are spending the day together on Saturday. I don't know what we'll do, but I suppose it doesn't matter."

Esther pressed her palms together and brought them to her lips, offering a quick prayer to the Lord for His blessings. "I am so happy for you."

"We want all the juicy details," Lizzie said with a slight lisp. *No dentures this morning.* "Did he kiss you at the end of the date?"

"*Nee.* Not on the lips anyway." She smiled, so Esther assumed that must not have been a bad thing. "We agreed to get to know each other better before we let that happen again. But I think he wanted to kiss me. There was a twinkle in his eyes." She turned to take a pancake from the griddle. "And I sure wanted him to kiss me, but I think getting to know each other better is more appropriate, and any kissing will mean more if there are real feelings behind it." She carried the platter of pancakes to the table and placed it next to the sausage and homemade bread.

Lizzie rolled her lip under. "Well, give us something—*any* details. We live for this kind of thing."

"Speak for yourself." Esther rolled her eyes. One day she was going to take a good look at the type of books Lizzie read.

Rose pulled out her chair at the end of the table. They prayed quietly but quickly. "Tell us about him." Lizzie straightened as she flashed a toothless grin.

"You said he was shy. I guess he was, a little." Rose slathered butter on her pancakes. She never used syrup, only lots of butter. "At first, he didn't say a lot, but . . . let's be honest . . ." She laughed. "My nervous chatter probably didn't give him much of an opportunity. But I tried to ease him into conversations to learn more about him, and it didn't take long before he seemed comfortable. He doesn't talk as much as I do." She rolled her eyes. "Most people don't, I suppose. But he smiled a lot, and I like that. We like a lot of the same things, except he doesn't like bananas." She held her fork halfway between her mouth and the plate, frowning a little. "I've never met anyone who didn't like bananas."

Esther ate quickly, although once again she wasn't very hungry. "I'm so happy that things went well. He must have thought so, too, since he asked to spend the day with you on Saturday."

Lizzie cleared her throat, and when Esther looked at her, she raised an eyebrow. "You're dressed as if you're going somewhere."

Esther wiped her mouth with her napkin. "*Ya*, I am. I'm going to see Gus. His vacations are about to come to an end. I'm going to make sure he knows how I feel about this. I thought he felt remorse for his actions, but now he's gone and done it again. At daybreak, I'm going to call a driver to take me to Bedford. I've already called the hospital, and the woman who answered confirmed he was there." She shook her head. "I was tempted to tell her over the phone about Gus's fake illness, but I want Gus to be accountable for his actions and to know how I feel."

Lizzie slapped a hand to her forehead. "Just let him live there! It's peaceful without him around."

"What he's doing isn't right." Esther lifted her chin.

Lizzie stared at her long and hard, then slouched into her chair and folded her arms across her chest. "Esther." She narrowed her eyebrows inward. "I don't like all this. You care too much about that horrid man. And I'm pretty sure he gave you flowers, and"—she growled under her breath—"I don't like any of this."

Esther sighed. "Please don't insinuate that there is anything more than friendship between me and Gus." She shook her head. "And right now, that friendship is on the line."

"You're too *gut* for that man, to even be friends with him." Lizzie sat taller and forcefully stabbed a bite of sausage.

Esther glanced at Rose, and the girl only shrugged. For once, she didn't have anything to say.

After a few more bites of food, Esther excused herself and went to her room. She didn't want to talk about Gus anymore.

∞

Rose finished her pancakes, then started clearing the dishes. Usually, Lizzie or Esther helped, but Lizzie was slumped in her chair, her arms back across her chest again.

"Do you think Esther cares more for Gus than she's letting on?" Rose spoke in a whisper, even though the door to Esther's bedroom was closed.

"I think Esther is a *gut* woman who cares about everyone." Lizzie dropped her arms to her sides as she shook her head. "But I know *mei schweschder*, and Esther's thoughts about Gus and whoever sent those flowers are wearing on her."

Rose placed a stack of plates in the soapy dishwater before she turned to Lizzie, leaning against the counter. "Maybe after she tells Gus how disappointed she is, she'll feel better. But she might not ever find out who had the flower arrangement delivered. I know you think it was Gus, that he's lying about it"—she reached for a dish towel, dried her hands, and draped it over her shoulder—"but that doesn't really make sense. If Gus sent the flowers, he wouldn't have been concerned about a stalker and been found sitting on the porch claiming to protect us."

She grinned. "*Ach*, well . . . claiming to protect me and Esther anyway."

Lizzie rolled her eyes. "I don't need Grumpy Gus Owens to protect me from anything. And neither does Esther . . . or you. We need to detach ourselves from his life. He only rents the cottage due to the promise we made to our *mudder*."

Rose knew the story of how Gus came to rent the cottage. Gus's mother had been best friends with Esther and Lizzie's mother. After Gus's mother had been killed in a buggy accident, he'd been sent away to live with relatives. Amish by birth, Gus chose not to return to the faith, and according to him, he hadn't lived a very good life. When he returned home fourteen years ago, decades had gone by. Esther and Lizzie's mother was still alive, and Gus had asked her not to reveal his true identity out of respect for his mother and the fact that he wasn't proud of the man he was. Esther and Lizzie had held true to their mother's dying wish—to let Gus live in the cottage for the rest of his life. No one in the community knew Gus used to be Amish when he was a young boy. Rose had only recently learned this information from Lizzie. Apparently Lizzie wasn't supposed to tell anyone, so Rose agreed not to share about Gus's history.

But every time Rose recalled the story and the part about Gus being ashamed of the man he was, she sensed that there must be remorse. Rose agreed with Esther. Buried beneath the grumpiness there was a tinge of goodness in Gus that needed to be nurtured. Most people just didn't have the patience to tolerate the man's rude and obnoxious behavior. Even Rose avoided him when she could. But Esther was possibly the kindest woman she'd ever met. Rose often wondered what life would have been like if Esther—or even Lizzie—had been her mother. It was sad that neither of them was able to have children.

Rose went back to washing the dishes. She didn't think anything she said would change Lizzie's opinion about Gus. She didn't know how things had become so volatile between the two of them. She wasn't sure if it was personality clashes, which Gus had with everyone, or if it was something more. Lizzie despised the man more than most.

"Will you be going with Esther to the hospital again?" Rose glanced over her shoulder.

"*Nee.* I only went the first time for Esther, in case Gus was seriously ill." She rolled her eyes. "Because, despite everything, if he had been Esther would have been upset." Lizzie chuckled. "Although a part of me is tempted to go. I'd enjoy seeing Gus get kicked out of his vacation accommodations."

Rose wondered what Esther would say. Would she simply state the truth to the hospital staff? How would they react? Or was she hoping Gus would own up to his lies after learning how upset Esther was? As the scene unfolded in her mind, one thing was for sure. Gus Owens was going to be livid. Rose would make it a point not to be around when he returned home.

Esther paid the driver before she traipsed to the bench in front of the hospital where she and Lizzie sat before. Visiting hours didn't start until eight o'clock, and it was only seven thirty in the morning. She should have asked about that on the phone.

She had a half hour to speculate about how things would play out.

It had rained sometime during the night, and the showers brought cooler temperatures. She should have known it would rain since she went to bed with achy knees. It would warm up during the day, but right now she was basking in the post-rain aroma that filled her senses, giving her a brief respite from the task at hand.

She smiled at two nurses who passed by her and wondered if either of them had tended to Gus. It was unlikely. There were bound to be many nurses on staff.

Esther took a deep breath. Gus was going to be very angry with her when she foiled his vacation plans. But with every step forward that Gus had taken toward being a better person, this was a huge setback, and Esther's disappointment in him fueled her decision to be here. Normally it wasn't her way to meddle in the affairs of others, unless it was related to matters of the heart. She and Lizzie couldn't resist the temptation to play matchmakers, which circled her thoughts back to Rose. Smiling, she hoped things worked out for the young couple.

Finally, she forced herself to consider her options for telling the staff that Gus was taking advantage of them. Would he be tossed out immediately? Perhaps Gus would deny that he was faking anything. He might yell and scream at Esther, which would be embarrassing. When it came to Gus, there was no way to know.

She glanced at the time on her mobile phone, the one she and Lizzie shared to call drivers or in case of an emergency. Her ponderings had killed some time. It was five minutes until eight, so she hoisted herself from the bench and made her way to the entrance of the hospital, unsure whom she should talk to. Perhaps she should visit Gus first and give him an opportunity to make things right on his own.

Esther breathed in the unwelcome odors of the hospital as she approached the information desk not far from the main entrance. "I'm here to see Gus Owens."

A woman about Rose's age studied a computer in front of her. "Sure. He's in room 226." The woman pointed to the elevators. Esther wondered if Gus had a preference for the second floor. She decided to go see him and give him an opportunity to confess to the staff.

She passed the nurses' station. The two women didn't seem to notice as she walked by, both of their heads down as they flipped through a stack of papers.

Esther dragged her feet, wishing she didn't have to do this. When she reached room 226, the door was closed so she knocked, not wanting to catch Gus in a compromising position. Last time, she'd heard laughter. But all was quiet. *Maybe he's napping.*

She eased the door open. *Wake up, Gus. Vacation is over.*

But the room was empty. She recognized Gus's red-checkered shirt draped over the back of a chair and his worn-out brown running shoes next to the bed. She couldn't recall Gus actually running anywhere. He was obviously somewhere in a hospital gown. Whatever ailment he had concocted, it must allow for the freedom to roam the halls. Esther was unsure whether to wait or go to the nurses' station.

After a few minutes of standing in the room, she left and went to where she'd seen the two nurses. They were still there, but this time they looked up at her as she approached them.

"Can I help you?" the older of the two women asked. Perhaps she was training the younger lady.

"I'm looking for Gus Owens. I was told he is in room 226, but he isn't in there right now." Esther paused as her chest tightened, deciding it was better to just get this over with. "He isn't really sick," she said barely above a whisper.

The older woman, possibly ten or fifteen years younger than Esther, took off a pair of black reading glasses and set them on the desk in front of her. "Excuse me? How are you related to Mr. Owens?" She eyed Esther's dark-green dress and black apron.

"I'm his . . . landlord. He rents a cottage from me and *mei* sister."

The same woman said, "Ma'am, if this is about a rental dispute or something like that, you'll need to speak with Mr. Owens."

Esther shook her head as her stomach began to churn. "*Nee*." She swallowed hard and leaned closer. "I have become aware of the fact that Gus—Mr. Owens—is taking advantage of a situation. You see, he isn't really sick."

The woman held up a finger and moved to a computer nearby. After a few seconds, she asked, "What is your name, ma'am?"

"Esther Zook."

"I'm sorry, Mrs. Zook, but you aren't listed as someone authorized to receive information about Mr. Owens. You can ask him to add you to the list of people who can receive updates about his condition." She sighed. "Actually there isn't anyone on that list right now."

Esther shook her head. "*Nee, nee.* That's what I need to tell you. Mr. Owens was here a week ago. He told me he was on vacation, that he had faked his illness so that he could stay in the air-conditioning and have as much food and pie as he wanted." She paused as both women scowled at her. "It isn't *mei* place to be here, and maybe I should have talked to Mr. Owens first and given him a chance to be honest about his intentions. But I fear he is doing the same thing again, pretending to be sick when he's not." Esther's stomach clenched. *What if a person goes to jail for a deception like this?* It was too late to take it back, though. "I felt like someone should know." She stood taller and raised her chin, even though she was questioning what she'd just done. "Maybe I should have stayed out of it," she said softly.

The same older woman turned her attention back to the computer. "I see Mr. Owens has a long history of visits here, but he hasn't required overnight care until the visit you mentioned from a week ago."

Esther was aware Gus had been to the hospital for tests and checkups in the past. He told her so when he brought her to her own medical appointments a year or so ago.

"I'm sorry I can't tell you more. Mr. Owens is probably not in his room because he was scheduled for some tests this morning." The woman eyed Esther up and down again. "That's really all I can say. There is a waiting room down the hall and around the corner if you'd like to wait for him to return. I can let you know when he's back in his room."

Any regret about telling the nurses the truth left Esther. Whatever tests Gus had conned the staff into giving him only made his deceptions worse. She shivered as she thought of the tests she'd had in the past. Esther was terrified of medical issues, and here was Gus, opting to have examinations just to maintain his lie.

"The man is not sick." Esther spoke more firmly this time. "Gus Owens is lying to you. He is faking an illness so that he can stay here and have a break from the heat this time of year. The cottage he rents does not have air-conditioning." She paused, shaking her head. "I admit that with every year, it becomes harder and harder to endure the summers, but for Gus to fake being sick is just despicable. It's not fair to other patients who might need your care and treatment from the doctors. I could not in *gut* conscience allow him to keep going with this."

"I've had enough." The younger woman slammed her palms against the desk, her face ablaze with reddening anger. "My father *died* of leukemia. I assure you, it's not something you can fake, and—"

"Shelley," the older woman interrupted. "Please . . ." She hung her head, shaking it as she frowned.

"I'm sorry, Loraine, but"—the younger woman's bottom lip trembled—"I thought you Amish were all godly and . . . to say that Mr. Owens, that nice older man, is faking a terminal illness, it's just beyond my comprehension. You don't sound like a friend at all. No wonder he doesn't have you down as someone we are authorized to give information to."

Nice older man? Esther blinked her eyes in confusion as she considered the possibility that they were looking at the wrong file. *Leukemia? Terminal illness?* This had to be a case of mistaken identity.

The older woman—Loraine—began to scold the younger woman, but Esther didn't hear much of what she was saying.

Gus came around the corner, dressed in a hospital gown and seated in a wheelchair. A man pushed him along and held a rolling pole that had Gus hooked up to wires and tubes.

Esther's feet somehow took her down the hall as a knot built in her throat. Loraine called after her, threatening to call security. They probably thought Esther was crazy, evil, or both. She stopped in front of Gus.

"Esther?" He was pale. His beard needed tending to, but that was normal. He said her name again, but she was too stunned to lift her jaw back into place. "I guess I have some explaining to do." He scratched his forehead.

Loraine was quickly by Esther's side. "Mr. Owens, do you know this woman? She said she is your landlord." The woman turned to Esther and shot her a look of contempt. "But she's made some hideous claims about you."

Gus lowered his eyes to his lap, and when he looked up, it was to look at Esther. And there were tears in his eyes. "She's my friend," he said softly in a shaky voice.

Terminal? Leukemia? A tear rolled down Esther's cheek.

"Now, now, Esther." Gus hung his head again, discreetly

swiping at his eyes. "I guess we need to have a talk," he said as he looked up at her.

Esther sniffled, brushed away a tear, and walked alongside the man pushing Gus down the hallway to room 226. Thankfully, the two women went back to what they were doing. Esther couldn't even look at them.

When Gus reached for Esther's hand, she took his and squeezed it. Gus had been there for her through a round of terrifying tests with a diagnosis of a stomach ulcer.

This was much different. Esther's knees were weak, her temples pounding, and her heart . . . in shambles. Maybe she cared about Gus Owens more than she cared to admit, even to herself.

Chapter 11

Esther waited outside Gus's hospital room while the attendant got him settled in bed, which only took a few minutes.

"You can go in now," the young man said with a smile as he came out of the room. "He's a character."

She wasn't sure what he meant by that, but on shaky legs, she opened the door and stood just inside the room.

"Why didn't you tell me?" She clutched her black purse with both hands, a part of her wanting to turn and run so she could go cry by herself. The other part of her wanted to rush to Gus and throw her arms around him. Instead she chose not to move.

Gus pointed to a chair next to the bed, which instantly made Esther wonder who else might have visited.

"I thought I could get through this without a big fuss." Gus's jowls hung lower than usual. "But it ain't looking like that."

Esther didn't want to use the word *terminal*. Did Gus even know that was the prognosis?

"After taking care of me when I had all *mei* medical tests, didn't you think I would tend to you?" Esther's bottom lip trembled.

"I drove you in my truck. You just needed rides." He rolled his eyes.

Gus seemed exactly the same to Esther. She recalled what the nurse had said—*nice older man*. Maybe when your life is in the hands of others you tend to be more vulnerable, thus kinder.

"It was more than that, and you know it." Esther thought back to the times when she was afraid. Gus had comforted her in his own way, a bit gruff sometimes, but he'd been there for her.

"I didn't want you all upset like you are now." He turned his head away from her. "I don't like to see you cry."

Esther's heart was in a state of confusion, thumping madly, and possibly cracking at the same time. "I'm all right, Gus. Now tell me what you know." She forced her lip to be still and kept her voice steady.

He slowly moved his head until he was facing her. "I'm dying."

Gus made the statement so matter-of-factly that Esther's chest contracted again.

"You don't know that. Only God decides when it is our time."

"Well, your God seems to have made a decision where I'm concerned. And He blessed me with some sort of rare blood type, which only complicates my situation." He rested his arms across the white cover draped over his enlarged belly. One hand had an IV atop his wrist, and there was a gadget on the forefinger of his other hand that seemed to be monitoring something. The machine by the bed beeped continuously, which only added to the fear brewing inside Esther.

"First of all"—she considered how best to say what she was thinking—"we have had this discussion before. My God is *your* God too. He will not abandon you in your time of need, and—"

Gus chuckled. "I will debate that until my last breath. If that were true, then where was He all my life?" He waved the hand with the IV dismissively. "Don't answer that. It was a rhetorical question. I know where He was. Absent. And it's too late for me to reach out to an entity that I don't know." Pausing, he held his palm up, the tube dangling from his wrist. "Don't make me your charity case when it comes to God. I've told you before, and I'll tell you again—there's a spot in hell saved especially for a man like me, probably on the front row nearest the furnace." The color in his face was coming back. "You're the only friend I got, Esther, so let me go in my own way, and don't push your religious stuff on me." Sighing, he said, "It's too late for me."

The Lord's calling was impossible to ignore. It wasn't their way to minister to others, but Esther could hear God speaking to her. *Bring him to Me.*

She put a hand to her trembling lips. Did she imagine the voice in her head? If not, was it confirmation that Gus was going to die? Did God expect her to guide Gus into a relationship with the Lord so he would go to heaven?

"It's never too late," she said as she locked eyes with Gus, blinking back tears.

The nurse—Loraine—came into the room. She smiled at her patient, then squinted an evil eye toward Esther before she turned back to Gus. "Mr. Owens, is everything okay in here? Is there anything you need?"

"Thank you for checking on me, Loraine." Gus smiled at the nurse. "I'm doing just fine, and I appreciate you."

Esther put a hand over her mouth when her jaw dropped.

"Well, Shelley and I can be here in less than a minute if you need us. Just push the red button." Nurse Loraine cut her eyes at Esther before she turned back to Gus, smiling. "The cafeteria has chocolate pie today. Do you want me to set aside a couple of slices for you?"

"That would be wonderful." Gus flashed her a big smile. "Don't tell the others, but you and Shelley are my favorites." He winked at Loraine. "Prettiest ones in the bunch too."

Loraine giggled as she waved him off and left.

Esther lowered her hand and gave her head a quick shake. Maybe she'd fallen, hit her noggin, and lost her mind. She rubbed her forehead. "Who are you and what have you done with Gus Owens?"

He frowned before he let out a heavy sigh. "On the off chance my seat isn't closest to the furnace, I'd like to go out on a good note."

Esther shook her head. "Gus, why can't you treat everyone as nice as you just treated that nurse?"

He shrugged. "Hadn't been much of a point 'til now."

Esther grinned. "Welcome back. That's the Gus I know and—" She stopped abruptly as she realized what she'd almost said. And in her own way, she did love Gus. But helping the man find redemption was a tall order.

Gus raised an eyebrow as if he was waiting for her to finish the sentence. Instead, she wanted to circle back to something he had said. "You said you have a rare blood type. How does that complicate your situation?"

"There's a blood shortage, in case you haven't heard." He rolled his eyes again, and Esther had to remind herself that Gus was ill. Otherwise, she would have reprimanded him for his curt tone and eye rolling. "I'm AB negative, and only one percent of the population is. Aren't I lucky?" He took a breath, then started coughing and reached for a glass of water on the bedside table.

"So, what does that mean?" Esther tapped her foot nervously as she chewed on a fingernail, something Lizzie usually did, not her.

"It means that on a normal day, there isn't enough blood, and there surely isn't enough of the kind I need." He held up a finger. "But even if there was, my age is working against me. I've only got a five percent chance of remission if the chemo works." Rubbing his beard, he said, "I don't even know if I'll do it. I might lose all my hair, Esther."

She wasn't sure when Gus started worrying about his looks. "You should have told me about all this." She put a hand to her chest. "This is not something you should go through alone. Does . . . does Heather know?" Esther bit her bottom lip.

"No. My daughter and I don't have a relationship. I haven't seen her since I gave her the money from my little part in that movie." He strummed his fingers against his belly. "I don't want her to know."

"What if she shares your blood type? Wouldn't that help

you have a better chance at recovery?" Esther didn't know much about leukemia, just that it was cancer of the blood.

"I don't want her to know." He glared at Esther. "I'll be mad if you tell her, and since I'm the one who is gonna die, you have to respect my wishes."

Esther dabbed at her eyes with a tissue she took from her apron pocket.

"See." Gus shook his head. "This is why I didn't want you to know. I don't need a bunch of crying, especially when it's you." He paused, scowling. "Although I doubt my passing will bring forth tears from anyone else."

Esther didn't know if Gus had touched lives she was unaware of. But Evelyn's husband, Jayce, was friends with Gus. The boy would take this news hard.

"Let's face it, I'm in stage four and my liver is enlarged. I'm a goner." He gazed into her eyes, which felt strange coming from Gus. Her heart swelled a little. "Do you think they got chocolate pie in that heaven you believe in?"

Esther smiled for the first time since she'd arrived. "I suspect heaven has anything a person wants."

Gus groaned. "I'm guessing no pie where I'm going."

She couldn't decide if he was hinting for her to help him, or if he would reprimand her based on his earlier comments. "Probably not where you *think* you're going. But, Gus, you can change course at any stage in life. In our faith, we believe that you have to live a *gut* life and believe that Jesus is the Son of God. You have to accept Jesus as your Lord and Savior. Redemption is always within reach. That hot seat you refer to doesn't have your name on it."

He stared at her for a long time. "I haven't always treated you very good. Why have you continued to be around me, or should I say *tolerate* me?"

Grinning, she said, "I like a *gut* challenge." She stood up slowly, keeping most of her pressure on her right leg. "I would like to be put on your list of people the doctors and nurses can talk to about your condition. Would that be all right?"

"I guess so." He lowered his head and fidgeted with his hands before he looked back at her. "Esther, when drool starts running down my face, or I can't feed myself . . . stuff like that . . . I don't want anyone to see me."

Esther knew in her heart that she would see this through with Gus, that she would wipe the drool from his face, feed him, and tend to whatever else he needed. But she nodded in agreement.

The man was a mess and had been intolerable to most people for as long as she had known him. But she saw something in Gus that he didn't see in himself. Remorse. Despite what he said, he was sorry for the things he'd done in his life that made him feel unworthy of God's love. And that was the beginning of redemption. With nurturing, Gus's relationship with the Lord could grow into something beautiful, and that's what Esther wanted for him.

"I will see you soon," she said. "How long will you be here?"

He shrugged again. "Who knows? I didn't think I'd still be here now."

"Very well." She gazed with a new sense of purpose at the miserable man in the bed. Esther believed in miracles. And doctors were wrong sometimes. But without a way to know Gus's destiny, she was going to do her best to show him how to have a relationship with God. She didn't care if ministry to outsiders was discouraged.

She left Gus's room and shuffled down the hall, which smelled of disinfectant. The two nurses, Loraine and Shelley, glared at her when she walked toward the elevator. She was tempted to explain about the conversation she'd had with them, but tears were building toward a full-blown meltdown.

After she'd called her driver and gotten in the car, she quietly cried in the back seat all the way home.

∞

Rose stood next to Lizzie in the living room looking out the window at Esther. They'd seen the driver drop her off, but she hadn't come into the house. She was just standing in the yard with her head down.

"Should we go out there and see if she's okay?" Rose leaned closer to the window.

"*Nee*. Let's give her a minute. She's processing something."

They waited, and a few moments later, they both quickly settled themselves on the couch as Esther slowly started toward the front door.

"Uh . . ." Lizzie slowly stood up when Esther shuffled into the room. "Did everything go all right at the hospital?"

"*Nee*, it did not." Esther sniffled, then pulled a tissue from her apron pocket.

Rose stood up to move toward her, but supposed she should let Lizzie handle this.

"Did Gus yell and scream at you? Did he get thrown out?" Lizzie turned toward the window, and Rose followed her gaze. "His truck isn't there," Lizzie said after she looked back at Esther. "Did he go to jail?"

Rose squeezed her eyes closed, cringing. Lizzie had asked the last question with a little too much enthusiasm. When she opened her eyes, the sisters were facing off, both with their hands on their hips.

"*Nee*. He did not go to jail." Esther covered her face with both hands, and when she finally showed her face, it was streaked with tears. "Gus is dying."

Lizzie grunted. "I know you're kidding. Gus Owens is too mean to die."

"It's true," she said in a tense, clipped voice. "He has leukemia, with very little hope of surviving."

Rose plopped down on the couch. It was hard not to think of her father in that moment. Despite everything the man had done, she was sad when he died. Gus probably had more good in him than her father did. If she said anything right now, it would surely turn into rambling. But a lot was going through her mind.

Lizzie looked at the floor and rubbed her forehead. Rose wasn't sure if it was because she didn't know what to say, because she didn't want to face Esther—who was openly crying now—or because she disliked Gus so much that she didn't care.

"I'm sorry you are hurting." Lizzie dropped her hands to her sides before hanging her head again.

They were all quiet. After a while, Esther stopped crying. "Gus doesn't know the Lord, and I want"—her voice was shaky—"I want to help him be at peace, to have a relationship with God. There is redemption for everyone if they seek it."

Rose silently prayed that Lizzie wouldn't say something cruel, which wasn't usually her nature. But when it came to Gus, there was no telling what might come out of Lizzie's mouth. Thankfully, Lizzie remained quiet.

"I think it's nice that you are willing to do that for Gus." Rose stood up. "I will help any way I can." She wasn't sure what she could do. Esther was the only person Gus seemed to like—and Jayce.

Esther attempted to adjust her prayer covering, but her hands were shaking. Lizzie reached up and straightened it for her, then tucked a few loose strands of hair behind her ears.

At first glimpse, Esther and Lizzie were as opposite as could be. Esther was tall and heavyset, slowing down due to arthritis in her knees. Lizzie was a tiny bundle of energy. If she had any ailments, Rose didn't know about them. Unless you counted her dentures.

Esther was refined and carried herself with dignity. Lizzie was a spitfire who said what was on her mind, didn't usually follow all the rules of the Ordnung, and had been known to cause trouble from time to time.

Rose loved her sisters, but she didn't share a bond with any of her siblings the way Esther and Lizzie did. Even though Lizzie despised Gus, she was putting Esther's feelings first, knowing her sister was in pain.

Esther cleared her throat. "Rose, I would like to have a gathering here tomorrow afternoon, after folks have time to get off work.

Maybe around six o'clock. Gus doesn't want his daughter to know about his condition, but I would like to invite Naomi and Amos and Evelyn and Jayce to come. We'll have light refreshments, and I will tell them about Gus. We are the only family he has."

Rose glanced at Lizzie, who was staring at the floor.

"I'm happy to handle all of that. I'll get word to Evelyn and Naomi, and I'll prepare the food. We are out of chowchow in the cupboard, but I believe there is more in the basement. I'll make sure to have a variety of snacks." She thought briefly if she should ask Benjamin to come, but he didn't know Gus, and this was a personal gathering. Rose would see him Saturday anyway.

"*Ach*, I forgot to tell you something." Rose flinched a little since this wasn't the best timing. "An Amish man from Shipshewana left a message on the answering machine. He wanted a room for a week, arriving tomorrow. I returned his call to confirm his reservation. Do you want me to call him back and see if he can arrive on Saturday instead? I think he is coming here for work."

Esther shook her head. "*Nee*. A new face might provide a distraction. If necessary, we can have our meeting outside by the garden."

Rose wasn't sure how much sleep Lizzie was going to lose over this news about Gus, but another person in the house might help to distract Esther.

"I'm going to lie down for a while." Esther's ashen complexion and swollen eyes were a testament to how much she really did care for Gus.

Lizzie stared at Esther's closed bedroom door for a long while before she turned to Rose. "Hon, I'm going to take a nap."

Rose nodded.

After Lizzie closed her bedroom door, Rose thought she heard a sound from inside. She tiptoed across the room until she could make out faint whimpering. Glancing back and forth between the closed doors of Esther and Lizzie's bedrooms, she finally inched closer to the sound. Rose put a hand on Lizzie's door, unsure whether to knock. She was also unclear whether Lizzie's sadness was for Esther or for Gus. Or both.

Chapter 12

Esther woke up, surprised she had slept away most of the day. It was already late afternoon. She'd missed lunch, but even though her stomach growled, food didn't sound good right now. She shuffled to the bedroom window and stared at the cottage as she tried to envision a world without Gus in it.

There would be no more constant bickering between their renter and Lizzie. Guests at the inn wouldn't have to put up with Gus's unpleasantness. Esther wouldn't have to reprimand him for calling her "Woman" or for calling Rose "Rose Petal." There would be no more instructing him on the right and wrong way to treat people. Esther wouldn't be taking him pie or leftovers because she felt sorry for him. No more mail deliveries to him. Gus's character flaws were many, and Esther had no trouble creating a mental list.

But overshadowing Gus's shortcomings were occasional

random acts of kindness that had always given her hope that the real Gus was buried beneath a life she knew nothing about.

Esther recalled having an MRI last year. She'd been so scared that she couldn't be still for the procedure. It was Gus who held her hand and convinced her that everything would be all right. And as much as he complained about his cats, it was easy to see how much he loved Whiskers and her two grown kittens.

When a film company had stayed at the inn, Gus saved the life of the star actress by jumping in the water inside Bluespring Caverns. And during that time, Gus became pals with one of the crew members, who happened to be Jayce.

Gus Owens was a work in progress, a project that Esther now feared she would never see come to fruition. Instead, she had been called to lead Gus to the Lord, and the task felt much larger than teaching him to be kind to others. Maybe the undertakings went hand in hand. To love and be kind brought a person closer to God.

She snapped out of her ponderings when Edgar Thompson started the lawnmower and began in the same place he always did on Thursday afternoons. First, he'd mow Naomi and Amos's yard, and then the space in the middle of the three houses. Afterward, he would do the cottage, and end by mowing around the main house.

Esther took a deep breath. She needed a distraction from her own thoughts, and maybe chatting with Edgar would close a window of suspicion regarding the delivery of the flowers. No matter how much she tried to convince herself that the identity of the sender didn't matter, it did.

When she walked into the living room, Rose was dusting the items on the mantel—a small figurine of a dolphin that Esther brought back from a vacation with Joe decades ago, two silk ivies in a vase, and two silver candleholders that had belonged to their mother.

Rose stashed her blue feather duster in the pocket of her apron. "You know . . ." The girl seemed lost for words, which was rare.

"What is it, dear?"

Rose chewed on her bottom lip, then sighed. "*Mei daed* was not a *gut* man. It's a terrible thing to say, but it's true." She cast her eyes down. "But I loved him, and I was sad when he died."

This was the most Rose had ever shared about her family, other than that she had multiple siblings. Esther waited to see if she would share more. She seemed to be carefully planning what she would say, which was also unusual for Rose.

"But Gus isn't a bad man. He says and does rude things sometimes, but I've seen the goodness in him that you've spoken of so often." She shivered. "He scares me sometimes when he's so gruff, but I think he'd jump in front of a train to save a person he cares about. I don't know if that makes sense. He's different from *mei daed*. And maybe his life has shaped the man that he became, but perhaps Gus has always been waiting to be set free." She locked eyes with Esther. "Do you think that in death he will be free of whatever torments him? Do you think people change when they get to heaven? Or do they repeat the same patterns as on earth?" She paused as her gaze drifted away from Esther, carrying Rose to the place she went sometimes. "But if a person behaved badly on earth, maybe they don't go to heaven."

Esther recalled what Gus had said about his front seat in hell. But Esther also didn't think Rose was talking about Gus anymore. Only one word came to mind. She didn't know if it applied to Rose's father, but she knew the word to be associated with Gus and the charge she'd been given to help him attain the goal.

"Redemption," she said softly to Rose. "I believe that if someone is truly sorry for the sins they have committed and is trying to live a good life, God readily opens His arms to that person if they have accepted Jesus as their Lord and Savior."

"That's what you're hoping for Gus, isn't it?"

This was the most calculated, thought-out conversation Esther had ever had with Rose. There were no rambling sentences or jumping from subject to subject before Esther could process what she was saying. Rose was becoming a better listener.

"I think miracles happen, and I will be praying for one for Gus so that I will have more time with him, to peel back the layers, to get to the real Gus you mentioned." She smiled. "He's in there. We just don't see him much. But equally as important, whether it is his time to leave us or not, I will be praying Gus finds redemption." Esther blinked back her own tears as she watched a tear slip down Rose's cheek.

"Esther?"

She edged closer to Rose and put a hand on her arm. "*Ya*, dear. What is it?"

"I prayed for redemption for *mei* father before he died. But I did not pray for a miracle. Sometimes I wonder if I will be turned away from the gates of heaven for not praying for *mei* own father to get well."

Esther rubbed Rose's arm. "*Mei* sweet *maedel*, only God grants miracles. We can pray to Him, ask Him to grant a miracle. But in the end, everything that happens is *Gott*'s will. If you didn't pray for your father to get well, it isn't your fault he died. You understand that, *ya*?" Esther wanted to ask what her father had done for her to feel this way, but she would accept whatever Rose was comfortable telling her at present.

"I guess." She swiped at her eyes. "I'm sorry you're hurting over Gus's news. It makes me sad too."

"I'm all right, Rose. It was just a shock, and I needed to process the information. And I needed to pray about it. But I'm okay." She grinned. "There are a lot of things I can't control in this world, but I can take a stab at figuring out who sent me flowers. I'm going to go have a talk with Edgar."

Rose lifted up on her toes. "Lizzie will be so excited. She calls him suspect number two."

Esther shook her head, then laughed, which felt good. "I know she does. Wish me luck."

After Esther went outside, Rose sat on the couch, leaned her head back, and covered her eyes with her hands, wishing she hadn't shared so much with Esther. Her father was a taboo subject, and Esther probably thought her father had laid hands on her. But the abuse Rose suffered from her dad had nothing to do with any physical harm. Most of the time, she was able to push it from her mind.

Lizzie swung her door open and bolted out of her bedroom. She was dressed, but her long gray hair lay flat against her back, and her mouth was agape. "I saw Esther from the window! She's going to go talk to suspect number two, isn't she?" Lizzie clapped her hands together as she scurried to the window in the living room. "We might as well be peepers—or Peeping Toms, like the *Englisch* say. Seems we are always spying on someone."

Rose sidled up to Lizzie and noticed dark circles under her eyes. It seemed Esther's effort to solve the flower mystery was a nice distraction for everyone.

Lizzie stomped a foot. "*Ach*, I can't see Esther's face, but Edgar is sporting a big grin." She snapped her head in Rose's direction. "What do you think that means?"

Rose shrugged. "I don't know. Maybe he sent the flowers and he's glad that she asked him about it." She gasped. "What if he asks her for a date? Do you think she would go? I bet it's been a long time since Esther was courted. Probably decades. I think it would be exciting, especially since she's so upset about Gus. It would give her something else to focus on. But . . . he's *Englisch*."

Lizzie laughed. "Hon, you're as bad as we are—a true romantic at heart. I'm almost certain Esther isn't in the market for romantic love, but who wouldn't like to know they have an admirer? And it would put to rest any worry about her having a stalker."

"Here she comes." Rose took a big step backward, wound around to the couch, and plopped down. Lizzie did the same, quickly picked up a magazine, and began thumbing through it.

Esther walked into the living room, her expression giving away nothing. "First of all," she said, "Lizzie, don't act like you're reading that magazine because you don't have your glasses on and you can't see a thing." Then her accusatory eyes landed on Rose. "I saw you with Lizzie at the window."

"Tell us." Lizzie tossed the magazine on the coffee table. "It's Edgar, isn't it? He's in love with you. He sent the flowers, didn't he?" She sprang to her feet. "Suspect number two!"

Rose chuckled at Lizzie's behavior, but Esther held her expression, revealing nothing as she sat down in the rocking chair and kicked it into motion.

Lizzie scowled. "Was it Edgar or not?"

Esther crossed one leg over the other and raised her chin. "Well . . . as for your suspect number two . . ."

Rose put her hand over her mouth, stifling laughter. Esther was intentionally dragging this out, and Lizzie was so red in the face, she looked like she might burst.

"Esther Ann Zook." Lizzie thrust her hands to her hips. "Is Edgar interested in romance?"

Esther batted her eyes at her sister. "*Ya*, he is."

Lizzie gasped so loudly, Rose feared she might choke. "I knew it."

"*Ya*, Edgar is very interested in romance . . . with *June Livingston*." Esther laughed.

"You mean, that *Englisch* woman who works at the funeral home?" Lizzie's nostrils flared. "Are you sure?"

Esther nodded. "*Ya*. I didn't even ask him about the flowers. He told me he had been seeing her and asked if he could do the yard earlier in the day next week so that he could take her to a family gathering."

Lizzie groaned as she shuffled back to the couch and sat. "Before Edgar retired and started mowing yards, he was a taxidermist." She shifted her dentures from side to side. "Guess they have something in common: death." Lizzie scrunched her face up and shivered.

Esther stood up abruptly. "I think I'll lie down." She didn't look at Lizzie or Rose.

"You just got up," Lizzie said as she stood, then followed her. "Esther, I shouldn't have said that. I'm sorry."

"*Nee*, it's fine." Esther gently closed her bedroom door behind her, leaving her sister staring at it.

Lizzie hung her head and went back to the couch. "Rose..."

"*Ya?*"

"At our age, Esther and I have attended a lot of funerals, more than we can count. And with our husbands and parents being exceptions, I can't recall seeing Esther this upset about a person facing death."

Rose folded her hands in her lap. "I heard you crying in your room." She squeezed her eyes closed, thinking maybe she shouldn't have said anything.

Lizzie didn't speak for a few moments, then she looked at Rose. "One day, I'll go, or Esther will go before me. No matter who goes first, it will feel unbearable. She isn't just *mei schweschder*, she's *mei* best friend. Esther is the best woman I've ever known. But, it's not just that." She smiled a little. "We have fun together. Always have. Even when we were married to Joe and Reuben, we still made time for each other and did a lot together. Esther is all the things I should be. She doesn't have a bad word to say about anyone."

"I think you complement each other." Rose wanted to tell Lizzie how much she would have cherished either one of them as a mother, but that would lead into a conversation she didn't want to have.

Lizzie patted Rose on the leg. "Hon, that's kind of you to say." She stared long and hard at her before she spoke. "But I assure you . . . *mei* tears were not for Gus Owens, they were for *mei schweschder*. When she hurts, I hurt." She stood up. "I need pie. Join me if you'd like."

After Lizzie left the room, Rose thought about what Lizzie had just said. And for reasons Rose couldn't wrap her mind around, she was pretty sure Lizzie was lying. Maybe Lizzie would stick to her convictions throughout this situation with Gus, but Rose couldn't help but wonder if her emotions ran deeper than she let on. Love and hate were closer together than people thought sometimes. If anyone knew that, it was Rose.

She laid her head back against the couch cushion again and closed her eyes, willing any thoughts about her parents to be replaced with thoughts of Benjamin. Saturday would be their third date, and she hoped to learn more about him. Even though he'd said he liked the person she was and how talkative she could be, Rose needed to tone things down, if only a little, and be a better listener. Benjamin might tire of her ramblings. Her father certainly had . . . more than once.

Squeezing her eyes closed even more, she pushed the vision

of her father from her mind's eye and replaced it with Benjamin's face. She wondered what he was doing right now.

∽

Benjamin lay in bed Thursday night thinking about Rose and wishing she had a cell phone. Misuse of mobile devices was common in most Amish communities since they were permitted for business and emergencies only. Benjamin tried to follow that rule, but if Rose had a phone, he would be calling her right now. It had only been twenty-four hours since he'd seen her, but visions of her had whisked in and out of his mind since he left her. Each thought brought forth a smile.

Her childlike enthusiasm was refreshing. Women he'd been out with in the past tended to be reserved, which meant they behaved the way a proper Amish woman should act in their opinion. It wasn't just that Benjamin was shy. Those types of women bored him. He didn't think he'd ever get bored with Rose around.

He startled when his cell phone buzzed on the nightstand. Yawning, he reached for it, but when he saw the caller ID he was suddenly wide awake.

"*Wie bischt?*" He sat up in bed. "Is everything okay?"

"Did I wake you up?" Rose asked. "I'm quite sure I shouldn't have called so late, but I just needed someone to talk to. Evelyn and Naomi are usually busy with their families right now, or they might already be asleep. I'm calling from the phone in the barn. You left your business card on the kitchen table." She paused. "Did I wake you up?" she asked again.

"*Nee*, not at all. I was just lying here thinking . . . about you actually." He wasn't sure if he would have been able to say that to her face, but it slipped out easily over the phone. He'd wondered if she might find the card.

"What were you thinking? Were you wondering what we'll do on Saturday? I've given a little thought to that since you aren't familiar with the area. I'm really open for anything."

"Me too." He wanted to tell her that he would be happy in her presence, no matter what the agenda was for the day, but he chose to hold on to that thought. "You said you needed someone to talk to. Is anything wrong?"

"It wasn't a *gut* day. Esther found out that Gus Owens—the man who rents the cottage by the inn—has leukemia and is probably going to die. He's a very grumpy fellow who doesn't really get along with anyone, except for Esther and a man named Jayce. He's very hard to be around, but Esther took the news hard. It just got me thinking about some things. Gus has a grown *dochder*, but they don't have anything to do with each other." She paused for longer than Benjamin would have expected. "I remember you saying your *daed* died four years ago. Prior to his passing, were you close to him?"

"*Ya*, I was. *Mei schweschdere* were too, but probably not as close to him as I was. Maybe because I was the only *sohn*." When she didn't say anything, he asked, "Were you close to your father?"

"*Nee*, not really."

Benjamin recalled Rose's reactions at supper when her family was mentioned. He rubbed the back of his neck, unsure how to respond. "Maybe because you had a lot of *bruders* and *schweschdere*?"

"Maybe." Another long pause. "Tell me about your father. Was he stern? Did he play an active role in your upbringing? Was he a happy man? Did he laugh a lot?"

He cherished the memories of his father. "*Ya*, he was a happy man most of the time. Things got him down, just like the rest of us, but he had a robust laugh that I can still hear in my mind sometimes. We did a lot together. On Saturdays, we usually worked half a day out in the fields, then spent the afternoons down at the pond fishing. He taught me what it meant to be a man, about hard work, and to always respect women." Benjamin loved how easy it was to talk to Rose—he felt very comfortable sharing with her—but he sensed there was a purpose for her inquiries.

"That's lovely to hear. You respected him, didn't you?"

"*Ya*, very much. He was a *gut* man." He rubbed the back of his neck again. "Rose . . . do you want to talk about your father?"

"I thought I did, but *nee* . . . not really, I suppose. I think I'd rather talk about possibilities for Saturday. I'm afraid there isn't a lot to do in the town of Montgomery. There are restaurants, as you know. I think there is a museum, but I've never been to it. Do you have a preference for an indoor or outdoor activity?"

She'd quickly directed the conversation away from her father, but talking about his father had taken him back in time. "Do you like to fish?"

It took her a while to answer. "I've never fished. *Mei bruders* did. That was another thing *mei daed* thought only the boys should do, but I don't remember *mei* father ever going with them."

She sighed. "I can remember how much trouble they got into when they didn't bring home a big stringer of catfish, though."

Benjamin's father never would have scolded him for not catching fish. And both of his sisters loved to go fishing. "Have you ever wanted to go?"

"*Ach, ya.* I would *lieb* to go fishing. Is that something you might want to do Saturday?"

"*Ya,* if you'd like to. I know there must be several lakes nearby. Or ponds at least." Benjamin thought about how fun it would be to see Rose fishing for the first time.

"I have the perfect place," she said. "There's a pond tucked almost out of sight at The Peony Inn. You might have seen it. I've never been down there to fish, but I've seen Gus go there many times toting a fishing pole and carrying a stringer of fish to a little building back behind the cottage. I guess that's where he cleans them. I could make us a picnic lunch, and we could fish, and . . . am I talking too much?"

"Rose, I could listen to you talk all day long."

There was a long pause, then Rose let out a squeal.

"What's wrong?" Benjamin was on his feet in seconds.

"Mice. I'm in the barn, and two mice just scurried across the ground."

Benjamin laughed. "Sorry, it's not funny."

Rose giggled. "It's a little funny. You would have thought so if you'd seen the way I jumped and scooted across the room. I almost yanked the phone cord from the wall."

And from there, Rose started talking about how she used to sleepwalk.

"You danced in your sleep?" Benjamin laughed as he tried to picture Rose dancing like the English.

Laughing, she said, "And I sang. Or so I'm told. I don't remember, but I think it was unnerving for Esther and Lizzie the first time it happened at the inn. It took them a while to tell me about it. It hasn't happened in a long time. Lizzie insisted that if I drank a warm cup of milk before bed I'd fall into a deeper sleep and wouldn't waltz around at night. It seems to have worked."

Benjamin fluffed his pillows behind his back, then crossed one ankle over the other. "I've got a picture of you dancing in *mei* mind."

She laughed. "It's probably not a very pretty picture. I'm sure I looked like a crazy person."

"Not at all. It's a beautiful picture." Benjamin closed his eyes and recalled their first night together and the way they had kissed.

She was quiet. "I'm looking forward to Saturday."

"Me too. Do you have a fishing pole? I'm guessing not since you haven't been to the pond. I have extras I can bring."

"That would be *gut*. I don't have one. I've always meant to go fishing at the pond, but just haven't. It seemed like it would be more fun with another person."

After another mouse scurried near Rose's feet, they said their goodbyes.

As Benjamin snuffed out the lantern on the nightstand, he thought about his father and the good man that he was. He wasn't so sure about Rose's father.

Chapter 13

Friday afternoon, Esther opened the door for their guest, the man who would be staying for a week. He was a young Amish fellow, maybe a little older than Rose and very nice looking. He didn't have a beard so he was unmarried. If Rose wasn't already smitten with Benjamin, Esther would have seen him as an opportunity to do a little matchmaking. But Rose needed a certain type of person, and considering she was going on her third date with Benjamin tomorrow, things seemed to be progressing nicely.

"*Wie bischt*, and welcome to The Peony Inn." She pushed the screen door open, and the tall man stepped over the threshold carrying one small red suitcase. "And what brings you to Montgomery?" It was a bit nosy, but Esther liked to have a feel for the type of people staying under their roof. Some people were very evasive. Others were happy to share.

"I'm here for *mei* great-aunt's funeral."

Esther struggled not to react. There'd been too much talk about death lately. "I'm sorry for your loss. May your aunt rest in peace."

"*Danki.* She was old. Just her time. *Mei* parents weren't well enough to attend, so they asked me to come." He sighed, as if the trip might be a burden for him.

Rose walked into the room and approached the man. "*Wie bischt.* I'm Rose, and if there is anything you need during your stay, please don't hesitate to ask." She motioned toward the dining room. "I've set out appetizers and iced tea if you are in need of a snack." She pointed to the stairs. "And your room is the second one on the right."

"You're the woman I spoke to?" The man sauntered closer to Rose after she nodded, then he grinned. "You're even prettier than you sounded on the phone."

Rose blushed immediately. "*Danki.*"

"I'm Lloyd." He turned to Esther and raised an eyebrow.

"*Ach, mei* apologies. I should have introduced myself. I'm Esther Zook. *Mei schweschder* and I own the inn." Esther's mind had been in a fog lately.

"I'm going to take *mei* suitcase upstairs, then I'd love some of those snacks you mentioned." The fellow slowed his stride when he passed by Rose, so close he nearly brushed elbows with her. "Maybe you'll join me," he said over his shoulder as he took his first step up the stairs.

Rose nodded and smiled, but not with the exuberance she usually displayed for guests. Cheerfulness came easily for Rose, but there was no twinkle in her eyes.

After the door closed upstairs, Rose shook her head. "Something about that man makes me nervous. He looked at me . . . funny."

Esther had to agree but didn't want to alarm Rose. "He probably just thinks you're very pretty and that was his attempt at flirting."

"Well, I didn't like it," Rose said firmly. "But I'll be polite and have a quick appetizer with him." She marched to the dining room.

Esther went to the kitchen and opened the refrigerator. There were plenty of appetizers on platters for their gathering later. Esther dreaded having to tell Naomi, Amos, Evelyn, and Jayce about Gus. Everyone had mixed emotions when it came to Gus. Jayce would take it the hardest, though. They'd already decided to meet at the picnic tables near the garden so as not to disturb their guest.

Lizzie shuffled into the room. "I heard a car door and saw that young man walking up to the house. What's his business here?"

Esther scowled. "He is here for a funeral. Can you please put your teeth in before everyone gets here?"

"Why? They've all seen me without them plenty of times," she sputtered, which often resulted in spitting.

Esther waved a hand in front of her face. "Because you unintentionally spit when they aren't in."

"Actually, I wasn't planning on attending that little gathering." Lizzie lowered her head a little but kept her eyes on Esther. "I'm guessing you're going to make me."

"I'm not going to *make* you do anything, but it would be nice if our entire family was together for this announcement." Lizzie considered their invited friends to be family also, but her sister didn't want to attend because the topic of discussion would be Gus.

Lizzie huffed. "I'll be there." She left for her bedroom. "And I'll put in *mei* stupid teeth."

Esther shook her head, but a sense of dread was circling all around her. She was going to present Gus's situation in the best light possible, hoping to come across as hopeful, despite what sounded like an imminent outcome.

She walked to the dining room so Rose wouldn't have to be alone with Lloyd.

∞

"Everything is done." Rose waved an arm across an elaborate spread of food. "I'm sure I made too much, but it's been a while since we've had a guest and I think I went overboard. But we will enjoy any leftovers, and Lloyd might be one of those midnight eaters like we've had in the past." Rose recalled the film crew who had stayed at the inn. Several of them were known to get up during the night for a snack.

"It will all get eaten. We can always take some of it to Gus." Esther paused. "I called to check on him this morning. They said he did well with his chemotherapy treatment, which normally doesn't require this long of a hospital stay—or a stay in the hospital at all—but they had trouble regulating his blood pressure.

He was also there because they were waiting on blood to arrive for a transfusion. I never realized there was such a shortage." Frowning, she said, "Maybe I should have visited him this morning, but it would have worn me out, physically and emotionally, and I want to be strong for our get-together. Anyway, he is scheduled to come home tomorrow as long as they are able to stabilize his blood pressure."

"*Ach*, that's *gut* that he doesn't have to stay in the hospital much longer." Rose had no idea how long a person could live with leukemia, especially if it was an advanced stage.

They heard footsteps coming down the stairs. Rose folded her hands in front of her and tried not to fidget.

"Wow. All of this for me?" Lloyd's eyes widened as he sauntered closer to the table. After he eyed the food, he looked Rose up and down and grinned. There was something suggestive in everything he did and said.

Esther cleared her throat. "You said you were here for a funeral? May I ask the name of your late aunt?"

Rose wanted to ask him why he was staying a whole week, but she waited for him to answer Esther's question.

"Mary Grace Troyer." Lloyd picked up a small plate and began filling it with chips, dips, pickles, and olives.

Esther tapped a finger to her chin. "Hmm . . . I don't believe I know her. Again, so sorry for your loss."

"*Danki*." He glanced at Rose again, but she looked away. Even if she hadn't met Benjamin, she could already tell that Lloyd wasn't someone she'd be interested in, no matter how nice looking he was. He had beady, dark eyes, and it felt like he was undressing her every time he looked at her. His presence gave her chills, even though it was surely seventy-five degrees in the house.

She folded her arms across her chest and stood taller. "Why are you staying for a week if you are only here to attend a funeral? It seems like you would be anxious to get home after something like this." She paused, opting to adjust the curtness in her voice. "I, too, am sorry for your loss."

"I, uh . . . needed some time away, so I thought I'd represent our family at the funeral and consider it a mini vacation too." His dark eyebrows arched above his black button-like eyes as one corner of his mouth tipped into a grin. Then he winked at her. "I'm glad I booked a week."

Rose wasn't looking forward to the next seven days. She enjoyed conversation with most everyone, but this man made her nervous.

"*Ach*, there is one thing . . ." Their guest frowned, shifting his weight from one foot to the other. "I saw a few mouse droppings underneath the bed."

Rose glanced at Esther, then back at Lloyd. "Oh dear. *Ach*, I'm so sorry. I thought I swept your room thoroughly, but I must have missed that. I'll take care of it right away." She could feel her face turning red.

"Do you have a mouse problem here?" He set his plate on the table and grimaced. "Because I can't stand the furry little creatures. If you've got some sort of infestation, I don't think I could sleep through the night."

Rose glanced at Esther, unsure what to say. There were plenty of mice in the barn, but she hadn't seen one in the house since she'd been there. *And why would a guest look under the bed?*

"Since we are in a rural area, we do get an occasional mouse indoors, but I haven't seen one in a very long time," Esther said. "I'm sure you don't have anything to worry about."

"*Gut.* I can't stay in a place with mice." Lloyd picked up his plate and started to eat again, his beady eyes studying Rose.

She excused herself, and Esther followed her to the mudroom in the back of the house.

"There's something about that man, Esther," she said, whispering. "He is very handsome, but to use one of Lizzie's words, he's rather *creepy*. I don't like the way he looks at me."

"*Ya.*" Esther frowned. "He looks at you like prey that he's getting ready to pounce on." She shook her head. "There haven't been many Amish men whom I didn't like, or at least tolerate, but this new guest leaves me feeling a bit unsettled. We will keep an eye on him."

"*Ya*, okay." She twisted the string of her prayer covering as she chewed her bottom lip. "I feel like I will need to lock *mei* bedroom door at night. Maybe we are just being silly and he's just very flirtatious, but I don't think I would have returned his interest even if I hadn't met Benjamin."

Esther rubbed her arm. "Let me know if he gives you any trouble. I'm going to start getting the food together for our gathering this afternoon." She lowered her arm and briefly hung her head before she looked up at Rose. "I hope everyone will still want to eat when they hear about Gus. Or maybe they won't be very affected by the news."

"Don't rule out a miracle, Esther. And I think everyone will be saddened by this news. Gus can be intolerable, but as we discussed earlier, there is good in him. I do think Jayce will take Gus's prognosis rather hard. It was a surprise to me that they became such good friends, but maybe it shouldn't have been. Jayce didn't get along with his father, and Gus doesn't speak to his daughter. Maybe they each found something in the other that they needed."

"Very well said." Esther gave a taut nod of her head.

"If not a bit wordy," Rose said before she grinned.

Esther stared at her. "I've noticed that it's easier to keep up with you lately, with what you're saying. I don't want you to change, Rose. Truly. Lizzie and I are old, and if the truth be told, probably a little hard of hearing. So, as I've told you before, we just had trouble keeping up with you sometimes. But something has changed. You seem . . . more relaxed." She smiled. "Maybe that has something to do with Benjamin?"

It didn't, but Rose nodded anyway as she forced a smile. Rose was working through some things on her own, issues that required a great deal of concentration. She was considering things before she spoke, in an effort not to say too much but also to open up to the people she loved. Some days, she wanted so badly to tell Esther and Lizzie—and now Benjamin—about her childhood. But would talking about it make it better or worse? It would forever be a memory she couldn't shed. But maybe it didn't have to define her.

"I need to change clothes." Rose eyed her soiled black apron. "Or at least *mei* apron, then I'll be in the kitchen to help you."

"No rush."

After Esther left the mudroom, Rose went upstairs. On the way, she said a prayer that all would go all right when they gathered outside soon. Or as well as could be expected.

∞

Esther waited until everyone had filled their plates with snacks, then they bowed their heads in prayer. There was a nice breeze underneath the oak tree where the two picnic tables had been for years.

"I left the girls with the babysitter we use sometimes." Naomi glanced around at everyone before she looked back at Esther. "I sensed this gathering was more than just a get-together. You have something important to tell us, don't you?"

Naomi had lived with Esther and Lizzie, and the girl could usually pick up on their moods. "*Ya*, I'm afraid I have some news." Esther was the only one standing as she took a deep breath. She'd practiced what she would say, but at this moment, nothing sounded right. "It's about Gus."

She glanced at Lizzie, who didn't look up. Then her eyes landed on Jayce, who had stopped chewing, then quickly swallowed. "What about him?"

"It's with a heavy heart that I must tell you that Gus has an advanced stage of leukemia. His prognosis is grim." Esther let her eyes drift to each one of them. There were concerned expressions, but Jayce's gaze clung to hers as deep lines of worry formed across his forehead.

When no one said anything, Esther said, "We have all had

our run-ins with Gus." She glanced at Lizzie, whose head remained down. "But we are the only family he has. I didn't want you to find out from anyone else." She bit her bottom lip when it began to tremble.

Jayce laid his fork on his plate, and Esther's heart hurt for the boy. "What do you mean? How grim?"

Esther wanted to sugarcoat the situation, but honesty would be best—mixed with a large dose of hope. "Gus is considered terminal." She held up a finger. "But only *Gott* knows the outcome of these things, and I believe our Lord provides miracles. I'm just letting you all know because I'm sure Gus will have more hospital stays in his future. He's receiving chemotherapy right now. He tried to keep the news from us, but I . . . I guess you could say I stumbled upon it."

"We will all do whatever we can for Gus," Naomi said as she glanced at Amos, who nodded. Their sentiments were echoed by Evelyn.

"Wait." Jayce's forehead began to bead with sweat. "I don't understand. I mean, he looks okay. I noticed he's lost a little weight, but—" He blotted the sweat on his forehead with his napkin before he laid it on his plate. Jayce was known to finish off three or four times the normal amount of food a man can eat, but he'd clearly lost his appetite.

Esther shifted her gaze to Lizzie, hoping her sister would offer up something positive to say, but Lizzie merely stared at her plate.

"I know you take Gus pie and leftovers," Evelyn said. "But I will start taking him more food as well. He'll need more healthy meals, I would assume, as opposed to those dinners that come in a box."

"I will do whatever I can too." Naomi blinked back tears. "He's a grumpy fellow, but I can't imagine him not being with us."

Amos put an arm around his wife. Esther put a hand to her heart, touched by the reactions coming from their small group. Jayce was rubbing his forehead with both hands.

"Gus will be home from the hospital tomorrow. I plan to talk to him about what he might need." She sighed. "I don't know much about leukemia, but I learned this morning that there is a shortage of blood. Apparently his situation is more dire due to the fact that he has a rare blood type."

Jayce cleared his throat. "I know a little bit about this." He lowered his hands to the table, and Evelyn placed her hand on his. "When I lived in Los Angeles, I worked with a man who had leukemia. We all gave blood in his name, and some of us donated platelets. He didn't have a rare blood type, and he didn't necessarily get our blood, but he got credit for the blood and platelets that we donated. Most of the time, he was assured a sufficient amount of blood for his transfusions because of our donations." He paused and took a deep breath. "In Gus's case, I would think that if any of us had Gus's blood type, he'd get it directly from us since it's not common. Either way, I'm going to find out *mei* blood type and plan to donate. Someone with leukemia usually needs blood transfusions often."

"I'm willing to find out *mei* blood type too." Naomi squeezed her husband's hand after he nodded and said he would also. "Either way, I'll donate blood to help out," she said.

After Evelyn said she would donate blood, Esther said she would also, even though all things medical terrified her. Rose also chimed in that she would give blood.

Everyone looked at Lizzie, who had slouched down on the bench so far that her chin was almost in her food.

"Lizzie?" Esther said when it didn't appear her sister was going to say anything.

"What?" Lizzie didn't look up, but she sighed. "Fine. I will too."

Esther wasn't surprised that Lizzie was the last to commit. "I think that is all we can do, along with prayer, of course. And knowing Gus, he isn't going to want us to feel sorry for him. I think we should try to carry on as normally as possible."

As Esther had feared, everyone else seemed to have lost their appetites along with Jayce. She had. Even Lizzie wasn't eating.

Jayce thanked Esther for the food, even though his plate was full, then he excused himself. His wife followed him to their buggy.

Esther wanted to go to the boy, to try to ease the pain he must be feeling, but Evelyn would help him through this. Esther only had God to turn to. And she planned to pray a lot—for more time to help Gus seek the redemption she believed he wanted, despite what he said. And for a miracle. Life without Gus would feel . . . off.

Chapter 14

Saturday morning, Benjamin walked alongside Rose down to the pond toting two poles, a tackle box, and a container of night crawlers. The worms were almost guaranteed to at least snag a bite.

"What kind of fish is in the pond?" He nodded to the fairly large body of water in front of them.

"I don't really know." She carried a picnic basket as she stayed in step with him. "I would think catfish, maybe bass, or crappie? I'm so excited. I hope I catch something." She lifted her eyes to the sky. "There are just enough clouds to keep us from being too hot. And the sunlight peaks through every now and then and keeps it from being a dreary day. What kind of bait will we use? I remember *mei bruders* used to use live bait like minnows or worms."

Her radiance and enthusiasm were contagious. Benjamin had a bounce in his step that he hadn't had in a long time. "I brought worms."

"Eww." She scrunched up her nose.

Benjamin chuckled. "I'll put them on the hook for you."

She shook her head. "*Nee*, I want the whole experience. I'll bait *mei* hook and even take off a fish if I catch one."

Benjamin smiled, knowing she meant every word. "I'll just sit back and watch."

She set the picnic basket on the bench that faced the pond. His mouth watered when she opened the two lids on top of the wicker basket. There were all kinds of containers, along with a thermos. "*Ach*, that's a lot of food."

"We have a guest staying at the inn, and Esther also had people over late yesterday afternoon. There were lots of leftovers." She started pulling out Tupperware. "I didn't even ask you if you wanted to eat first. I wasn't sure what you liked, so I brought a little of everything."

He leaned closer, lowering his head above the basket. "Where are the carrots?"

She crinkled her nose again and lifted up a small plastic container. Holding it with two fingers at arms length, she said, "Exclusively for you."

He laughed. "I was actually kidding, but I'll happily eat them." His stomach rumbled. "Are you hungry?"

"You certainly are." She giggled. "I can hear your stomach growling."

Benjamin put a hand on his stomach. "I didn't eat much breakfast since I figured we would have an early lunch." He'd arrived at the inn at ten o'clock, like they'd agreed on. She didn't even have everything unpacked when they heard movement to their left.

"No, no, no." A large man with a gray beard and ponytail walked up to them carrying a fishing pole and tackle box. "Rose Petal, this ain't gonna work."

"Good morning, Gus." She stopped what she was doing, straightened, and folded her hands in front of her. "It's nice to see you, and I'm glad you're home from the hospital." She nodded at Benjamin. "This is *mei* friend, Benjamin."

"Yeah, okay." The older man scowled at him before he turned his attention back to Rose. "First we had Naomi and Amos canoodling down here. Then Evelyn and Jayce." He rolled his eyes. "And now it's you two."

"I've brought lots of food if you'd care to join us." Rose smiled, unruffled by the man. "I have dips and chips, chicken salad, tuna salad, vegetables, and—"

"I don't need any food." The older man sighed. "Food is the *last* thing I need. Peace and quiet is what I need. Fishing gives me that." He took two steps forward. "Maybe since I'm dying, you could schedule your canoodling around my fishing schedule?" He paused as he drew gray bushy eyebrows into a frown. "Which would be *now*, by the way."

Wow. Rose had been right when she said Gus was grumpy, but in light of the circumstances, Benjamin held his tongue. He wondered, however, if fishing and lunch would lead to the canoodling Gus mentioned. Then he reminded himself that he and Rose had agreed to hold off on anything physical, at least for now. But Benjamin still had a hard time not staring at her mouth and recalling their first kisses.

"Gus, I have heard Esther tell you several times in the past that the pond is for everyone to enjoy." She shrugged. "And basically, we were here first, but we don't mind if you'd like to join us. We're planning to eat then start fishing afterward. I've never fished before, so Benjamin is going to teach me. I'm even going to put *mei* own worms on *mei* hooks, and—"

"Oh, good grief. I'm going to go see Esther about this." Gus stomped off toward the main house.

"It was nice to meet you, Gus," Benjamin said as the older man walked away.

Gus mumbled something, but Benjamin didn't catch what he said. Probably just as well. If the man hadn't been terminally ill, he would have felt the need to defend Rose, to ask Gus to be a little kinder.

Rose slammed her hands to her hips. "See what I mean." She shook her head. "He's like that most of the time. But I've always been nice to him. And especially now, I'll continue to treat him with kindness. I'm always hoping some of it will rub off on him." She lifted the thermos from the picnic basket. "I think he makes excuses to see Esther. We all think he's sweet on her. *Ach*, well . . . everyone but Esther thinks that. But Esther did take his leukemia diagnosis very hard." She drew in a breath. "Lizzie is another story. She and Gus fight like crazy." She shriveled up her nose again. It was cute when she did that. "Lizzie has actually kicked him in the shin before, more than once."

"She's so tiny." Benjamin recalled how different the sisters were in appearance. Esther was a larger woman.

"Don't let her fool you. She's a tough lady. And unpredictable. Esther is more refined." Rose laughed. "They are opposites, but they *lieb* each other very much. I wish I was close to *mei schweschdere* like that." Her expression fell right away, like it always did when she mentioned her family. "I *lieb mei schweschdere*, but we just weren't close like that."

Benjamin sensed again that she wanted to talk about her family, but she never elaborated on anything.

Rose spread a red-and-white checkered blanket on the ground, and after they'd each filled a plate, they sat down, each with a glass of tea.

"The yardman, Edgar, he sprays for ants down here by the pond, but I'll leave the picnic basket on the bench, just to be safe." She nodded at his plate. "I see you got a little of everything . . . even carrots."

Benjamin chuckled, then picked one up and pushed it toward her.

"*Eww, nee*. Get that orange thing away from me." She pointed to the picnic basket. "Don't make me pull out a banana."

He tried to make a face like she did, but he suspected he probably looked silly since she laughed. He was going to ask what her aversion was to carrots, but then his eyes landed on her mouth again, and he lost his train of thought.

Gus's fishing supplies landed with a thud on the front porch before the screen door closed at the main house.

"Oh dear." Rose's eyes widened. "I don't think he even knocked. And we have a guest staying there."

∞

Esther rushed from the kitchen to the living room when the screen door slammed shut and Gus began bellowing out her name.

"Gus." She put a finger to her lips. "No yelling. We have a guest staying with us, and he's upstairs."

"Well, we need to talk." He looped his thumbs under suspenders that weren't nearly as tight against his belly as they used to be. Why hadn't she noticed that he'd lost weight?

Sighing, she motioned for him to follow her to the kitchen. Luckily, Lizzie had gone to take food to some shut-ins around their area.

"You will keep your voice down." She pointed to a chair. "Sit. Do you want *kaffi*?"

"No. I don't want coffee. And I don't need to sit down. I need to know why two more people are occupying space down by the pond during my fishing time. I already missed several days of fishing because I was in the hospital. Now Rose Petal and her beau are down there and claim to be fishing."

Esther sat at the table and tapped it with her first finger. "Sit."

"Oh, good grief." He pulled out the chair and groaned as he sat. "I'm dying, Esther. Do you really have to reprimand me? Can't a man on his way out at least enjoy a little fishing? And another thing"—he cut his eyes at her from across the table—"you must have told your entire clan that I'm sick. Why would you do that? They don't like me. But they must feel sorry for me because when I got home this morning, I had four casseroles in the refrigerator, two chocolate pies on the table, and two loaves of homemade bread on the counter. And a whole bunch of dips and chips and other stuff." He scowled. "Esther, I can't eat all that."

Esther gleamed on the inside. "Well, the pies are from me. And obviously Evelyn and Naomi made the casseroles, which can be divided into portions and frozen. Rose is responsible for the appetizers. I'm not sure who gets credit for the bread." When he opened his mouth to speak, she said, "Hush. Now you hear me out. It is not that any of our little group doesn't like you." She cleared her throat when he frowned, both of them knowing Lizzie wasn't included in that statement. "But they don't like the way you treat them sometimes, and there is a difference. They were all saddened by your diagnosis, and everyone is going to donate blood so that you won't be denied a transfusion when you need one."

"*Everyone?*" He leaned back in the chair and folded his hands across his stomach.

"*Ya*, Gus. Even Lizzie."

"Well, surprise, surprise." He lowered his head for a couple of seconds before he looked back at her. "Esther, I don't want you giving blood. You're terrified of all that medical stuff. Although I'd rather have your blood flowing through my veins as opposed to the others."

"It doesn't work like that unless one of us has your exact blood type, which is unlikely since it's not common. But each time one of us gives blood, we can give it in your name."

He stared at her for a long while. "Why would you all do that?"

"Because despite what you think, Amos and Naomi and Evelyn and Jayce all care about you." She raised a palm to shush him when he opened his mouth to speak. "And yes, in her own way, Lizzie cares about you too."

Esther waited for an argument from Gus, but a dazed look of despair spread over his face. "What did Jayce say?"

She cleared her throat, struggling to keep her emotions in check. "He was visibly upset."

Gus turned his head away from her. "Hmm" was all he said.

"Can I make a suggestion?" Esther raised an eyebrow.

"Well, if I say no, you'll do it anyway." He waved a hand dismissively. "So go ahead."

"You are capable of being nice to people. I saw that with the staff at the hospital. And when I questioned you about it, you said you'd like to go out on a *gut* note." She shrugged. "Why not be kind, the way you were with those nurses, to the people who care about you? The day you returned from the hospital, you were showered with food. And everyone in our little family—and yes, Gus, we are a family—is planning to give blood on your behalf." She slouched into the chair and grinned. "It might put you farther away from that front row by the furnace you spoke about."

He was quiet, which was unusual.

"I'm sure you have a lot on your mind, Gus. But you should be grateful to have friends, especially now."

"I've told you. You're my only friend. And I reckon Jayce is too." His slumped into the chair. "Um, by the way. Did you find out who sent you those flowers?"

"*Nee*, I didn't. And I'm not going to worry about it. We don't need you sitting on the porch in an attempt to protect us. I don't feel like the flowers were sent with any ill will intended. Would I like to know who sent them? *Ya*, I guess I would. But I'm not going to dwell on it."

His scratched his beard. "I still think I need to stay closer, to keep an eye on you—and even Rose Petal." Esther sighed, but didn't correct him. "So don't let your crazy sister come at me with a baseball bat if I'm on the front porch again."

"We will be fine, and you startled us, or Lizzie wouldn't have been wielding a bat."

"Whatever. She'll use any excuse to get at me," he grumbled under his breath.

Crossing her arms, Esther squinted at him from across the table. She was going to have to play hardball with Gus if she was going to get any results. That's the way it had always been, and it seemed more important now. "Do you want to stay friends with me, Gus?"

His mouth fell open, then he snapped it closed. "You gonna bail on me, Esther? It would be nice to have a couple of friends on this earth before I'm hauled away to the firepit."

"Rule number one." She held up a finger. "There is no more talk about going to hell. I believe in positive affirmations, and that's what we will start with. Repeat after me . . . I love the Lord, and I'm going to heaven."

"We both know that ain't true." He ran a hand through his matted gray hair tied back in the usual ponytail.

"Say it."

He groaned. "I love the Lord, and I'm going to heaven." He rattled it off fast and laced with insincerity, but at least he'd said it. "You're gonna try to save me with your religious stuff, and I told you I don't want any of that."

"I think you do." She hoped her expression was firm enough to make her point.

"Well, you're wrong. It's too late for me anyway."

Esther didn't hear any regret in his voice. "Rule number two," she said as she held up two fingers. "You will not say that again—that it's too late for you."

"I know what you're doing, and it's what I asked you not to do. I don't want to be your charity case." He sighed. "I will try to be nicer to people. But don't expect me to go all religious on you. Ain't happening."

We shall see. "Fair enough. Being nicer to people is a start. And Gus . . . that includes Lizzie too."

He lifted himself to a standing position, shaking his head. "I figured it would."

Esther stood up also. "How lovely it would be if you thanked Evelyn and Naomi for the casseroles, and Rose for the appetizers."

"Good grief. Dying is gonna kill me." He turned to leave.

"Do you want me to go with you?"

Gus slowly turned around. "If I thought it was because you enjoyed my company, I'd say yes. But no one enjoys my company. You're just afraid I won't go say thank you to Naomi."

She tried to hide her amusement. "Perhaps it's a little of both."

He stared at her long and hard. "Okay."

Esther's heart warmed as she followed him out the door. "Naomi is on the porch. The twins are usually napping about now, so this would be a *gut* time to go say *danki* to her."

Gus stomped across the yard taking long strides. For a man who was dying, it hadn't seemed to slow him down. Esther was about six feet behind him when he reached the porch of Naomi and Amos's house. He didn't even go up the stairs.

"Welcome home, Gus." Naomi leaned the broom she'd been using against the house. "Is everything okay?"

Esther finally caught up to him and stood beside him. "*Ya*, everything is fine," she said before she nudged Gus with her elbow.

"Thank you for whatever food you left for me at my house. And I'm sorry I've been mean in the past." Then he spun around and headed toward his cottage.

Naomi's mouth fell open. "I have no words," she said to Esther in a low voice as Gus walked away. "I know you told him to say that, but I'm still a little flabbergasted."

"I told him he should thank you for the food. The apology that came after that was all him." Esther stuffed her hands in the pockets of her apron. "Baby steps," she said before she turned to go back to the inn. Evelyn and Jayce didn't live on-site, so maybe he would drive to their house. Facing Jayce was going to be much more difficult for Gus.

He stopped where Rose and Benjamin were fishing down by the pond. Esther couldn't hear what was said, but when Rose's mouth fell open, she supposed he had thanked her also.

When Lizzie returned and pulled her buggy up to the barn, Gus never looked her way, and Lizzie didn't pay him any mind either.

∞

Rose finally lifted her jaw. "*Ach*, wow. That was a first." Gus had thanked her for leaving the appetizers at his house. Even though he had grumbled about something to do with fishing as he walked away, it was still shocking. "I'm sure Esther had something to do with him expressing his gratitude."

Benjamin grinned as he pointed to her fishing pole. "You've got a bite."

Her eyes grew huge. "Do I pull the pole out of the water now?" She had it clutched so tightly with both hands that her knuckles were turning white.

After setting down his pole, he went behind her, wrapped his arms around her, and held the pole with his hands atop hers. "Feel how the fish is hitting on your bait? You want to wait until it latches on for sure and takes off with your worm, then you'll yank the rod upward. It's probably a catfish since I put on weights to fish at the bottom, and . . ."

Rose didn't hear anything else he said as she stood perfectly still. The feel of his arms around her and the spicy scent she'd come to associate with him had hypnotized her as she floated a foot off the ground. She'd already caught her fish. At least, she hoped so.

"He's got it! Now!" Benjamin's loud voice in her ear pulled her back down to earth and she did as he said. She could feel the weight of the fish tugging on the end of the line.

"I've got it. He's huge." She glanced over her shoulder and almost knocked into his chin. "I should pull it in now, *ya*?"

He eased away from her, grinning. "Slowly reel him in. He's all yours."

Rose heeded his advice and began to turn the crank on the fishing pole. She missed his arms around her, but she couldn't wait to see what she'd caught. "It must be huge. This one is a fighter." She giggled. "Are they all fighters? I wouldn't know. But I'm sure it's big. Do you think it will be big enough to clean and eat? I like fried catfish."

She could feel the fish coming near the surface, so she turned the spinning handle even faster until she was able to yank the fish out of the water. Her jaw dropped. When she turned around, Benjamin had a hand over his mouth, but he was laughing too hard to hide his amusement. "We might need a few more of those to make a meal."

She eyed the small catfish that couldn't have been more than six or eight inches long. Not even as long as her shoe. "He felt enormous."

Benjamin walked to her side, eased the hook out of the fish's mouth, then set the little fellow free. "We'll let him grow some more," he said, still grinning. "*Ach*, well . . . it was your first catch."

He was staring at her mouth again, which he seemed to do often. Rose didn't mind. She was probably guilty of the same thing.

As he slipped another worm on her hook, he let go of the line. "I thought I'd help you out with that worm."

She laughed. "Why? Because the worm I put on looked like a beehive by the time I got through wrapping it around the hook? I wanted to make sure it stayed on. I used to hear *mei bruders* come back and talk about all the big ones that got away. I didn't want *mei* big one"—she laughed again—"to get away."

"Well, it didn't." He picked up his fishing pole, and they both sat on the bench. "Fishing takes a lot of patience. We might be here all day."

"I'm okay with that if you are." She turned to face him, fighting off the urge to look at his mouth. They'd done things out of order. The kiss should have been something to look forward to, but she already knew how good it felt, which just made her long for it again.

"I'm perfectly fine with it." He eased an arm around her, and Rose laid her head on his shoulder.

They didn't catch any more fish. But they talked. Actually, Rose did most of the talking, but once again, she was careful. She enjoyed Benjamin's company, and even though he insisted that he loved listening to her jabber—Rose's words, not his—she was on alert, careful not to say too much. She wasn't sure when the demons of her childhood began to surface. They had to have always been there. Maybe her chattering had kept them at bay. But living with Esther and Lizzie had shown her what a normal family could feel like, and it had her analyzing her life. One topic bullied its way into her mind lately—could she be a good mother? Or would she be like her own mother, a woman so subservient that she allowed Rose's father to rule his household any way he saw fit?

As the sun began its descent, they sat quietly on the bench for a while, having packed up all the fishing gear.

Benjamin turned to her and said, "I need to ask you something." He flinched a little. "And it's okay to say no."

"You can ask me anything." They were close enough for him to kiss her. She wondered if that was the question.

"*Mei mamm* wants to cook supper for you Wednesday night." He rubbed his forehead. "We haven't been seeing each other long, and I know you met her at worship service, but she wanted me to ask you. She said she'd like to get to know you better." He paused, smiling. "I told her I was still getting to know you, but she's a *gut* cook."

"I'd love to come for supper Wednesday."

What better way to learn about a man than to see him interact with his mother?

Chapter 15

Benjamin escorted Rose to the front door of The Peony Inn. "I had a really *gut* time today. It was fun watching you catch your first fish, and the food was wonderful."

"We were together a long time, but the day seemed to fly by. It's time for me to start cooking supper, but it feels like we just ate lunch." She did that thing with her nose again. "I mentioned earlier that we have a guest. He arrived yesterday to attend a funeral that is being held Monday, but he isn't leaving until Friday. I'll be glad when he's gone. I locked *mei* bedroom door last night. And I'm glad I did because I heard footsteps in the hallway late at night. I usually wear earplugs because Lizzie snores so loud, but I didn't put them in because this man—Lloyd—makes me nervous. I don't like the way he looks at me, and when I heard footsteps, someone turned the doorknob to *mei* bedroom. It had to be him. I could hear Lizzie snoring downstairs, and Esther rarely comes upstairs because of her knees. I was going to tell you earlier, but I didn't want to start our day with that subject." She wrapped her arms around herself and shivered.

Benjamin's jaw tensed. "Did you tell Esther and Lizzie?"

"*Nee*, but Esther didn't have a *gut* feeling about him when he arrived. She and Lizzie stayed close to me last night during supper, and again this morning at breakfast. I'm sure it will be fine." She paused, sighing. "You know how sometimes you just get a gut feeling about a person, but other times, you can just sense something isn't right? That's how I feel about Lloyd."

"I don't like the idea of you staying upstairs with him by yourself, especially if you think he tried to get in your room. And you don't even have a phone to call for help." His stomach roiled at the thought of someone trying to hurt her.

"I'm sure it will be fine. I probably shouldn't have said anything. All I'd have to do is scream, and Lizzie would come running up the stairs with the baseball bat she keeps under her bed." She chuckled. "I'll be fine."

From the little he knew about Lizzie, he wasn't surprised that she had a baseball bat, but he wasn't sure everything would be fine. "I'll be right back."

He returned with his cell phone. "*Mei* work calls come mostly on the landline we have in the barn. This is supposed to be for emergencies." He winked at her. "And for women who call me from out in a barn at night." Benjamin pushed it toward her. "Take it. You won't be able to call me. *Ach*, well, I guess you could if I go out in the barn." He grinned briefly. "But I'll feel better knowing you have a way to call someone for help."

"Are you sure?" She hesitated but took the phone. "I would

feel safer, I think." Shrugging, she looked down. "I am probably being silly. Maybe it was Esther checking to make sure I'd locked my door like I said I would."

Benjamin gently cupped her chin and raised her eyes to his. "I don't think you're being silly. I believe in those gut feelings. You just have to hit 9-1-1 for the police. I'm sure you know that but—" He still had hold of her chin, and their eyes were locked. Her lips were slightly parted. "I want to kiss you."

"I know. You stare at *mei* mouth constantly." Grinning, she said softly, "Honesty. The best policy, they say."

"Do you want me to kiss you?" Benjamin lowered his hand but kept his eyes on hers. He had caught her looking at his mouth too. Or he thought he had. He hadn't been shy or nervous around Rose since he'd started getting to know her. But right now, his heart rate was skyrocketing.

She tapped a finger to her chin. "Hmm . . . I suppose that would be all right." There was a heartrending tenderness in her gaze that said *permission granted*.

In less than a second, he claimed her lips with the same passion as the first kisses, but this time it was backed up by more than physical attraction. As he cupped her cheeks and drew her closer to him, there was an intimacy so sweet and tender that Benjamin felt even more protective of her than only a few moments ago. He eased out of the kiss and rested his head against her forehead. For a moment they just stood there until Benjamin broke away and touched the phone in her hand. "Please keep this close by tonight," he said, looking into her eyes.

"Okay," she said softly.

He kissed her gently. "I've never met anyone like you."

She stared at him for a long while, a sober expression on her face. "I'm a *gut* kisser."

Benjamin bent at the waist and laughed. "*Ya*, you are," he said when he straightened. "Or maybe not." He shrugged. "Let me see." His lips quickly recaptured hers, and he was more sure than ever. He was falling for Rose.

As he forced himself to ease away from her, he said, "There's no worship service tomorrow, but I'll try to call you from our phone in the barn first thing in the morning. I suspect I'll be missing you by then."

"Watch for mice," she said as she raised an eyebrow and grinned.

He tipped his hat. "Will do, ma'am."

Rose stood on the porch until Benjamin's buggy was out of sight, then she went inside the house. Lloyd was sitting in one of the rocking chairs that faced the porch window.

"*Wie bischt*," he said coolly as he propped an ankle up on his knee. "Is that your boyfriend?"

Rose froze. *Where are Esther and Lizzie?* She heard noise in the kitchen. "*Nee*," she said as she scurried in that direction. Lloyd couldn't have seen her kissing Benjamin unless he had gotten up and gone all the way to the left side of the window. Maybe he only saw them pull up in the buggy and Benjamin walking her to the door.

Lizzie was taking a roast out of the oven, surrounded by potatoes and onions, no carrots. "Sorry I'm late and you had to start supper."

After Lizzie set the large pot atop the stove, she raised her apron and blotted the sweat on her forehead. Then she smiled, minus her dentures. "You must have had a *gut* day."

"*Ya*, I did. His *mamm* wants to cook for me Wednesday night." Blushing, she looked down and wiggled her toes. "And he kissed me again," she said in a whisper.

Lizzie lightly clapped her hands together. "I knew it. I knew he was the one."

Rose tapped a finger to her teeth. "Did you forget something?"

"*Nee*, I didn't." Lizzie pressed her lips into a straight line. "Those dentures are giving me fits." She glanced toward the living room, then leaned closer to Rose's ear. "I don't much care what that man thinks. He gives me the creeps, always loitering nearby but not making himself known. I'll be glad when he's gone."

"I'm locking *mei* bedroom door at night," Rose whispered. "I think I heard him jiggle the doorknob to my bedroom. Benjamin loaned me his mobile phone in case I need to call for help."

Lizzie's jaw dropped before she snapped her mouth closed and pressed her thin lips together, the lines on her forehead growing deeper. "*Ach*, we're not going to have that in this *haus*." She shook her head. "There's a baseball bat under *mei* bed for people like Lloyd."

"*Nee*, I don't want any violence. I might have imagined what I heard." Rose wanted Lloyd gone, but she didn't want him in the hospital. "Lizzie, can you meet me in the barn right after dark? I think I might know a way to get Lloyd to leave on his own."

"The barn? What in the world for?" Lizzie frowned. "There are mice out there, especially at night."

"Exactly," Rose answered, grinning.

"Well, I don't know what you're up to, but I'll be there." Lizzie nodded toward the pot on the stove. "If you can carry that roast to the dining room, I'll get the bread and chowchow."

"Of course." She positioned two pot holders on either side of the roast. "You can still include the carrots, even though I don't like them. I know they are usually served with roast."

"We work around my dietary preferences, and Esther can't eat certain things because of her stomach ulcer. So we can work around your dislike of carrots." She chuckled. "I still remember the day you first arrived and carried on about how much you didn't like carrots." Lizzie stared at her, so Rose waited to lift the pot. "You seem so much more relaxed. To put it bluntly, you don't talk as much." She held up a hand. "You know I say that with *lieb*."

Rose's lack of communication had more to do with childhood thoughts assaulting her lately. "I guess I'm just happy." That part was true, too, and when she was with Benjamin, she did tend to be more relaxed. Although the timing of her childhood recollections was inconvenient. She wanted to bask in the happiness she felt when she was with Benjamin all the time, without unwanted thoughts slipping into her mind.

"*Ach*, you'll end up leaving us too." Lizzie sighed. "But I'm very happy things are working out with you and Benjamin. And I get credit."

Rose smiled. Sometimes matchmaking seemed like a competition between Esther and Lizzie. "*Ya*, you do."

"The food smells wonderful." Lloyd sauntered into the room. Despite the compliment, his flat expression was hard to read—until he eyed Rose up and down and grinned. "Can I do anything to help?"

"*Nee*, just have a seat in the dining room. Everything is ready." Rose lifted the pot and followed behind him. After she set it down, she went back to the kitchen.

"I guess we should eat with him," Rose said, flinching. "By the way, where is Esther?"

"She went with Gus to go see Evelyn and Jayce. The boy obviously took the news about Gus hard." Lizzie paused, but her eyes didn't reflect the venom usually visible when it came to their renter. "And apparently, Gus wanted to thank Evelyn for the casseroles she left in the refrigerator."

"He thanked me for the appetizers I put in his refrigerator. And before that, I saw him talking to Naomi. I guess he is making the rounds and thanking everyone." Rose went to the sink to wash her hands.

"Not everyone," Lizzie said as she took a bowl of salad from the refrigerator.

"What do you mean?" Rose said as she dried her hands.

"He didn't thank *everyone*. I left him two loaves of bread on the counter. And I got up extra early to bake them." Lizzie frowned. "And before you say anything, I did that for Esther. She'll wear herself out trying to do for that man. If she knew he didn't have bread, she would make him some."

Rose tipped her head to one side. "You don't fool me, Lizzie. You care about Gus, whether you admit it or not."

With the salad bowl in her hands, Lizzie shook her head. "*Nee*. I care about *mei schweschder*."

Rose took the salad dressing from the refrigerator and followed Lizzie to the dining room, sure that she wasn't being completely truthful about her feelings for Gus. He had been a fixture around the inn going on fifteen years. They would all feel the loss.

Esther sat on the couch by Evelyn. Jayce remained standing across the room while Gus cleared his throat and looked at Evelyn.

"Thank you for the casseroles you left at my home. And I'm sorry for being mean over the years." Gus frowned, and before Evelyn could respond, Gus said, "Jayce, let's talk on the porch." He motioned for the boy to follow him.

After the men were outside, Evelyn's eyes widened. "Wow. You've come a long way with him."

Esther smiled. "I encouraged him to thank everyone for the food they left at the cottage. But I didn't tell him to apologize for being mean. He added that on his own, and he also told Naomi the same thing."

"Jayce is taking Gus's illness very hard." Evelyn sighed. "They give each other a hard time, but there is a strong bond between them. I think it has to do with the night Jayce slept on Gus's couch, long before we were married. He was upset about his father, and he told me recently that on that night, he told Gus he wished he were his *daed*. So despite their playful sparring, if Gus doesn't receive the miracle we are praying for, Jayce is going to be very hurt."

Esther didn't want to think that far ahead. She was going to keep praying for the miracle and working with Gus on how to treat others more kindly. She'd noticed that Evelyn had been whispering, and suddenly she knew why. From their spot on the couch, they could hear everything being said out on the porch. Both women stayed quiet.

"Doctors don't know everything," Jayce said.

"Well, kid, they seem to in my case."

"I had a friend when I was growing up who recovered just fine from leukemia. Having the disease isn't a death sentence."

Esther glanced at Evelyn, then looked back at her lap. They shouldn't be eavesdropping, but they were so close to the window, it was impossible not to hear.

"Kid, I'm seventy-six years old. I've got stage four leukemia, along with a bunch of other issues that surely would have killed me soon enough anyway." Gus paused. "And I don't believe in miracles, just in case you were going to throw that in."

"Well, if it's all right with you, I'll be praying for one anyway. You're like my—"

Esther took a tissue from the pocket of her apron and dabbed at her eyes after Jayce couldn't even finish his sentence.

The men were quiet for a while, then Gus cleared his throat.

"I'm only doing this chemo to buy myself a little more time," Gus said. "Esther thinks she can transform me." He paused. "She can't, but it seems important to her to try."

Esther caught the tear sliding down her cheek with the tissue, and she was touched when Evelyn reached for her hand and held on tightly.

"I need you to do something for me after I'm gone. Now, listen, because this is important. I'm telling you now in case I get all slobbery and can't talk or something later."

"What is it?"

"I need you to look in on Esther, make sure she's okay. I reckon Rose Petal will run off with her new beau, and Esther will be stuck with just that crazy sister of hers, along with whatever renters stay at the inn. And don't let any weirdos rent my cottage."

"I promise to make sure Esther *and* Lizzie are okay. I would have done that without you asking me to anyway."

"Yeah, okay, whatever. That's all I wanted to say."

"Well, what if *I* have things to say?" Jayce's voice cracked, and Esther's heart was breaking.

"Let's don't do this, kid. Don't get all sappy on me." There was another long pause. "I gotta go."

"Wait. That's it?" Jayce's voice quivered, and it sounded to Esther like he was about to cry.

She wanted to go outside and give him a hug, but when she looked over her shoulder, she could see between the partially opened blinds. Gus had beat her to it. She inched over so Evelyn could see Gus hugging Jayce.

"You'll be all right, kid." Gus patted Jayce on the back.

"I'll still be praying for that miracle."

Esther and Evelyn quickly turned away from the window when Gus and Jayce moved toward the front door.

"Let's go, Esther," Gus said as he walked into the room.

Esther sniffled, hugged Evelyn and Jayce, and followed Gus to his truck, unable to hold back her tears as she climbed inside the cab.

Gus got in, closed his door, and frowned at her. "Now, Esther, I can't be having this all the time, you crying and carrying on." He stared at her, scowling even more. "So, stop."

Esther wiped her nose, raised her chin, then looked straight ahead as Gus started the truck. She stayed quiet until they were back at the inn.

"I will continue to pray for a miracle," she said firmly before she exited the truck and slammed the door.

She didn't stop when Gus called her name. By now, there was a flood of tears spilling down her face.

∞

Rose was glad Lloyd said he had to be somewhere and left right after supper. Lizzie met her in the barn as planned after dark. She suspected Lloyd would leave first thing in the morning, if not sooner.

After she had bathed and changed into her nightclothes, she locked her bedroom door and took out her keepsake box from under the bed.

She fluffed the pillows behind her, stretched out her legs, and placed the box in her lap. As she stared at it, her fingers drumming against the stained oak, Rose recalled her brother making it for her and giving it to her on her sixteenth birthday. Abram was probably the most sentimental of all her siblings.

Finally, she unhooked the small latch and gingerly opened the keeper of her memories, which was about the size of a shoebox. There were letters from her mother and siblings, all of which she'd written back. There was an angel pendant hanging on a broken silver chain. An English friend had given it to her when she was a teenager. She used to wear it tucked beneath her dress, until her father saw it one day and yanked it from her neck. There was a small rock she'd painted to resemble a ladybug because someone in school told her ladybugs were lucky. She pawed around other memorabilia, but it was her mother's very first letter that she wanted to reread. It had arrived about two weeks after Rose left Ohio.

Wie bischt, Rose.

I hope you are doing well with Big Roy and Katie Marie.

Rose recalled the short time she'd spent with her cousins before she moved to the inn and began working for Esther and Lizzie. Her cousins didn't really have room for her.

Although I don't understand why you left. I'm lonely here in this big *haus* by *mei* self. Some folks call you selfish for not considering how your leaving might affect me. Of course, I tell them that I am fine without you. But you are gone, presumably in search of a husband since you couldn't find one here. I hope you find what you are looking for.

Mamm

Rose had written her back, apologizing for her selfishness and for leaving. She'd wished her mother well and asked her to write back often. Looking back, she wasn't sure why she'd made the request. The letters between Rose and her mother were infrequent and formal. She had more communication with her brothers and sisters, and she enjoyed hearing about their children.

As she had done so many times in the past, she took her notepad and a pen from the drawer of her nightstand. Then she thought about all the things she wanted to say to her mother. She practically had the words memorized, but each time, she'd thrown away the letter and opted for polite formality. Not this time.

Dear *Mamm*,

Wie bischt. I hope this letter finds you well. I have decided to tell you the real reason why I chose to leave home, although in my heart, I feel you must know why. I left because I couldn't face you any longer without voicing *mei* true feelings, which would have surely gotten me kicked out of the *haus* anyway. It seemed easier at the time to just leave with my emotions unresolved. But I am realizing that if I am going to move forward and rid myself of the emotional scars I carry with me, then I need to tell you how I feel as part of *mei* own healing process.

She paused as she thought about the timing of her actions again. Was this something she needed to put behind her before she could move forward? Sighing, she went on.

I often wonder if *mei bruders* and *schweschdere* have ever talked to you about the things that went on when we were growing up, but I have not asked them. The only reason I knew discipline in our *haus* was different than in other families is from the few times we were allowed to sleep over at a friend's house. Away from home, it was obvious our family wasn't living the right way, despite your proclamations that everything *Daed* did was to right our wrongs in the eyes of *Gott*.

But, *Mamm*, if you apologize for allowing those things to happen, I will forgive you. And in the process, perhaps I will heal, and you and I can have a closer relationship.

I *lieb* you,
Rose

She tapped the pen to the pad for a few seconds. What if she was wrong about her mother? What if her mother had suffered at the hands of her father and Rose and her siblings just never saw it? It seemed unlikely that they wouldn't have noticed something during all their years at home. But she decided to add a P.S. anyway.

P.S. *Mamm*, if *Daed* treated you badly, please tell me. I don't want to accuse you for your lack of intervention if you also suffered at the hand of *Daed*.

She put the letter in an envelope and addressed it to her mother, but she didn't seal it. Tomorrow, she would read it again and decide whether or not to mail it. Her chest tightened just thinking about actually sending the note.

After snubbing out her lantern, she lay back, closed her eyes, and thought about more pleasant things to lull her to sleep. *Benjamin. The kisses they shared. The fun they had fishing.*

But her heart skipped a beat when she heard footsteps in the hallway, much too heavy to be Lizzie's or even Esther's. Lloyd must have returned from wherever he'd gone. Rose fumbled for Benjamin's phone on the nightstand. It was still half charged, and it lit up when she held it to her chest, her heart pounding. She'd gotten Amos's and Gus's phone numbers from Esther's address book she kept in the kitchen. She could barely read the numbers in the dark. Getting the police involved in anything was always a last resort. Still, Amos probably kept his phone off at night, and she hated to bother Gus since he was sick.

As he'd done the night before—now she was certain it was him—he turned her doorknob. She wanted to scream for him to go away, but he went to his room, and she heard the door close behind him.

Despite her attempts to recapture her visions of Benjamin, she was wide awake and alert. Hopefully her and Lizzie's plan would work and Lloyd would leave first thing in the morning, if not sooner.

Chapter 16

THE NEXT MORNING, ESTHER WAS SIPPING HER COFFEE IN THE kitchen when Lizzie and Rose came into the room together. Lizzie refused to look at Esther, and Rose plastered on a smile that couldn't have looked more fake if she'd tried.

"You're up early," Rose said as she scurried to the cabinet where the pots and pans were stored. "I'll get started on breakfast for our guest."

Lizzie kept her head down as she poured herself a cup of coffee.

Esther ran her finger along the rim of her coffee cup. "Don't rush to start breakfast."

Rose slowly turned around to face Esther, and Lizzie eventually did also.

"Our guest left at about five this morning." Esther raised her chin. "I woke up when I heard loud steps coming down the stairs, and I met Lloyd in the living room."

"She did it!" Lizzie pointed to Rose, whose mouth fell open.

"You helped!" Rose fired back, a skillet in her hand, dangling at her side.

Esther wasn't sure what was funnier—the way the man bolted out the door earlier, or Lizzie and Rose blaming each other now. "I've never seen a man get out of this *haus* so fast. He said his room was infested with mice and that he couldn't spend one more night here." She paused, tapping a finger to her chin. "How did that happen? And how are we going to get rid of the mice you two turned loose in his room?" She pointed a finger back and forth between Lizzie and Rose, landing on Lizzie. "You're a bad influence on Rose." Esther's chest hurt from stifling laughter.

"Me?" Lizzie set her coffee on the counter, then put a hand to her chest. "It was her idea."

"And there aren't any mice. Only droppings." Rose glanced at Lizzie and grinned. "A whole lot of droppings." She turned to Esther. "And I'll clean it all up right away. But, Esther, I just don't think I could have spent one more night upstairs with him nearby."

Esther finally couldn't hold it. She almost spit from coughing when she started laughing. "He was a *creepy* fellow, wasn't he?"

Lizzie and Rose laughed along with Esther, which felt good. It had been a hard week.

Esther and her clan—as Gus called them—met at the hospital midmorning on Tuesday. They'd hired a driver, but Gus wanted to take his own truck so Jayce rode with him.

Esther's stomach churned with nervous anticipation as they awaited the results of all their blood tests from the day before. Evelyn, Jayce, Naomi, Amos, Lizzie, Esther, Rose, and the patient all sat in a small room around an oblong table. Esther had been surprised that the test was mostly painless, just a prick on the finger.

Gus hung his head and was unusually quiet. Naomi had left the twins with a sitter, which was probably best. The girls wouldn't have anything to do in this small room. Evelyn and Naomi carried on with some initial small talk, but everyone was quiet and waiting now.

When the doctor walked in, he introduced himself and asked if everyone understood Gus's condition. He reiterated that there was only a slim chance that the chemotherapy would work, but that it was certainly worth a shot. Gus would have three more treatments.

Esther thought Gus's hair looked a bit thinner, and his middle was shrinking daily. She took a deep breath and put a hand across her roiling stomach.

"First of all, thank you all for coming and for agreeing to give blood. Even if your blood doesn't go directly to Gus, he will get credit in his name, and it will also help other patients who are in need of blood transfusions. It's shocking to most people how often we run out of available blood and patients have to wait to have much-needed transfusions." The young doctor, who didn't look old enough to be a physician, turned to Gus. "You are a lucky man to have such good friends."

Lizzie snickered, but quickly put a hand over her mouth. Thankfully, she had her dentures in today.

Gus cleared his throat but didn't say anything.

Dr. Meadows tapped a folder to his hand. "We have some very good news that shocked most of the staff. Less than one percent of the population has Gus's blood type, and one of you is an exact match. That means that your blood and platelets can go directly to Gus, eliminating the wait time for a supply to come from somewhere else. It increases his chance of beating this, which I remind you, still remains very low. Which one of you is Elizabeth Glick?"

Esther brought a hand to her chest as her eyes widened. She was afraid to look at Lizzie, but she finally did and saw her sister's jaw hanging open.

"Me. I'm Elizabeth Glick," Lizzie said slowly and cautiously.

"You're the one," the doctor announced proudly. "An exact match."

The color drained from Gus's face as he looked up at the white-tiled ceiling. "This can't be happening." He shook his head, then nodded toward Lizzie. "Does that mean that woman's blood will be running through my veins?"

The doctor scratched his head. "Uh . . . yes."

Lizzie raised her hand as if she were in school. "So, let me get this straight. If I give *mei* blood to Gus, and whatever those other things were that you mentioned, I'm helping to save his life?"

The doctor immediately shook his head. "No. But you would

be bettering his quality of life for the time that he has left and eliminating some of the suffering that would be worse without his blood type on hand for a transfusion. Leukemia patients, especially at this stage, require blood transfusions often."

"You might as well infuse me with poison." Gus hung his head as he stood up.

Lizzie flashed her pearly whites. "If you want *mei* blood, you can ask me nicely."

"Esther, do something," Gus said, his fists beginning to clench at his sides. "Tell that wacky sister of yours to shut her mouth."

The doctor held up a hand. "Whoa. I'm not sure what's going on in here, so I'm going to step out of the room and let you all discuss it." Frowning, he said, "And please keep your voices down."

After the doctor left, Esther stood up. "Lizzie and Gus, just hush." She turned to her sister. "You will not torment Gus about this." Then she looked at Gus. "And you will be gracious and accepting of Lizzie's blood in an effort to help you feel better. There will not be another derogatory word said about it. And I mean it." Esther's voice shook as she spoke, and her voice was louder than normal.

Gus shuffled out of the room, shaking his head.

"I'll ride home with him and see if I can get him to calm down." Jayce kissed Evelyn on the forehead and left.

Esther glared at Lizzie, who was chewing her bottom lip, then she giggled. "Gus Owens is gonna have to kiss *mei* feet. This will be fun."

"He's dying, Lizzie. Shame on you!" Esther rushed out of the room and didn't stop until she was outside in tears.

Evelyn, Amos, Naomi, and Rose went directly to the van that was waiting for them. Lizzie found Esther on the bench they'd sat on before.

"You gotta admit," Lizzie said as she put a hand on Esther's knee. "*Gott* does have a sense of humor. Can't I just have a little fun with this?" Amusement flickered in her sister's eyes. "You know, something like, 'Gus, tell me what a wonderful person I am and I'll let them siphon blood out of me to prolong your existence.'"

Esther huffed as she stood and went to the van.

"Wait, Esther! I'm just kidding. Of course I'll be nice."

Esther wasn't sure about that, and she'd about had it with this feuding between Lizzie and Gus. She didn't respond as she climbed into the van.

It was a quiet ride home. The driver dropped off Evelyn, and when they arrived back at the inn, Amos and Naomi walked to their house. Gus's truck was at the cottage.

Esther put a hand across her stomach as she trudged inside with Lizzie and Rose following. It was not surprising that her ulcer was acting up.

"I'm sorry," Lizzie said as soon as they walked in the house. "I will do better to mind *mei* manners where Gus is concerned. You're right. He's sick, and I should be more considerate of his situation."

Esther sat down on the couch and propped her feet up on the coffee table. She hadn't bothered to drop her shoes by the door. It wasn't a steadfast rule to do so since they often had a lot of people going in and out. Today, she was just anxious to get off her feet.

"I appreciate that, Lizzie. This is emotionally hard enough without you and Gus bickering."

Lizzie hung her head. "I know."

Rose gave her a sad smile. "I'll go prepare lunch. Is there anything special you'd like?" Her soft voice was sympathetic.

"I'm not hungry, hon. I think I'll go lie down." Lizzie shuffled to her bedroom and closed the door behind her.

"What about you, Esther? I have a batch of egg salad in the refrigerator, or I can prepare a hot meal."

"I'll get myself an egg sandwich in a while. You go ahead and eat if you'd like." Esther needed her stomach to settle before she considered eating. And she didn't have much of an appetite.

Rose sat beside Esther on the couch. "Can I ask you something? I know this might not be the best time and that you have a lot on your mind, and—"

"Ask me whatever you want." Esther yawned, hoping Rose's inquiry didn't require an in-depth answer.

"Did something happen between Lizzie and Gus? I mean, we all know how Gus is, but Lizzie borders on hostile when it comes to him." Rose tipped her head to one side.

"*Nee*, I don't think there was any specific event. They just have personalities that don't jive—worse than the rest of us when it comes to Gus." She paused in recollection. "They care about each other more than either will admit. It's almost like a game with them." She cut her eyes at Rose. "A very irritating game that gets on *mei* nerves. But I've seen instances when one or the other has softened. For example, when Lizzie found out that Gus's mother died when we were children, she sincerely told Gus that she was sorry for his loss. She hadn't remembered the event until we found out Gus's background not long ago. And there have been other sentimental moments between them, but it's rare."

Rose nodded. "I see. Well, I hope they will be kinder to each other during this difficult time. I'm going to pray for a miracle related to Gus's medical condition, but I'm also going to pray that Gus and Lizzie will get along better."

Esther wanted to take a nap, but Rose gnawed on a fingernail. Something else was on the girl's mind.

"I believe that *mei* being here is a miracle," she said with her eyes cast down.

Esther fought off a yawn. "I think it's wonderful about you and Benjamin."

Rose lifted her eyes to Esther's, but only half smiled. "It is wonderful about Benjamin, but that's not the miracle I'm speaking of."

Esther waited. Again, she was noticing more and more how Rose seemed to be thinking out her thoughts before randomly speaking them.

"You and Lizzie are *mei* miracles. You've shown me what real love feels like, what it means to be a family. You refer to our little group as a family, and I feel blessed to be a part of that."

Esther needed to tread lightly, but she had continued to wonder about Rose's family. The girl's comments about her past were becoming more frequent but never shed any light on what things were like when she was growing up.

"And we are blessed to have you in our family." She waited for Rose to respond, but she started chewing on her fingernail again. "Rose . . . you do know you can talk to me about anything, *ya*? Even your family back home in Ohio." Esther wasn't sure if she should have said that last part.

Rose nodded, then stood up, barely smiling. "Maybe I will someday."

After Rose went to the kitchen, Esther lifted her tired body from the couch and decided to join her for a sandwich. Maybe Rose would open up a little more about her family.

Rose was laying out bread, egg salad, and chips when Esther came into the kitchen. "Did you change your mind about eating? Can I make you a sandwich?"

"*Ya*, that would be nice. *Danki*. I think my ulcer is acting up a bit. Or maybe I'm just hungry." Esther pulled out a kitchen chair. "I was going to take a nap, but I probably wouldn't be able to sleep with all this grumbling going on in *mei* stomach."

Esther picked up the letter addressed to Rose's mother. "It's nice that you keep in touch with your family."

Rose had reread the letter to her mother several times and decided to mail it, knowing she might not ever hear from her mom again. "*Ya*, I try to." She finished putting together the sandwiches, then carried the plates to the table and went back for the bag of chips. After she was seated and they prayed, Rose glanced at Esther. The woman had dark circles under swollen eyes.

Everything with Gus was taking a toll on her. Rose didn't want to add to her worries, but if she didn't talk to someone soon, she felt like she would explode.

"Hon, are you all right?" Esther asked before she took a bite of her sandwich.

Rose's stomach tightened as she considered telling Esther a little about her upbringing. "*Ya*, I'm okay." She began to tear the crust off of her bread.

Esther nodded at her plate. "You only do that when you are deep in thought or upset about something."

"It's a little of both, I suppose." She took a deep breath as she eyed the letter. "After I send that to *mei mamm*, I might not ever hear from her again."

Esther briefly stopped chewing.

"I didn't grow up in a normal Amish household. At least, I don't think I did. *Mei daed* . . . he, um . . . was very stern with us. Strict." She'd opened the jar of memories, mostly ones that haunted her. Esther would have questions, and Rose wished she could put the lid back on the jar.

"I think most parents discipline their children?" Esther's statement sounded more like a question.

"I know." Rose had never spoken to anyone about the things that went on in her house, and it was proving more difficult than she thought.

"Hon, something is tormenting you. Maybe if you talk about it, you will feel better. And if you don't want to discuss whatever is bothering you, I will respect that too."

"I-I think that most *kinner* get spankings." Rose paused as her heart raced. How much would she have to tell Esther to make herself feel better? *Definitely not all of it.* Maybe she needed someone to tell her that the things that happened weren't normal and that it wasn't her fault.

Esther offered a gentle smile. "I know that Lizzie and I got our fair share of spankings." She'd stopped eating. Rose had her full attention.

Sweat beaded at her temples. "As I told you before, *mei daed* wasn't a *gut* man. And our spankings were more like beatings." She shuddered as she said the word while tearing her crust into tiny pieces. "It was worse for *mei bruders*, I think. I have five *bruders* and two *schweschdere*. It seemed at least one of them always had a black eye or a broken rib, or"—she shrugged as she kept her eyes on the fragments of bread crust—"some other injury." When she finally looked up, Esther had tears in her eyes. "Us girls were punished a lot too." She cast her eyes down as a blanket of shame fell over her. "We got into mischief sometimes, and I'm sure we deserved to be punished." She squeezed her eyes closed and wished she'd never started this.

"What did that man do to you, Rose?" Esther's voice was somber and calm, but her eyes were glazed with fury.

Rose lowered her eyes to her plate. Her bread crumbs looked like specks of sand. "It's probably not what you're thinking," she said softly.

"Did your father lay his hands on you and your *schweschdere*?" Esther's voice shook as she asked the question.

"Not in that way." She could feel her face burning with embarrassment, and the knot in her throat caused her to feel like she might choke. "He just did things." It would be easier to tell Esther about things that hadn't happened to her. "Helen, *mei* oldest sister, was in charge of keeping the bathrooms clean, but when she started dating, she was home less and less." She paused as the scene unfolded in her mind. "*Mei daed* came home from working in the fields. When he found Helen, he grabbed her by the hair and took her into the downstairs bathroom, the one he and *mei mamm* used. *Mei mamm* lined up me and *mei schweschdere* and made us watch. He lifted the lid and stuck her face in the commode. I thought he was going to drown her, but he lifted her up gasping and spewing toilet water, then he did it again . . . and again . . . and again." Rose wasn't sure when she'd started crying, but it was a faucet she couldn't turn off. When she looked at Esther, the poor woman had her hand over her mouth as tears trailed down her cheeks. "There were other things. Many other things."

"Rose, your father sounds like a monster. No child deserves that type of reprimanding. Ever." Esther paused to blot her eyes with her napkin. "And shame on your *mudder* for making you and your *schweschdere* watch." She squinted her eyes. "Unless . . . did your *daed* treat her badly too? Was she afraid of him?"

Rose shrugged. "I'm not sure. I don't think so. I never saw him treat her badly, but she also never stood up to him." She swiped at her eyes with her hands. "Shouldn't she have done something, tried to make him stop? All she ever did was tell us that if we behaved, our father wouldn't be forced to discipline us."

Esther sniffled. "*Ya*, hon, she should have intervened if she was able."

Rose envisioned the expression on her mother's face each

time someone was reprimanded. Flat and uncaring. "I'm sure we were bad sometimes, but—"

"Stop." Esther shook her head. "You were *kinner*. You did not deserve the punishment your *daed* doled out. None of you did, and you have to know that, Rose."

She locked eyes with Esther, barely able to speak. "I feel shame. I worry that I won't be a *gut mudder*. What if I'm like her? I have her genes. What if I marry a man who is cruel to *mei kinner*? And yet, all I have ever wanted to do was be a *mamm* and to be everything she wasn't."

"Rose." Esther got up and walked around the table. She hadn't even eaten half her sandwich. She sat down next to Rose and cupped her wet cheeks in her hands. "Shame is the work of the devil. You must let that go to be able to heal. You and your siblings did nothing to deserve that type of abuse, and you shouldn't feel any shame." Esther pulled her into a hug and rubbed her back. "You poor dear. *Danki* for sharing that with me. You will be a wonderful *mudder*. I'm sure of it."

Rose eased out of the hug. "I'm sorry. You already have so much on your mind and so much worry in your heart. But for some reason, I felt like I needed to tell someone, to know that it was real, that it happened." She stared into Esther's loving eyes. "It did happen. I know it. All of it, from the time we were young until everyone left the *haus* to marry. Everyone else married young. I don't think *mei schweschdere* loved the men they married. They only provided an escape for them. I think both of them have grown to *lieb* their husbands over the years, though. They have six beautiful *kinner* between them. *Mei bruders* all chose brides early, too, and have lovely families. But after everyone was gone, *mei daed* had grown old, and he was sick. After he died, I couldn't look at *mei mamm* without wanting to lash out at her. But she was all I had. Coming here was an escape for me too." Rose's throat hurt from crying and talking at the same time. "She told me I'd never find a husband. She said my nonstop chattering wouldn't be tolerated by any man." She hung her head. "Maybe she's right."

"*Ach*, child." Esther dabbed at her eyes again. "That's not true. And you have Benjamin." She cupped Rose's chin and smiled through her tears. "And you have me and Lizzie, and Evelyn and Naomi. Even Gus. Family is who you make it."

Rose pointed to the letter. "For the first time, I've questioned *mei mamm* in that letter. I'm giving her a chance to apologize." Blinking her eyes, she said, "I will forgive her if she does." She paused, sighing. "I feel like I've had this bottled up for so long, and I don't really understand why it's coming to the forefront of *mei* mind. I think it's because I sense Benjamin really likes me, and I feel the same way. And I think I need to talk about all of this so that I can move forward with my life. But what if he gets tired of *mei* chattiness? I've tried to be less talkative and spend more time listening to others. Or at the least, I've tried to organize *mei* thoughts before I speak. But sometimes, everything just comes out of *mei* mouth all at once, and I think that's because—" *No, I'm not ready to tell her.* She shrugged. "I don't know."

"God bless you, dear sweet *maedel*." She pulled Rose into a hug again.

Rose decided that was enough for today—all either of them

could handle for now. Maybe someday she would tell Esther how exactly she'd suffered at the hands of her father. But not today.

"Did Gus die? What happened?" Lizzie had snuck up on them. "He's gone, isn't he? That's why you're both so upset." Tears formed in the corners of her eyes as she brought a hand to her mouth.

Esther and Rose exchanged confused glances.

"*Nee*, Lizzie, *nee*. Gus isn't gone." Esther kissed Rose on the forehead and walked back around the table to where Lizzie was standing. "Rose and I were just having a conversation about something totally unrelated to Gus. And everything is fine now."

"It doesn't look fine," Lizzie spat as she blinked back tears. "I'll be right back." She raised her chin, spun on her bare foot, and headed back to her room.

"She doesn't like people to see her cry. Remember what I said about Gus and Lizzie caring for each other more than they let on?"

Rose nodded, still lost in her confessions. "I *lieb* you, Esther. I wish you or Lizzie had been *mei mamm*. It's a terrible thing to say, but it's true."

"I *lieb* you too, sweet *maedel*. Lizzie and I both would have been honored to be your *mamm*. But we are your family now, and you can come to us about anything."

"I know." Rose felt a sense of peace about that. Not complete peace. Maybe she never would feel that until she told someone what her father had done to her. In some ways, it wasn't nearly as awful as what he'd done to her siblings. In other ways, it felt worse.

Chapter 17

Benjamin sat out in the barn talking to Rose for over an hour, but he could hear her yawning on the other end of the phone. After she and Lizzie had gotten rid of their "creepy" renter, Benjamin had brought over a charger and let her hold on to his cell phone a little while longer so they could talk without her having to sit in a barn full of mice. She had sounded tired the whole time they were talking, but she'd had an emotional day. She told him all about it, how Lizzie was a match for Gus's transfusions and how Gus would have preferred his blood to be compatible with someone else in the group.

"It sounds like you had a hard day. Tomorrow will be better. *Mei mamm* is really looking forward to supper tomorrow night. I am too." Benjamin hoped his mother didn't embarrass him. She tended to gush, especially when it came to anything resembling romance. He'd watched his sisters endure her over-the-top cheerful attitude that could have been mistaken for a drunken person at times. But he had the best mom ever, so he shouldn't complain.

"I'm looking forward to getting to know your *mamm* better too."

"Do you want me to pick you up? I'm happy to do that."

"*Nee*. If we're having supper at four or five, I'll easily be able to get home before dark."

"You need to go to sleep. I can hear you yawning." Benjamin stifled a yawn of his own.

After they said good night, Benjamin lifted himself down off the workbench where he'd been sitting in the barn. And as he made his way into the house, he smiled. Finally, he'd found someone who was sweet, animated, smart, beautiful, and interesting. He was hopeful about the future. And interestingly enough, his ease at being around Rose seemed to transform him around others. In general, he felt more relaxed with people.

Rose didn't think she'd felt so emotionally zapped since she left Ohio to come to Montgomery. Everything related to Gus had them all upset today but telling Esther about her childhood and teenage years was even more draining. She couldn't imagine having that conversation with Benjamin. From everything he'd told her about his family, they sounded wonderful. She'd avoided most of his questions about her family, but if things continued to go as well as they had so far, Rose needed to tell him about her past. She owed him that. Benjamin might share her fears about whether or not she'd be a good mother based on her own childhood. She'd wanted to be a wife and mother for as long as she could remember. Now that someone seemed to really care about her, it frightened her as much as it excited her.

Yawning, she snuggled into her pillow and lay atop the covers. She couldn't wait until fall arrived. But they would have at least one more month of warm temperatures, then September would be here to cool things down.

October and November were when most weddings took place. She allowed herself to dream about that possibility—becoming Benjamin's wife. It was much too soon to be having such thoughts, but thinking about it made her smile. If she could keep her past from threatening her future, she might have a real shot at happiness.

Esther dove into the slice of apple pie like it was medicine for an ailment. Eating for comfort wasn't helping her waist, and the heavier she got, the harder it was on her knees. She wasn't what most folks would call overweight—just thicker.

She glanced over her shoulder when she heard someone coming. Lizzie crossed through the living room in her robe, barefoot and with a scarf over her head. She pointed her flashlight at the dimly lit lantern on the table.

"I wasn't sure if it was you or Rose in the kitchen." She rubbed her eyes, then squinted at Esther. "What are you doing up at this hour?"

Esther wasn't even sure what time it was. She glanced at the clock on the stove. *Two in the morning.* "I couldn't sleep. I've been tossing and turning most of the night, catching a few winks here and there." She nodded to the pie. "It seemed a snack was in order."

Lizzie sat across from Esther, yawning. "I know you're upset about Gus, and I'm going to make a real effort to be nicer to him."

"I appreciate that, but"—Esther recalled her conversation with Rose—"I'm more upset right now about what Rose tearfully shared with me."

"I wondered what was going on when I walked in on the two of you, but you said everything was fine." Lizzie frowned. "It's not, is it?"

Esther finished savoring a bite of pie, then she told Lizzie about her conversation with Rose. "Her father sounds like an awful man. I think these types of things catch up to a person eventually. It's so sad that Rose worries about being a *gut* mother. I don't think I've ever seen that girl be unkind to anyone, and she's wonderful with Naomi's twins. But her tragic childhood is catching up with her and spilling out like poison. Maybe once she's told someone everything, she'll be rid of those ugly memories for good. But . . . she didn't tell me the one thing that I think disturbs her the most. Rose talked a little about the abuse her siblings were subjected to, but she never told me what her father did to her, only that it was nonsexual."

Lizzie puckered her lips as she shook her head. "Maybe we don't want to know."

Esther had thought the same thing. "*Ya*, but if she ever decides to tell one of us, we will need to be strong and help her get past it."

Nodding, Lizzie reached for the pie, cut a tiny slice and set it on a nearby paper plate. "Do you think I have to change *mei* diet when I start saving Gus's life?"

Esther groaned a little. "You're not *saving* his life. You are prolonging and helping his quality of life for however long he is with us."

"I weighed myself. I need to fatten up. You're not supposed to give blood at *mei* age unless you weigh at least a hundred and ten pounds. I weigh a hundred and fourteen." She smiled. "That's what the pamphlet from the hospital said, so I gotta eat more pie."

Esther shook her head, grinning. "I probably have a hundred pounds on you."

"I told you. We're adopted." Lizzie stuffed her mouth with a large bite, then gummed it to death.

Esther chuckled softly. "As we've discussed, our facial features tell another story."

"I also read that if I give platelets, they take your blood out of you, steal the platelets, then put your blood back in you. Seems odd to me." She paused to enjoy her pie. "Gus has lost weight. His face is thinner. But he doesn't look like a dying man."

"He's only at the beginning of his treatments. I suspect that as he continues the chemotherapy, it will take a toll on him."

"Well, if he looks and feels fine, why not wait until he's sicker before making him suffer through those treatments?"

"I think it's all about timing. And even if Gus was in pain, I'm not sure he'd tell us. He's much too prideful." Esther wanted another slice of pie, but as she put an arm across her stomach, she decided against it. "Lizzie, it's nice that you're researching about the procedures."

She stood up. "Of course I am. They're taking *mei* blood and platelets. I want to know what's going on," she said with a mouthful of food.

Esther put a hand to her forehead. "Please don't eat like that when other people are around."

Lizzie opened her mouth wide and revealed all there was to see, like a small child might do. Esther couldn't help laughing. It had been such a horrible day.

"Ha-ha. Made you laugh." Lizzie grinned a toothless smile. "I'm going back to bed, and you should too."

Esther rose from the table, yawning. "I suppose you're right. Tomorrow is a new day."

Rose was up earlier than usual and started breakfast. After she'd fantasized about becoming Benjamin's wife the night before, she'd fallen into a deep sleep and felt rested this morning.

Lizzie walked into the kitchen a few minutes later. "Ugh," she said, scowling. "I ate enough for two people yesterday, and I even had pie in the middle of the night, but I still didn't gain any weight. If *mei* weight falls too low, I might not be able to give Gus blood."

Rose smiled on the inside, recalling what Esther had said about Lizzie and Gus caring for each other more than they let on. But Rose knew better than to tell Lizzie how nice it was that she was taking this so seriously. She'd only deny it.

"You're in luck then because I'm making those Belgian waffles you like so much."

"*Gut*. I'll be eating plenty." Lizzie poured herself a cup of coffee and sat down at the kitchen table and began reading the newspaper. Occasionally, she glanced at Rose, but would quickly refocus on reading. Rose couldn't help but wonder if Esther had told Lizzie about Rose's childhood. The sisters were close, so Rose suspected she might have. If so, Rose was glad Lizzie wasn't bringing up the subject.

After her chores this morning and after lunch, she would have the afternoon to focus on this evening. She was nervous and excited to spend time with Benjamin's mother. She wasn't going to let negative thoughts bombard her mind.

Benjamin couldn't stop looking at the clock in the kitchen. He'd had two plumbing projects to keep him busy most of the day, but now he was antsy and ready for Rose to get here.

"It's almost four, Benny. She'll be here soon." His mother opened the oven to check something that was cooking.

"You didn't make anything with carrots, did you?"

"*Nee*, I made that chicken casserole that you and your sisters rave about. Your father wasn't a huge fan of casseroles, as you know. That's why I didn't make it when you were growing up. But after he passed, I decided to mix things up a little when it came to cooking." His mother chuckled. "I wouldn't put carrots in anything I made this evening because you told me not to at least three times."

Benjamin scratched his cheek. "*Ya*, I guess I did."

"You really like this woman, don't you?" His mother set the spoon she was holding on a plate on the counter. "Do you think she's the one?"

"I don't know." If he were being honest, he would tell his mother that he had already fallen hard for Rose. But she would be more wound up than she already was. His mother had cooked and cleaned all day while humming and smiling. Benjamin wasn't sure who was more excited about Rose's visit—he or his mother.

"She's here." His mother pointed out the kitchen window.

By the time Rose got out of the buggy, Benjamin was walking toward her. He kissed her tenderly before he tethered her horse.

"What a lovely way to start the evening," she said as she put a finger to her lips, her eyes melting into his.

He quickly kissed her again. "I won't be able to do that for a while with *mei mamm* around." Winking at her, he took hold of her hand and they walked to the door. He slowed his stride and gently pulled her to a stop before they reached the porch steps. "I know you've met *mei mamm*, but you've never really been around her. I feel like I should warn you about her."

Rose's stomach churned as her eyes probed his. "Warn me about what?"

He grinned. "Nothing bad, but *Mamm* is probably the happiest woman on the planet, and she can be a little wound up when it comes to anything, um . . . romantic."

"Hmm..." She tapped a finger to her chin as a warmth filled her. "Are we romantic?"

"I hope so. I don't just kiss women randomly." Chuckling, he started up the steps. "Well, maybe I did once. This woman named Rose put a spell on me when I first met her. I kinda kissed her before I really knew her."

"*Ya*, you did." Rose giggled as she recalled those first kisses that had sent her into a wild whirlwind of hope, which had led to anger, which had progressed to where they were now.

"Come on. Don't be afraid."

Rose wasn't scared, but she was anxious and hoped she didn't start rambling about silly things.

Benjamin stepped aside and held the screen door open. "Welcome," he said smiling.

Rose wasn't sure whether to hug Catherine or not. In general, their people weren't outwardly affectionate, but Lizzie and Esther hugged almost everyone. Rose had that tendency, too, now that she lived with the sisters.

"*Wie bischt*, Rose." Catherine rushed across the living room with a big smile on her face. She was an attractive woman with brown hair and beautiful green eyes like Benjamin. Tiny lines feathered from the corners of her eyes, and her laugh lines were abundant. She was like a burst of fresh air as she closed the space between her and Rose, gently pulling her into a hug. "Welcome to our home."

"*Danki* for inviting me." Rose started walking alongside Catherine when she looped her arm in Rose's.

"I've been so looking forward to spending time with you this evening. I've prepared a chicken casserole that *mei kinner* always *lieb*." She winked at her. "No carrots."

Rose glanced over her shoulder at Benjamin, who grinned and shrugged.

When they went into the dining room, Rose's eyes widened. There was a gorgeous layout with crisp white napkins next to blue-and-white china. Crystal water glasses were full at each of the three place settings, and there was a beautiful arrangement of orchids in the middle of the table. The dining room at The Peony Inn was beautiful, but it didn't have a view like this. Colorful flowers in potted plants were in full bloom on a deck just outside the room. Three large windows were side by side along one wall. Rose thought about Naomi and Amos, both painters. They would love to paint this scene, she was sure.

"You have a beautiful home, and the view in this room is stunning." Rose instinctively walked to the large window.

"I tinker with flowers," Catherine said modestly as she motioned for Rose and Benjamin to sit down.

After they'd prayed, Catherine stood up and filled Rose's plate with casserole, salad, and buttered bread. It was way more than she would ever be able to eat.

"So, tell me about your family. What made you move from Ohio all the way to Indiana? I'm sure Benny told you that we used to live near Bedford, but the allure of a smaller and quieter community brought us here. I'm not as close to *mei kinner* and their *kinner*, and I have to hire a driver to visit, but that's the only downside." She smiled, waiting for an answer.

Rose couldn't tell her that she'd moved here in hopes of

finding a husband, which was partly true. And she didn't want to say that she could no longer face her mother. Revealing any information about her childhood was out of the question.

"I have relatives here, Big Roy and Katie Marie Kaufman. I stayed with them for a while before I moved to The Peony Inn to work for Esther and Lizzie." Rose doubted that was a solid enough answer to please Catherine. "I *lieb* working there, and even though Esther and Lizzie aren't blood related to me, they are like family."

"Do you have siblings back home?" Catherine added extra butter to her bread, the way Rose liked to do. "I'm sure you know Benny has two *schweschdere*."

"I have five *bruders* and two *schweschdere*. They're all married. After *mei daed* passed, it was just me and *mei mamm*." She tore the crust off one side of her bread, then remembered what Esther said—how Rose did that when she was concentrating or upset. It was an odd habit, so she forced herself to stop. "I just needed a change."

Catherine tipped her head to one side like she might not understand, but she didn't push any further. "Benny tells me that you went fishing for the first time." She brought a hand to her chest. "I was shocked you had never cast out a line. Benny fished with his *daed* most Saturdays, and the girls enjoyed fishing too." She turned to her son. "Do you remember when Bethany caught that huge fish and ended up falling in the water?"

Benjamin laughed. "Bethany is the oldest of *mei* two *schweschdere*," he said to Rose. "She was about twelve when it happened. *Mei* younger *schweschder*, Miriam, was screaming so loud that me and *mei daed* ran to the pond. We thought Bethany was drowning when we saw her head bobbing up and down." He chuckled again.

"She never let go of that fishing pole, and that catfish was going *ab im kopp*, dragging her farther out in the pond. *Daed* and me jumped in the small bass boat we kept out there, and we pulled her—and the fish—in." He looked at Rose. "It was a big fish, about five pounds."

"A tad bigger than the fish I caught." Rose felt herself blushing.

"It doesn't matter." Catherine smiled. "You caught one on your first try, and that's impressive."

Rose listened in awe as Catherine and Benjamin—Benny as she called him—reminisced about a childhood that sounded magical compared to hers. If she kept seeing Benjamin, some day he would want to know about her life growing up. But for now, she loved listening to stories about a normal, loving family. Catherine lit up the room when she reflected on times past. Rose wanted to be the type of parent Catherine was. She wanted to give her children those types of memories, ones to be fondly reflected on years later.

Rose didn't have to worry about talking too much. Catherine had plenty to say, and Rose found herself wishing Catherine had been her mother, the same way she'd wished that about Esther and Lizzie. She suspected Catherine wouldn't want someone with her background as part of her family. Rose was jumping ahead of herself again. She and Benjamin hadn't even known each other that long. But if his kisses were any indication how he felt about her, then his feelings mirrored Rose's.

Benjamin didn't seem as shy around her anymore, and Rose tended not to ramble as much as she used to. It felt like a good balance, but it was more than that. He was kind, thoughtful, and handsome—everything Rose always thought she wanted in a husband. Right now, she felt fearful of disappointing him. Maybe her bad memories should all be crammed back in the jar and never released. Did she really have to tell anyone else about her childhood? More and more, she was deciding that no was the answer. She thought about how torturous it had been to have the discussion about her family with Esther.

By the time they finished eating, and Catherine had told plenty more stories, Rose tried to picture growing up like Benjamin, Bethany, and Miriam. How different her life might have been.

After they'd had dessert—pecan pie and apple pie—Rose offered to help Catherine clean the kitchen, but she wouldn't hear of it.

Rose wanted to get home before dark, plus her mind was running on overdrive. She thanked Catherine for the meal and said she should go before night fell.

"It has been so nice getting to know you, Rose." Catherine hugged her. It was a real hug, not the light pat on the back kind of hugs some people gave. She wasn't sure Benjamin's mother knew any more about her than she did when Rose walked in the door. But Rose had learned a lot about Benjamin and his family, and she'd commented and asked questions. Perhaps that's what Esther and Lizzie meant about being a better listener. It wasn't about how much Rose talked or didn't talk, but about balancing a conversation.

After Rose thanked her for the wonderful meal and conversation, Benjamin walked with her to the buggy. She had stayed longer than she meant to, but if she set the horse in a steady trot, she could still get home before dark.

Her emotions were all over the place. The more she recalled

her childhood, the more withdrawn she felt. It seemed cruel for God to introduce her to a man she believed she could love forever. But her feelings of unworthiness had crept up on her and overwhelmed her with doubt that she could be a good mother.

"I told you. *Mei mamm* is cheerful almost all of the time. Actually, she's animated the way you are, lively . . . all things I like." He chuckled as he untethered her horse. "Talk about marrying someone like your *mudder*."

Rose froze. She was sure the shock on her face was obvious when Benjamin locked eyes with her. "Wow. I mean . . . That just kind of came out," he said as he gave his head a quick shake. "Um . . . wow."

Rose knew more than anyone how something can unintentionally slip out, but it was usually backed up by an unconscious thought, which warmed her heart. "In some ways, I can see that your *mamm* and I are alike." She tried to pretend she didn't hear the part about marriage. "She enjoys a lively conversation too."

"Are you okay?" Benjamin held the reins and walked closer to her. "You didn't say much tonight, but that could be because *mei mamm* started telling stories, and when she does that, it's hard to get in on the conversation."

"I'm fine. I had a lovely time, and I enjoyed hearing about your childhood." *I'm becoming a better listener.*

When he kissed her good night, she wished she could stay in his arms forever. Her past was catching up with her, and she worried it was going to ruin everything. Logically, she knew her memories shouldn't define her, but as everything bubbled to the surface, she was forced to feel it and face it. Even the kiss—as wonderful as it was—felt different, like a prelude to this relationship ending before a new one could really get started. Fear was creeping into her life, and she knew the emotion blocked the voice of God and would only cause her emotional grief.

"Maybe we can spend the day together again this Saturday," he said when she eased out of his arms.

She forced a smile. "Maybe," she said softly as she gave him a quick wave before getting into her buggy.

By the time she got home, her heart was heavy and night had fallen earlier than she'd expected. Esther and Lizzie would already be asleep.

Upstairs, she slipped into her nightgown, took her hair down, and ran a brush through the long tresses. She lay atop her covers wondering if Benjamin had just had a slip of the tongue, or if he was hoping things were progressing toward marriage someday? She hoped it was the latter.

She glanced at the phone he had loaned her and picked it up. She held it for a while before setting it back on her nightstand. The conversation she needed to have with Benjamin wasn't one to be had over the phone, if she even chose to divulge her past.

As she lay back atop her covers, she tried to analyze what his reaction would be if they ever had that conversation. Would he be kind and understanding to her face, but secretly think that her past would prevent her from being a good mother someday? How could he possibly understand when he'd obviously had such an idyllic upbringing?

With her thoughts unresolved, she closed her eyes and prayed for guidance.

Chapter 18

BENJAMIN HAD TAKEN A SHOWER NOT LONG AFTER ROSE left, so he hadn't really had a chance to thank his mother for such a nice meal. "*Danki* for everything, *Mamm*. Supper was great," he said as he walked into the living room.

"I think Rose is lovely. Not as talkative as you said, but very easy to carry a conversation with." She stowed her knitting needles and yarn in the basket next to her chair. "And I enjoyed her story about how they got rid of their *creepy* guest."

Benjamin chuckled. "*Ya*, I can picture Rose and Lizzie doing that." After he stopped laughing, he said, "You didn't exactly give her a chance to say much."

"*Ach*, Benny, I did too."

It was more than that, though. Aside from the mice story and a few comments, Rose was unusually quiet, and it wasn't just because his mother had dominated the conversation. He could tell something was wrong as soon as she arrived. She was polite, but somewhat subdued. He'd written it off as her just being nervous to spend time with his mother. But the goodbye kisses weren't the same. They were wonderful, but different in a way he couldn't put his finger on. He wasn't sure how much of it was because he made the comment about marrying someone like your mother, or if it was something else. Was it even fair to try to rationalize it? No one could be in a chipper mood all the time.

He considered going out to the barn to call her, but decided against it. If something was on her mind or bothering her, maybe she needed time to sort through it.

His mother yawned. "I'm off to bed. When you talk to Rose, please tell her again how much I enjoyed her visit."

Benjamin gave her a quick wave. "*Ya*, I will. Sleep *gut*."

He wondered again about calling Rose, but maybe he would visit her tomorrow. He did need to get his phone back, but he hated to lose the convenient communication with her.

Rose was taking eggs out of the refrigerator the next morning when Esther shuffled into the kitchen. "Hon, unless you're having a craving for eggs, I say we just have some cereal." She pulled out a chair and sat.

Rose was glad not to cook this morning. She'd overthought things for way too long last night and hadn't drifted off to sleep until late. She slid the eggs back in the refrigerator and took out a carton of milk.

"I want to do something nice for Gus, but I imagine he has plenty of food still," Rose said. She needed a distraction from her thoughts.

"I never thought I'd hear the day when that man said he had too much food." Esther grinned. "I guess freezing portions had never occurred to him."

Rose put out Esther's homemade granola that Rose ate also, and she grabbed the box of Cap'n Crunch for Lizzie.

"*Ach, gut*. Cereal for breakfast," Lizzie said as she came into the kitchen and took a seat across from Esther. She patted the top of her cereal box. "I've missed you, Cap'n Crunch." She looked at Rose, then at Esther. "Did I miss anything?"

Rose shook her head. "*Nee*, not really. I was just telling Esther that I'd like to do something for Gus, but I just don't know what. He likely has enough food . . ."

"That's about all that pleases Gus," Esther said as the sun began to shine through the windows. "Food." She stood up and went to lift the blinds in the kitchen. Her body went rigid. "Gus's truck isn't there."

"He never goes anywhere this early." Rose said a quick prayer that Gus was all right as Esther hurried out the door to the barn.

Esther saw three messages on the answering machine, and her hand shook as she hit the button to listen to them.

The first one was at eleven thirty last night. *Esther, I'm in the hospital, but not in Bedford. They moved me to Bloomington. Don't worry. I'm fine.*

Next was a message left at four this morning. *Lizzie, I'm gonna need some of your blood.* There was a pause. *Good grief, I sound like a vampire.*

And the last recording had been left about an hour later. *Tell Naomi to feed the cats. Not sure when I'll be home.*

Esther tucked her chin and stared at the dewy grass tickling her bare feet as she crossed the yard. She stopped to collect her thoughts before she went inside.

"Did he leave a message?" Rose asked as Esther walked into the kitchen.

"*Ya,* he left three." She recited the messages. "Lizzie, you call the hospital in Bloomington to see what you need to do. When you're done and know more, I'll call a driver to take us there."

Lizzie began spooning her cereal, shoving big bites into her mouth so fast that milk dribbled down her chin.

Esther put her hands on her hips and shook her head.

"Don't look at me like that," she said to Esther between mouthfuls. "You know how easily I lose weight. I don't want to get there and not weigh enough."

Esther appreciated Lizzie's enthusiasm about her role in Gus's health care, so she didn't say anything else.

It was a while later when Lizzie returned from the barn. "They said I need to be there at eleven this morning. I asked what happened, and they said Gus showed up at the emergency room around ten last night. He was pale, running a fever, and weak. After some tests, they thought it best to move him to the Bloomington hospital. An ambulance took him there during the night. I asked how long he would be there, but they couldn't—or wouldn't—say. And I called a driver for us."

Esther put a hand across her stomach when it began to cramp. She'd learned to control her stomach ulcer most of the time. But stress occasionally set it off.

It was decided that Rose would stay to tend to things at the inn.

"Is there anything extra that I can do while I'm here? Perhaps I should get Gus's clothes from the cottage and wash them, maybe tidy up the place?"

"Gus isn't fond of people in the cottage, but in this instance, I think washing his clothes and giving the place a good cleaning might be a *gut* idea. He needs to be in a clean environment when he returns from the hospital." Esther put a finger to her chin. "I wonder if we should take him toiletries and extra clothes."

"Ew. I'm not going through his toiletries." Lizzie crinkled her nose. "We have extra toothbrushes, deodorant, and things like that upstairs for guests. Let's just take him some of that."

Esther nodded. She didn't want to rummage through his things either. Rose had cleaned Gus's cottage one other time when she'd first started and didn't know any better. She knew what she was up against.

They waited for Rose to run upstairs, and when she returned, she handed Esther a plastic bag. "There's a toothbrush, paste, lavender soap, a sample size deodorant, a hair brush, and some lotion that he might not use, but I put it in there anyway." She also gave Esther a slip of paper as she caught her breath. "I still have Benjamin's phone. He loaned it to me when I told him I was nervous about being by myself with Lloyd upstairs, and he let me keep it a bit longer. I don't know how long I'll have it, but here is the number." She wrung her hands together. "*Ach*, I hope Gus is okay."

"He's not okay, he's dying." Lizzie made the statement with little emotion attached to it, but hearing the words out loud tugged at Esther's heart.

"Hon, I'll call you as soon as we know something," she said to Rose before turning to Lizzie. "Do you have our mobile phone?"

"*Ya*, it's in *mei* purse. But it only has one of those little bars in the corner. We can charge it at the hospital."

Their driver arrived a few minutes later.

Lizzie didn't say much on the way to the hospital.

"Are you nervous about giving blood?" Esther asked when they were about halfway there. Bloomington was a little farther than Bedford, about an hour's drive from the inn.

"*Nee*. They just poke you in the arm and siphon it out from what I've read." Lizzie folded her hands atop her little black purse. "Robbing me of *mei* platelets bothers me more, but they didn't say anything about that on the phone."

"It's not too bad, giving platelets," their driver said. Henry had been carting them around on and off in his dark-blue passenger van for years. "Eat an antacid, though."

Esther and Lizzie exchanged glances. "An antacid?" Lizzie asked.

"Yeah, during the procedure you develop a weird taste in

your mouth, like metal. But that's about the only downside. At least it was for me when I donated platelets for a friend. Are you donating for anyone I know?"

"Gus Owens," Lizzie said as she rolled her eyes. Esther let it go. If that was the worst thing her sister did today, she could live with it.

"Yeah, I know Gus."

Esther waited for more, but that was it from Henry.

When they pulled up at the Bloomington hospital, Henry said, "I don't get to Bloomington much, so I'm going to do a little browsing around. Just call and let me know when you think you'll need a ride back. If it's too long, I might head home and come back later."

"*Ya*, will do," Esther said as they stepped out of the side door of the van.

When they walked in the main entrance of the hospital, they looked around until Esther saw an information desk. "There." She pointed to her right.

"We're here to see Gus Owens," Esther said. "*Mei* sister is also here to donate blood for him at eleven."

A petite woman with red hair got on her computer. "Are you family?" she asked above dark-rimmed glasses.

Esther hated lying, but they might not let her in if she said no, and Gus was family as far as she was concerned. "*Ya*," she said. "We are family."

"Mr. Owens is in ICU. It's only ten thirty, and I'm sure they will give you instructions about giving blood and what to expect when you get upstairs. Go to the fourth floor and take a right.

There will be a red button on the wall. Push it and someone will let you in."

Esther thanked her, and she and Lizzie walked toward the elevators.

"Since when did you take up lying?" Lizzie cut her eyes at Esther.

"Gus *is* family." Esther raised her chin as she pushed the Up button.

"Your family, not mine," Lizzie grumbled.

They had the elevator to themselves. "I expect you to be on your best behavior today. If Gus is in ICU, things might be worse than we think. Especially if he needs blood this urgently."

Lizzie stayed quiet.

They did as the receptionist downstairs had instructed, and two double doors swung open after they pushed the red button. They went to the first nurses' station and were told Gus was in room 406.

"This reminds me of when Joe was sick, even though he wasn't at this hospital." Esther glanced around at the small rooms, some with the shades open, others closed. The smell of ammonia hung in the air as machines beeped everywhere. Just the atmosphere caused Esther to shiver.

"*Ya*, it reminds me of when Reuben was sick too," Lizzie said.

They walked in silence until they reached room 406. "The sign says only one person can go in." Lizzie tapped the sign taped to the door. "While you see what's going on with Gus, I'll try to find out where I give blood."

Esther nodded as she eased the door open. A young nurse was standing by the bed.

"Good morning," she said. "I'm assuming you're a family member?"

"*Ya*, I am." Esther took in Gus's appearance. He was white as the walls in this sterile room, and the circles he always had under his eyes were darker and sunken in. Seeing him hooked up to so many machines made Esther's knees weak. He didn't look fine to her, as he'd stated in his recorded message.

"I brought you some toiletries." She held up the plastic bag. "Just a few things to get you by until you go home."

The young nurse refocused on a clipboard she had in her hand.

"Apparently, I ain't going home," Gus said, his breathing labored.

Tammy was the name on the nurse's tag. She cleared her throat and touched Gus on the arm. "Mr. Owens, we have you scheduled for a blood transfusion shortly. I believe your donor is due in the lab to give blood at eleven. You're going to feel much better after the transfusion." She patted his arm, smiling.

"It isn't gonna change the outcome." Gus turned his head to the side, not looking at either of them.

"I'm going to let you two talk." The nurse left, but Esther saw her sober expression just before she closed the door behind her.

"Gus? What's going on?" A suffocating sensation tightened in Esther's throat.

He still wouldn't look at her. "I started feeling all light-headed last night so I went to the ER. They sent me here to Bloomington pretty quick." Finally, he looked her way. "It's spreading faster than the chemo can get rid of it. There won't be any more treatments. It's in my lymph nodes, spleen, and liver."

Esther sat on the only small chair in the room. "You said in your message that you were fine. I-I don't understand." She clenched her jaw, hoping to stifle the sob building rapidly in her throat.

"They told me from the beginning that things could fall apart quick." He paused to take a deep breath. "I been thinking, Esther." His jowls hung lower than usual and his hair and beard had thinned—from the chemo, she supposed. "I might like to hear about that God you talk about. That seat by the furnace is looking less appealing with every breath I take. And I don't think I have a lot of breaths left."

Esther put a hand to her chest as her heart rate started to slow down. She even managed a small smile. It broke her heart that they were going to lose Gus, but there would be peace in knowing he had found the Lord before he passed. Although she wasn't going to stop praying for a miracle.

"Do you really believe that if I'm sorry for the stuff I've done that I might be able to get a seat where you're going when it's my time?"

Esther had never seen Gus openly cry before. Until now. He was fighting it, blinking his eyes a lot to keep the tears from spilling, but one rolled down his cheek anyway.

"*Ya*, I believe that," she said as she took a tissue from her purse and blotted her eyes. "And it makes me very happy to hear you say this."

Tammy the nurse came into the room and glanced back and forth at Esther and Gus, tugging at her ear. "I'm sorry. I know this is a bad time, but"—she studied the clipboard in her hand—"on the forms you filled out, you put down that you don't have any family."

Gus hung his head.

"He has a family. I am his family, Esther Zook." She reached up and barely tapped the clipboard the woman was holding. "And you'll need to list the rest of his family members, too, because I know they will want to visit him. Their names are Jayce and Evelyn Clarkson, Amos and Naomi Lantz, Rose Petersheim, and Lizzie Glick." She paused, her voice trembling. "Write all of those down. Did you get them?"

The nurse nodded. "Yes, ma'am. But I'm afraid Mr. Owens won't be staying here in the ICU for long. He's going to receive a blood transfusion, which will make him feel better for a while, but once someone reaches a—"

"They need to free up a bed for someone who can be saved," Gus said in a hoarse voice.

Esther reached for his hand, rough and wrinkled from years of living, like Esther's. She held on tightly. "Gus. You *are* going to be saved."

He squeezed her hand.

Chapter 19

Rose recalled the last and only time she'd ever cleaned Gus's cottage. It was worse today. The kitchen had dishes stacked in the sink and all over the counter. Three crusty, but mostly empty, cans of cat food were next to a takeout chicken box with the bones still inside. She was afraid to go in the bathroom, but she slipped on her rubber gloves and carried her pail of cleaning supplies to go have a look. Cringing, she decided she'd tackle the worst thing first.

When she heard a buggy coming in the driveway, she walked to the living room and looked out the window. Her heart flipped in her chest when she saw Benjamin. She got out of view and pressed her back to the wall next to the window as her body tensed. There was so much on her mind right now. Gus, her conversation with Esther about her childhood, and her relationship with Benjamin were all heavy on her heart.

Since Lizzie and Esther weren't home, he would knock on the door. When no one answered, he would leave. That would be best for now. "*Ach, nee.*" She remembered she had his phone. It was in her pocket so she wouldn't miss a call from Esther or Lizzie. Benjamin probably needed it back.

She pried herself from against the wall and went to meet him in the yard. He caught a glimpse of her leaving the cottage, and they met halfway.

"You, uh, seemed a little quiet last night. I-I just wanted to make sure you were okay." Benjamin stuttered a little and when his eyes avoided hers, he reminded her of the shy man she'd originally met.

"*Ya*, I'm okay." This wasn't the time to get into a heavy conversation. "But we found out this morning that Gus is in the hospital in Bloomington. He went there last night." She hung her head before she looked up at him, into his beautiful green eyes. "Esther or Lizzie is supposed to call me when they know more, but I'm sure you need your phone." She lifted the cell phone from the pocket of her apron.

"Keep it for now. *Mei* business cards have the landline number, so I don't get many calls on that phone." He rubbed his chin and finally locked eyes with her. "Are you sure there isn't something else going on?"

Rose bit her bottom lip. Should she tell him that she wasn't good enough for him? Or about her fears about being a good mother? He would want details. Once he heard her sad tale, would he look at her with pity? "*Nee*, nothing else is going on." She nodded over her shoulder. "I'm going to wash Gus's clothes and clean his cottage so he'll have a tidy place to come home to.

But . . . are you sure you don't need your phone? I'm not sure when they will call about Gus."

"*Nee*, you keep it." Benjamin shifted his weight from one foot to the other. "Did, um, you give any more thought to spending the day together on Saturday?"

With a heavy heart, she said, "I think I best wait and see how things are with Gus."

"*Ya*, sure." A muscle quivered at his jaw. "Did I or *mei mamm* do something wrong last night? She told me to tell you that she had a lovely time. I know she didn't give you a chance to talk much."

Instinctively, she touched his arm. "*Nee, nee*. I had a wonderful time, and your *mudder* is everything I wish mine ha—" She stopped herself. "Your *mamm* is lovely." She briefly looked over her shoulder. "I better get busy. Gus's cottage is a mess."

"*Ya*, I won't keep you. You'll let me know about Saturday?" An odd and lingering gaze passed between them, an unspoken knowingness that something had changed.

"*Ya*, I will." She leaned up and awkwardly kissed him on the cheek. "I better go."

She turned to go back to the cottage so he wouldn't see her eyes watering. All she'd ever wanted was to be a good wife and mother. Finally, she thought she'd met someone who put that possibility within her reach. Benjamin had calmed her with his soft-spoken, sweet words, but once she'd quieted down and couldn't hide behind all her chattering, it had left her with too much time to think. Her memories and fears were more tangled than ever now, but she couldn't bring herself to voice them, leaving her with little else to say.

On his way to repair a kitchen sink just on the outskirts of Montgomery, Benjamin had plenty of time to think and analyze. Something between him and Rose had changed. Her high-energy personality and animated ways had brought him out of a shell he'd lived in for way too long. But he felt himself regressing, and something was amiss with Rose too. He missed her merriment, her endless childlike chatter, and the way they balanced out each other's personalities. *What went wrong?* She'd been different the night before, and that was before she knew about Gus. Had she met someone else? He had to consider that. They hadn't been seeing each other long, and neither of them had mentioned that they were an exclusive item.

Whatever it was, it left him wondering if he should cancel the plans he'd made for them on Saturday.

Despite his worries, he took a few moments to pray for Gus. He didn't really know the man, and had only met him once, but Rose obviously cared about him if she was cleaning his cottage.

When Esther left Gus's room, she dried her eyes as best she could, then stopped at the nurses' station. "Excuse me," she said to the nurse, Tammy. "You said Gus wouldn't be staying here. Where will he be going?"

The woman sighed. "I'm sorry you found out about Mr. Owens the way you did. I can see how difficult this is for you.

I'm actually not sure where he will be going, but this sudden decline is going to require regular blood transfusions, and as his health deteriorates, he will require pain medications and close monitoring. There's a member of the hospital staff who's assigned to communicate with Gus about this level of care, but she isn't in right now. Mr. Owens will most likely be transferred to a hospice facility where they can keep him as comfortable as possible." She paused, frowning. "I'm afraid he's not a candidate for a marrow transplant due to his age and condition."

Esther sniffled. "*Danki* . . . I mean, thank you for the information. *Mei* sister is giving blood for Gus since she is an exact match. Do you know where I can find her?"

"Of course. In the lab on the second floor."

Esther stopped at the bathroom before she went to the elevator. She splashed water on her face and attempted to gather herself. When she finally did get on the elevator, Lizzie was waiting to get on when Esther reached the second floor.

After Lizzie stepped inside, Esther asked, "Do you want to go see Gus before we leave?"

"*Nee.*"

They were quiet on the short ride to the first floor, and when they exited the building, Esther called Henry, who was in the area and said he'd be there shortly.

"Did everything go all right giving blood?"

"*Ya*, it went fine." Lizzie had a bandage around the middle of her arm. "I had to eat cookies and drink juice before I could leave. When does Gus come home?"

"He won't be going back to the cottage." Esther told her

everything Gus had said, along with what the nurse communicated to her.

Lizzie was quiet for a while before she turned to Esther. "So he'll die in a hospital or in hospice?"

"*Ya*, I guess so. But, Lizzie, he wants to have a relationship with *Gott*, and I'm going to help him in that effort. I know that the words 'be saved' aren't completely in line with our teachings in the *Ordnung*. We are instructed to lead a good life, to believe Jesus is our savior, but that we won't automatically get to heaven just by believing without walking the walk also."

"Then I'm not sure how you're going to *save* Gus since he hasn't been walking the walk." Lizzie's comment wasn't said in a cynical way, but more with a hint of sympathy infused.

"We don't know what Gus's life has been like. He obviously thinks he has done things that make him undeserving of heaven. But he can't judge himself any more than we can judge him."

They were quiet. There was a bench a short walk away, but Henry had said he was close, and surprisingly, Esther's knee wasn't giving her fits today.

"We've witnessed several *gut* things that Gus has done over the years, despite his challenging disposition." Esther paused. "We don't know that the *gut* things don't already outweigh the bad things. Only Gus and *Gott* know that. But if it is a relationship with the Lord that Gus is wanting, then I believe that can lead to redemption."

"You're a *gut* woman, Esther. And there's Henry," Lizzie said as the blue van pulled into the parking lot.

"So are you, Lizzie." She nudged her sister with her elbow and grinned. "Most of the time."

"I just gave a bucketload of blood for that man," she said indignantly with her chin raised. "I hope he appreciates it."

"I'm sure he does."

Henry slid the side door open. "Everything go okay?" he asked as they climbed inside the van.

Esther wasn't in the mood to retell the details, and she sensed that Henry was only being polite. "*Ya.* Just ready to get home." She'd fill in Rose at home too.

Rose smelled of bleach and other cleaning solvents by the time she walked back to the inn. It had been a dirty job, but overhauling the cottage had kept her mind from wandering to places she didn't want it to go. And Gus would have a clean place to come home to.

She was opening the door when the blue van pulled in the driveway. *Why didn't Esther or Lizzie call me?* Rose waited on the porch for them, and as they got closer, she saw Esther's swollen eyes.

"I should have called, I know," Esther said wearily as she grasped the handrail and struggled up the porch steps. "I'll tell you everything inside when I can get *mei* feet up."

Rose let the sisters get settled on the couch, both with their feet up on the coffee table, then Esther relayed all the information the nurse told her and what Gus had to say.

"I'm afraid you cleaned the cottage for nothing." Lizzie looked wiped out and pale, her eyes barely open as she yawned.

"This is terrible. He won't see his home again," Rose said as she sat in one of the rocking chairs. "He won't see his cats either. He loves those kitties." She waited for Lizzie to make a snide remark about the animals, but she didn't. "This is awful. I wish there was something I could do for him. It's okay that I cleaned the cottage because it needed it. I was happy to do it for him, but now he won't see it." Rose was talking too much, something she hadn't done in a while. She recalled the calming effect Benjamin had on her. Even though she still had a lot to say, it seemed to make more sense when she was with him.

Lizzie crossed one ankle over the other. "I always figured Gus would outlast both of us." She glanced at Esther.

"*Ya*, me too." Esther stretched her arms above her head and yawned just as the grandfather clock chimed four times.

"We missed our nap," Lizzie said as she laid her head back against the couch. "Tell us some happy news, Rose. Something cheerful."

She hadn't had a chance to share details about her supper last night with Benjamin and his mother. Rose gave them a brief rundown. "I liked Catherine, his *mudder*, a lot."

"*Gut*. Always *gut* to get along with the mother-in-law." Lizzie raised her eyebrows playfully up and down.

Rose looked down at her lap. "*Ach*, I don't know that things will go that far."

"Why?" Lizzie asked as she folded her arms across her stomach. "Did something happen?"

Esther peeled an ear in Rose's direction.

"*Nee*. Not really. He came by today and told me to keep his phone since I still hadn't heard from you." She shrugged. "He wants to spend the day with me on Saturday, but I'm not sure I will. I mean, maybe I will, but I don't know. It just seems we're too different to really get any more serious than we are. I think our relationship will probably dissolve organically. It's okay though because—"

Lizzie swung her feet off the coffee table and planted them on the floor as she sat taller. "Child, what are you going on about? Dissolve organically? What in the world does that even mean? You've been head over heels for that man. Did he do something to cause you to change your feelings?"

"*Nee*, Benjamin is wonderful. And that's the problem. After meeting his *mudder*, it's quite clear that he came from a lovely family. They're close. His parents raised him and his sisters in a *haus* filled with *lieb*. He'll make a *gut* father someday, and I—"

"Stop!" Lizzie slapped her hands to her knees. "Don't you dare tell me that you don't think you can be a *gut mudder* and that you're sparing him a lifetime with you because you're damaged. That's baloney. You'd be denying both of you a lifetime of happiness."

"You are both exhausted," Rose said, sighing. "We will discuss this another time."

"*Nee*. I want to talk about it now." Lizzie spit her teeth out in her hand and scowled.

"Lizzie, hush." Esther rubbed her temples. "Quit badgering the child."

Lizzie shook her head. "From everything you and Esther have told me, you seem to have these feelings of unworthiness and shame. Rose, you have to let those emotions go and give yourself permission to be happy."

"I agree," Esther said softly.

"I'm not the *gut* person you think me to be." Rose was tired of hiding within herself, clinging to the one thing she hadn't told anyone. Her heart pounded in her chest like a bass drum as her lips began to tremble and sweat gathered like tiny rivers across her forehead. "Esther, I told you that I didn't ask *Gott* for a miracle when *mei daed* was sick. And I told you that I was sad when he died." She paused, squeezing her eyes closed and trying to rid herself of his face. "Maybe on some level I was sad. Sad that he was *mei* father. Sad for *mei bruders* and *schweschdere*, that we had lived the way we had." She opened her eyes and looked back and forth between Esther and Lizzie. "I hated him! I hated *mei* father. He was an evil man, a terrible man." She bent at the waist. "I have so much hatred inside of me, how could I ever be a *gut* parent?" Long overdue sobs poured forth, the last of the bottled-up emotions she'd been carrying around.

When she finally straightened, Esther and Lizzie were both crying.

"This isn't the time for this," Rose said, shaking her head. "Not today, after the news about Gus, not today when—"

"Rose?" Esther waited for Rose to meet her gaze. "What did your father do to you?"

Saying it out loud would mean it happened. Even though she knew it did, she would have to face it head-on. "He taped *mei* mouth shut with duct tape when I talked too much." She lowered her head. "Maybe it doesn't sound as bad as a beating, or some of the other things my siblings went through, but it was humiliating and painful when he ripped the tape off. Once when I had a stuffy nose, I begged *mei mamm* to take the tape off. I wrote it on a piece of paper that I couldn't breathe. She put some saline drops in *mei* nose and told me to blow *mei* nose. It only helped a little. But she said the tape would stay on. I knew not to talk too much, but it wasn't something I could help. Words just spilled out, and I had trouble organizing *mei* thoughts, and I never felt calm or at peace. I was always nervous. It's not like that when I'm with Benjamin. I feel free to talk all I want, but he has a calming effect on me, so *mei* words are better organized. But how could I subject him to someone with all of this bottled-up hatred? It's wrong in the eyes of the Lord, and I know in *mei* heart that it's wrong. I'm ashamed of *mei* feelings." Realizing how long she'd had her head hung, she lifted her eyes to Esther and Lizzie. Both women had their hands to their mouths. "I'm sorry. I'm talking too much again."

"Rose, how long did your parents leave the tape on?" Esther's face was drawn, and Rose wished so badly she hadn't said anything. "For an hour? Longer? It doesn't matter, Rose. You did nothing to deserve that."

"Sometimes he left it on for days. He would rip it off so I could eat, then he put it back on." She squeezed her eyes closed, and the memories were like venom flowing through her veins, slowly eating away at her if she didn't harness the hate and get rid of it.

Esther held her face in her hands. Lizzie's mouth hung open.

"Most of the time, I can keep the memories at bay, refusing to be anything but happy. But somehow everything came barreling to the surface when I realized how much I cared for Benjamin. I thought all I'd ever wanted was to be a *fraa* and *mudder*, to be everything *mei* own *mamm* wasn't."

"You can have all of that, hon. Genes don't make us who we are." Lizzie nodded at Esther. "I mean, look how different me and Esther are. I'm the cute, sweet, delicate one, and she's the large, matronly, boring one." She flashed a toothless smile at her sister.

"Cute, sweet, and *delicate?*" Esther's eyes widened.

Lizzie waved off her sister and refocused on Rose. "And you are a product of your environment."

"Exactly," Rose said softly. "And I'm afraid *mei* environment wasn't very *gut*. There wasn't love in the traditional way. *Mei* siblings, we all loved each other, but we were fearful all the time, and—"

"Stop," Lizzie said again as she held up a hand. "I'm not talking about the past. I'm talking about your environment right now. Today. What do you see?"

Rose looked back and forth between Esther and Lizzie and even smiled a little. "I see two *schweschdere*, who are very different, but who love each other very much."

"What else? Where do you live?" Lizzie settled back into the couch cushions.

"I-I live here."

"*This* is your environment. You live in a *haus* filled with love. We all love each other, and this is your life today—now. Yesterdays are gone, hon. Embrace the future, lean on the Lord, and make your world everything you want it to be. He wants that for you. And I believe sometimes *Gott* puts us through things, and it seems to us that it doesn't have any rhyme or reason, but there is always a purpose for our hardships."

Rose stood up. "I appreciate everything you are saying, and I love you both very much. But I think I have to work through this on *mei* own." She went to the couch and hugged each of them. "I'm sorry to have created more upset and worry on a day when news about Gus has everyone upset already." She glanced at Lizzie to see if she'd roll her eyes, but she didn't.

"Don't you apologize, *mei maedel*." Esther kissed her on the cheek, then began to cry again. "If anyone needs to say they are sorry, it is me and Lizzie." She shook her head hard. "We never should have told you not to be so chatty. It's who you are, it makes you the person you are, and—" She wept even harder.

"She's right, hon." Lizzie cupped Rose's face. "For that to have happened to you"—she brushed away a tear—"we never should have encouraged you to be anyone you aren't. I'm sorry."

"Please don't apologize." Rose shook her head. "You helped me to be a better listener and to actually *hear* what was being said without words swimming aimlessly around in *mei* head. I'm a better person due to the advice you have both given me. It's all about balance. Maybe what happened when I was a child fueled my chattiness as an adult, but I do feel I'm a better listener today. Please don't feel regret."

Both women were quiet and dabbing at their eyes.

"I'll be upstairs if you need anything." Rose hoped she wouldn't develop a headache. This was all too much for one day, and she suspected Esther and Lizzie felt the same way.

After Rose was upstairs, Esther and Lizzie fell back onto the couch. "I don't know if we actually helped that girl or not, but I would have told her to talk all the time if I'd known the abuse she suffered." Esther blotted the tears in her eyes again as Lizzie nodded in agreement.

Esther finally took in a deep breath and patted Lizzie on the leg. "I'm proud of how you handled this situation. Even if you did call me matronly and boring. I wasn't sure at first if you were pushing her too hard, but maybe she will reflect on some of the things you said and begin to heal."

"Rose has always been so cheerful and chatty. I don't like seeing her this way, so down and out." Lizzie pushed her lip into a pout. "I understand how life's woes can catch up with a person, but it's all landed on her hard. But I'll tell you one thing . . ."

Esther braced herself and clutched her apron.

"She is not going to let that Benjamin get away. I'm going to see to that. They seem so *gut* for each other."

"I'm going to have to agree with you, but all on *Gott*'s time frame." Esther yawned. "I'm going to go out to the barn and call Gus. And don't give me a hard time about it."

"Just use our mobile phone. I charged it at the hospital." Lizzie pointed to the kitchen. "It's on the counter."

"We're only supposed to use those for emergencies." Esther yawned.

"I guess this kind of is."

There was a sadness in Lizzie's voice that Esther felt in her heart. The entire day had been overwhelming. She'd pray that tomorrow would be better.

Chapter 20

Esther used the mobile phone to call from her bedroom. She didn't know you couldn't actually talk to a patient in ICU. She asked the person who answered the phone for an update on Gus, and the nurse on duty said he was feeling much better after the blood transfusion. "He will probably be moved into a regular room in the morning," the woman had said. When Esther questioned about hospice care, the nurse told her she didn't see it noted on his chart. Esther smiled before she ended the call. God was still in the miracle business, and Gus was going to be a recipient. Esther was sure of it.

But even her positive attitude about Gus couldn't squash everything that had happened today. She buried her face in her pillow and sobbed, even though she didn't think she had any tears left. Such sadness had wrapped around them, and Esther prayed hard for Gus's recovery. She asked God to ease Rose's pain. And she prayed for her entire family to be well and happy.

She had cried for a long while when her bedroom door opened. Lizzie walked in, crawled in bed with her, and draped an arm over her. Her younger sister used to do that when they were growing up, when Esther had a nightmare or was sad or afraid. Esther latched on to Lizzie's hand, and no words were necessary. Lizzie just held her while she cried.

∞

Rose stared at the phone when it began to buzz on the nightstand. She owed it to Benjamin to answer, to make arrangements for him to get his cell phone back. But she wasn't the same Rose he enjoyed spending time with, and she had no plans to spend the day with him. She'd meant what she said to Lizzie, that the relationship would just organically dissolve. There was no need for a messy breakup because Rose wasn't even sure what their status was.

"*Wie bischt*," he said after she answered. "Are you doing okay this evening?"

Rose was far from okay, and her insides twisted like knots tightening. "I'm all right. It has just been a long day."

"I know. You sound tired." He paused. It sounded like he might have yawned, which induced the same from Rose. "Did you decide about Saturday?"

She squeezed her eyes closed and thought about how nice it would be to spend the day with Benjamin—under different circumstances. Rose wouldn't be good company for anyone right now. "I think that, um, with everything going on with Gus, I need to stay close to Lizzie, and particularly Esther. Both of them are exhausted, so I'm going to do more to help out." She put her arm across her stomach and bent at the waist.

"Okay." He was quiet for a while. "I need to get *mei* phone back. Is there a time that would be convenient for me to pick it up?"

Rose opened her mouth to tell him any time was fine, but the formality in his voice made it clear they weren't just talking about the phone. This was an ending, and they both knew it. Benjamin's disadvantage was that he didn't know why. It seemed their parting of ways wasn't happening as organically as she'd predicted.

"Whenever it's convenient for you." Rose hoped he would give her a time so that she could plan to be gone.

"I have a couple of jobs tomorrow, but I'll come by in between them or when I'm done."

The formality was there again. They were setting a meeting, nothing more. "Okay," she said.

They were both quiet, as if neither wanted to hang up, but they didn't know what to say either.

Finally, Rose said, "I'll see you tomorrow."

Benjamin's goodbye was abrupt, and the line was dead before Rose had a chance to respond.

She buried her head in her pillow, racked with sobs. She'd just pushed away possibly her only chance for happiness. But Benjamin wouldn't be content with Rose until she was happy with herself. And she didn't know if or when that would happen.

Benjamin sat on the workbench for about ten minutes after he hung up with Rose. Gus's condition had surely upset the entire houseful of women, but his gut told him it was more than that. The call had been an unspoken goodbye, and Benjamin was angry and hurt. She could have at least told him what he'd done to run her off.

He lifted himself from the workbench and jumped down. Then he picked up the business card he'd taken out to the barn, knowing he might have to make a call after he talked to Rose. He tapped the card against his palm a few times and wondered if he should wait to cancel his reservation. Maybe she would change her mind when he saw her tomorrow.

After another few minutes, his anger began to settle, and the churning in his stomach eased up. Maybe she was more upset about Gus than she was revealing. Benjamin would give her some time. That was the right thing to do. He needed to make the call.

It rang three times before Sam Hanners picked up the phone. Benjamin took a deep breath. "Captain Hanners?"

"Speaking."

"This is Benjamin King." He closed his eyes and wished things were different.

"Yeah. You're the young Amish man who requested I take you and your girl on a spin down the river. There's a section at the far end of the east fork that's deep and will let me build up some good speed."

"Sir, I'm sorry to have to do this, but I'm going to have to cancel. Something came up with *mei*, uh . . . friend." He cleared his throat. "And she can't make it."

"That's all right, fella. The boat will still be here when you're ready, and good Lord willing, I'll still be here too."

Benjamin thanked him, and as he walked to the house, he pictured Rose with her eyes wide in amazement as they held on to the dash—and each other—going however fast Captain Hanners would have been able to go on the river. Where had Rose gone? *And would she be back?*

∞

Rose rode with Esther to go see Gus the following morning. It would keep her out of the house most of the day. Hopefully, Benjamin would pick up his phone while she was gone. She'd left it with Lizzie and explained that he might come for it. Also, she hated to see Esther make the trip alone an hour each way to the hospital in Bloomington.

"Henry, do you want me to call you again when we're ready? Or we can set a time now for you to pick us up." Esther picked up the chocolate pie she'd brought as she scootched across the seat in the van. Rose took the pie so she could step out.

"I'll just hang around the area until I hear from you. Nothing on my agenda today." Henry slid the passenger door closed.

They strolled toward the entrance and Rose glanced over her shoulder as the van pulled away. "Didn't you say Henry has been driving for you and Lizzie for a long time?"

"On and off, more so after his wife passed."

"Hmm."

Esther cut her eyes at Rose. "What do you mean, *hmm?*"

"He's a widow. He's *Englisch*. And you've known him for a while. I'm surprised Lizzie hasn't tagged him as suspect number three. He's a nice-looking man. And he seems kind. Maybe he's the one—" Rose stopped as she realized she was about to dive into nervous chatter.

Esther chuckled. "*Nee*, it's not Henry. And I'd almost forgotten about *mei* secret admirer. If I had a stalker, it seems he would have stalked by now, so I'll stick to referring to him as *mei* secret admirer."

"It's nice to hear you laugh. I know this is a hard time for you." Rose opened the main door to the hospital and stepped aside for Esther. They went to the front desk and were told Gus was in a regular room this morning, room 215. That news brought a smile to Esther's face. He hadn't been taken to a hospice facility.

"He's out of ICU," she said as she picked up her pace.

As they neared the elevators, Esther said, "I realize it's a tough time for you, too, but I think many of your worries are unfounded when it comes to Benjamin."

"I think I need to get myself right before I can be *gut* for anyone. And I don't understand *Gott*'s timing. From the time I left Ohio, I had managed to leave *mei* past mostly behind me. And now it has come back to haunt me at the worst possible time."

After the elevator door closed, they were quiet since there were three other people with them. But once they stepped out, Esther said, "You are allowing it to haunt you, Rose. I sympathize with your situation. I truly do. But shame and fear do not come from *Gott*. Love and forgiveness come from *Gott*."

"I know." *And what do I do with all this hatred I have for* mei *father?* She'd woken up around three this morning. All the covers were off the bed. Her house slippers weren't in their normal spot by the bed, and her hairbrush was on the floor. She had a funny feeling she might have been sleepwalking again, which seemed to only happen when she was upset. And it hadn't occurred in a long time.

When they arrived at Gus's room, Esther knocked on the door. "Should I wait out here?" Rose asked.

"*Nee*, I'm sure he will be happy to see you." She smirked. "Because you know Gus is always delighted to visit with anyone."

Rose grinned, glad that Esther was able to hold on to a fragment of her sense of humor during such a sorrowful time.

She held back as Esther moved closer to Gus. He was sitting up in bed, and Rose couldn't help but think he didn't look like a dying man. Thinner for sure, and all the tubes and beeping noises were unsettling. And there was an empty tray of food on the bedside table.

"*Ach*, you're looking much better today. More color in your face." Esther set the pie on a small table in the corner that had two chairs on either side. "And this room is so much nicer than that small space in ICU."

"I hope that's a chocolate pie." He scowled at Rose. "Why are you here?"

"I-I can wait outside." She rushed to leave, knowing she shouldn't be surprised at Gus's reaction, but it stung just the same.

"Rose made the journey with me so I wouldn't have to travel alone." Esther thrust her hands to her hips. "Which I appreciate, and you need to apologize to her."

His mouth took on an unpleasant twist. "If I'm being mean, it's because I have your crazy sister's blood traveling through my veins."

Esther pulled out a chair and sat. "That's ridiculous, and you know it. Lizzie's blood has put color back in your face. Do you feel better today?"

He scratched his head. His gray hair was pulled back in the usual ponytail, and his beard of the same color needed a trim. "I don't like being here, Esther. I ain't ever gonna see my home or my cats again. Whiskers will be especially lost when I croak. Stupid cat sleeps with me."

"I don't think you're going to . . . croak. You're not in a hospice facility, and release from ICU to a regular room is a *gut* thing."

"I'm only here because those hospice places are full." He started to cough, so Esther reached for the glass of water by the bed, but he shook his head. "Esther, we need to get busy with your God stuff. I have been practicing talking to Him. He ain't listening."

Esther twisted her hands in her lap. Perhaps this was too big a task for her, but she was going to do her best. "*Gott* always hears you, and He always answers. It might not be the answer you want to hear, but He will not forsake you."

"He's forsaken me for years, and as much as I'd like to avoid the hot spot, I don't see how I'm worthy enough to be considered for residency at the other place." He pointed his finger upward.

"Gus, none of us are worthy. We are all sinners finding our way and doing the best we can. Lesson number one: you forgive yourself and release any shame you are carting around." Esther thought about Rose, who should probably be in on this conversation. "The weight of your past will wear you down."

"I'm already worn down. I'm dying." Gus rolled his eyes.

Esther took a deep breath and blew it out slowly in an effort to remain calm. "I don't know what you have done throughout your life, and there is no need to tell me." She surely didn't want to know. "But you ask *Gott* to forgive you for those deeds."

"I've been doing that repeatedly all morning. But I don't feel any different."

"It takes time to develop a relationship with the Lord."

"Well, it's obvious I don't have a lot of time." He coughed some more.

Esther unzipped her purse and pulled out a folded piece of paper. "I've written down some scriptures from the Bible that I think might help you." She handed it to him, and he hesitated but slowly unfolded the paper and began to read.

> Revelation 21:4. He will wipe every tear from their eyes. Psalm 34:18. The Lord is close to the brokenhearted and saves those who are crushed in spirit. Psalm 147:3. He heals the brokenhearted and binds up their wounds.

Gus turned the paper over. Both sides were filled with scriptures Esther had carefully chosen. "And you think these will help me?"

"I do." Again, she considered this might be too big a project for her. "Gus, do you have a religious preference? Maybe you would prefer to have a member of clergy speak with you?"

"No." His voice held a rasp of irritation. "They've already sent more holy men in here than I care to count—Catholics, Lutherans, Baptists, Methodists, and others." He folded his arms over his stomach beneath the covers. "Esther, you giving up on me already?"

She rubbed the back of her neck. "*Nee*, I'm not giving up on you. But I'm not really qualified to help you find the Lord. There are people who specialize in ministry."

He gazed into her eyes so intensely that Esther could almost feel his fear. "You're the holiest person I know. If you can't help me, I'm a goner for sure." He rolled his eyes again. "I *know* I'm a goner, but . . . you know what I mean." He glanced around the room. "This place is so depressing. Everything is white. The walls are white, the tables are white, the sheets and blankets are white." He leaned his head over the side of the bed. "Even the floors are white."

Esther glanced at the tile before looking back at him. "It isn't ideal, but on *mei* next visit, I will bring you some flowers, if that's allowed, to brighten up the place."

"When is your next visit?" There was a faint tremor of emotion in his voice.

"I can't come every day, but I will visit often."

"How often?" His voice broke in a hoarse whisper as he reached for the water and took a sip.

"As often as I can. But remember, there are others who want

to visit you too. All those I listed as family, remember? Lizzie is putting together a schedule for everyone. You won't be alone, Gus. You have people who care about you. I know you don't know Amos as well as the others, but he would like to come see you also. And I know Jayce will visit as much as he can."

"I'm sure wacky Lizzie isn't on that list," he grumbled under his breath.

"Maybe if you stop calling her crazy and wacky, she'd agree to come see you. But from now on, you will not refer to her in that way, or I'm not coming back." She raised her chin and gave him the sternest expression she could muster.

His glare burned through her. "You'd do that? Quit coming?"

"*Ya*, Gus, I will quit coming if you are going to be unpleasant or speak ugly about people I love, and that includes Lizzie."

"Fine." His lips thinned with irritation.

Esther cleared her throat. "It would be nice of you to speak kindly to Rose, who is waiting outside. It would also be *gut* practice for you, a drill of how you should speak to everyone. I'll be your coach."

"Fine," he repeated before he let out a heavy sigh.

Esther went to the door and peeked her head outside. "Come in, hon. Gus would like to see you."

Rose blinked her eyes and looked a bit baffled, but she followed Esther into the room.

"Hey, Rose Petal." Even though his mouth was set in annoyance at first, one corner slowly lifted.

"How many times have I told you not to call her that?" Esther shook her head.

"It's okay." Rose moved closer to the bed. "I've never really minded. It's rather endearing, actually. So if you want to call me Rose Petal, I'm fine with that. And—"

"Got it." Gus held up a palm to shush the girl, then he frowned. "What's wrong with you? You're all pale and have dark circles under your eyes."

"I-I'm just working through some things." Rose folded her hands in front of her and avoided Gus's probing eyes.

"Well, don't take too long. Life tends to catch up with you. Before you know it, you'll be old and dying like me."

Esther wanted to ask Gus to quit saying how he was dying all the time, but he seemed to have Rose's attention.

"Is it about that fellow I saw you canoodling with at my fishing spot?" His eyebrows drew into a frown.

Rose glanced at Esther, who stayed quiet.

"A little. It's also about *mei* family and *mei* childhood. I'm analyzing some things." She looked away from him as her face turned red. Esther was surprised Rose had shared such personal details.

Gus shook his head. "Well, take it from me, let the past be the past. Don't dwell on it. Family is tricky." He waved a dismissive hand in the air. "Rose Petal, embrace the people you love, 'cuz you ain't gonna be around forever to tell them how you feel."

Esther's jaw dropped about the same time as Rose's. Esther smiled on the inside.

Gus was taking baby steps, but at least he was walking, and it was progress.

Chapter 21

Benjamin pulled up at The Peony Inn around lunchtime, hoping to catch Rose at home since she usually prepared the meals. Lizzie answered the door after he'd knocked several times.

"*Wie bischt*, Benjamin." She had a towel in her hand and was blotting her face. "Sorry it took so long to get to the door. I was splashing cold water on *mei* face. It's hard to believe we have another month of summer. I'm relieved no one has booked a room. Easier on us during this heat." She pushed the screen door open. "Come in. If you're looking for Rose, she went to the hospital with Esther, but she said you might be by to pick up your mobile phone." Lizzie motioned for him to follow her to the kitchen. "It's on the counter."

She picked up Benjamin's phone and handed it to him. "I think it's dead."

"That's okay. *Danki*." He wanted to ask Lizzie what was

going on with Rose, but the words wouldn't come. "Um . . . how is Gus doing?"

Lizzie shrugged. "He's dying, but otherwise okay, I guess. He has *mei* blood pumping through him, so I'm hoping it will make him nicer."

Benjamin held back a grin. "*Danki* for *mei* phone. Blessings to Gus. I guess I better go."

"Not so fast." Lizzie cut her eyes at him, frowning. "I thought you and Rose were a perfect match, and now there are problems, *ya?*"

"There seem to be." Benjamin stared at his phone as he moved it from one hand to the other. "Although I don't know what they are." He wasn't comfortable talking about this with Lizzie, but if the woman could shed some light for him, then he'd endure a conversation about Rose.

"The *maedel* is beating herself up about matters related to her childhood. She thinks that because certain things happened when she was growing up, she wouldn't be a *gut mudder*. When she started to care about you, everything seemed to come to the surface for the poor girl. Esther and I have talked to her, encouraged her to leave the past behind, but she's stuck there. And when she realized you had such a happy childhood—and she really liked your *mudder*, by the way—anyway, she's decided she isn't *gut* enough for you." Lizzie grumbled. "Then she said something about letting the relationship organically dissolve." She scrunched up her face and pressed her thin lips together. She didn't have her teeth in, he noticed. "What exactly does that mean, *organically dissolve?*"

Benjamin was still trying to absorb everything she'd said. "She said she cares about me?"

"*Ach*, you'd have to be blind not to see that." She edged closer to him. "I think she's in *lieb* with you, if you want my opinion." Benjamin wasn't sure why she whispered that since no one was home, but this was certainly good news. "If you feel the same way about her, I suggest you tell her to forget about the past and hook up with you."

He grinned. Lizzie talked like the English sometimes. But the cracks in his heart were already mending. "*Danki* for telling me."

She grunted as she raised her shoulders slowly before lowering them. "Well, do you care about her or not?"

"*Ya*, very much."

Lizzie pointed a finger at him. "Then you best get busy and get this fixed. Nothing worse than a failed matchmaking attempt, and Esther and I are very *gut* at what we do." She challenged him with her eyes. "Get busy."

"*Ya*, yes, ma'am." Benjamin thanked Lizzie again. "I'll talk to her Sunday after worship service." He left The Peony Inn with a bounce in his step. Whatever Rose had been through, they would talk it out together.

Rose was anxious to find out if Benjamin had been by while she and Esther were gone. Lizzie was sitting on the couch, her legs crossed, and kicking one foot when they came into the living room. She was pretending to read a magazine, but she was flipping the pages much too fast to be reading, or even studying the pictures.

"Was Benjamin here?"

Lizzie slammed the magazine shut and uncrossed her legs. "Glad you asked. *Ya*, he was." She giggled. "I fixed everything for you." She winked at Esther. "I'm the better matchmaker and the one who gets things handled."

Esther shook her head. "If you say so."

Rose's chest tightened. "What do you mean you fixed everything?"

"I told him how you've been beating yourself up about things that happened when you were a *kinner*, how you don't think you'll be a *gut mudder*, and that you're stuck in the past. And I told him how you think you aren't *gut* enough for him." She flashed a toothless grin of satisfaction. "He said he cares about you and planned to talk to you after worship service Sunday."

Rose's blood was simmering to a boil as she trembled from head to toe. "Please tell me you are making this up, that you didn't really tell Benjamin all of that?"

Lizzie narrowed her eyebrows, glanced at Esther—whose mouth had fallen open—then she looked back at Rose. "Of course I did. You want things fixed between the two of you, right?"

Rose covered her mouth with both hands after she gasped. "Lizzie, how could you? That was not your information to share!" She glared at this woman she loved, but her shock and horror were wrapping around her so tightly she couldn't breathe. "You have embarrassed and humiliated me. I can't even imagine what Benjamin must think." She could envision Lizzie telling

Benjamin her innermost secrets, and she probably did it just the way she described. "How could you, Lizzie? I am never telling you anything again!" She ran for the door and kept going until she was past the pond and out of sight.

Breathless, she dripped with sweat as she bent at the waist and tried to catch her breath. There was no way she was going to worship service Sunday, and maybe never again. She was so tired of crying, but she couldn't stop the tears from coming.

Esther put her hands on her hips as she stood in the middle of the living room. Lizzie slouched into the couch and wiggled her bare feet on the floor as she twisted the string on her prayer covering.

"Don't yell at me." Lizzie pouted like a child. "I thought if he knew everything then he would understand and talk to Rose. And Benjamin was happy I told him. I could tell."

"Maybe so." Esther sat beside her sister. "But Rose is right. It wasn't your place to say anything. That decision should have been left up to Rose, and you took away her choice. Now she has to confront a situation she might not be ready to delve into."

"You know how it goes, Esther. If people wait too long, life gets away from us, and it becomes too late."

Esther recalled what Gus said to Rose, a version of the same words Lizzie had just spoken. "I understand that, but it was still not your place to share Rose's personal life with Benjamin."

Lizzie huffed, then stood up. "I'll go talk to her."

"Let her be. Give the child some time." Esther blotted her

forehead with a tissue. "Besides, you'll have a heatstroke if you stay outside for long. I'm not surprised we don't have any rooms rented out. We should be used to no air-conditioning, but this is the worst summer I can recall."

"I was just trying to help." Lizzie's eyes were watery. "I'm going to lie down."

Esther sighed as her sister's bedroom door closed behind her. Lizzie didn't want Esther to see her cry, although she'd comforted Esther when she was in tears countless times. She sat on the couch and put her feet up, thinking she could probably stay in this spot forever. She closed her eyes and tried to pretend she was in Antarctica.

This situation would likely resolve itself by Sunday. Lizzie and Rose would have hugged and made up by then. Rose and Benjamin would hopefully work everything out too. After she said a prayer about it, she turned her focus to Gus. She prayed hard that God would keep working on that miracle.

By Sunday, Rose still wouldn't speak to Lizzie. It had only been a day and a half, but Rose's silence was making them all uncomfortable. She prepared the meals and kept up with her chores, but despite Lizzie's attempts to reconcile, Rose wouldn't hear of it. Esther was going to have a talk with Rose and tell her it was time to forgive Lizzie for her error in judgment. But when she walked into the kitchen to have the usual bowl of cereal before worship service, the room was vacant. No one had even made coffee.

"I overslept," Lizzie said as she met Esther in the living room.

"Put your teeth in."

"*Ach*, okay. I forgot."

While Lizzie went to get her dentures, Esther ambled to the foot of the stairway. "Rose, are you ready?"

After a few seconds, Esther called to her again.

"I'm not going to worship," Rose hollered from upstairs.

Esther struggled up three steps, hoping she didn't have to go all the way to the second floor. "Rose, if this is about Lizzie, or having to face Benjamin, those aren't *gut* enough reasons to miss church."

Rose emerged at the top of the stairs with a hand across her stomach. "I'm not feeling well," she said as she tucked long strands of brown hair behind her ears.

"What's wrong?" Esther suspected it wasn't anything physical.

"I threw up."

It was hard to argue with that, unless it was a bald-faced lie. "Can I bring you anything?"

"*Nee*, I just need to go back to bed." Rose spread her other arm across her chest as she flinched.

Esther stared at her. "All right. I hope you feel better. We will see you early afternoon."

Rose nodded before she went back to her room.

"Where's Rose?" Lizzie asked with her teeth in.

Esther shuffled toward the door. "She said she doesn't feel well, that she threw up and isn't going this morning."

"It's because of me." Lizzie slipped into her shoes.

"*Ya*, probably." She opened the screen door and held it for her sister. "And I'm sure she's afraid to face Benjamin."

"I thought I was helping." Lizzie shuffled her teeth back and forth before she stomped down the porch steps. She was already in the driver's side of the buggy by the time Esther had trudged across the yard.

"Maybe don't help so much next time." Esther climbed into the seat.

They were quiet on the way to the Millers, who were a young couple with a small home. Worship service would be held outside in the heat. But it was early and not too warm yet. Maybe she could convince Lizzie not to stay for the meal afterward. It would be blazing hot by then. And Lizzie and Rose needed to talk.

Rose's lie tore at her insides, but she wasn't ready to face Benjamin. She resumed the task at hand before Esther had called upstairs for her.

She continued to remove all the letters from her brothers and sisters from the keepsake box and put them in a pile on the bed, and she took out the broken angel necklace. She also salvaged two movie ticket stubs from when she and a friend had gone to see a movie during the early part of her running-around period. Luckily her father hadn't found out. They'd seen a romance movie, and although parts of it had embarrassed her, it was so tender and sweet that Rose wanted that for herself someday. Or she thought she did. But her only potential chance at happiness was ruined. Rose would have to forgive Lizzie. Her intentions had been good, just misdirected.

After she had all of the things she wanted to keep out of the box, she stuffed the letters from her mother inside. She closed the box and picked up the duct tape she'd found in the barn and began haphazardly wrapping it around the box until none of the brown showed at all. She slid it back under the bed, vowing to never read her mother's letters again.

She gathered up the letters from her brothers, sisters, and sisters-in-law, and eased them into the drawer of her nightstand so she could reread about their lives and continue corresponding with them. All her mother's letters had ever done was upset her, and since she didn't anticipate a response to the recent note she'd sent, she was committed to work on her own healing. Even if she had no idea how. But rereading her mother's insincere, often judgmental, and sometimes cruel letters would not help Rose to feel better about herself.

After retrieving a pair of tweezers from the bathroom, she got to work repairing the chain on the angel necklace. After it was whole again, she slipped it over her neck and tucked it beneath her nightgown. *Take that,* Daed. Hate was a strong word, and she wished she hadn't used it during her outburst with Esther and Lizzie. But to recover and let go of her past, she was going to have to find a way to rid herself of the extreme dislike she had for her father, and even her mother.

She lay back on the bed and closed her eyes. *Help me,* Gott, *to rid myself of such hateful thoughts about my own parents. Show me how to heal.*

She was drifting back to sleep when she heard a voice in her mind loud and clear.

Forgive them.

∞

Benjamin sat through worship service, but he didn't hear much of what was said. Rose had obviously chosen not to see him today, even though Esther said Rose was ill. Esther also said that Rose was very angry with Lizzie for telling him about her childhood. Benjamin could understand that, but he needed a chance to let her know that he'd fallen for her, and that her past didn't matter. But he was also wise enough to know that until Rose figured out a way to heal herself, she wasn't going to be back to the woman he'd grown to care so much about. Still, he wanted to help somehow.

"I'm in big trouble at home," Lizzie said as she sidled up to him following the service. "Rose isn't speaking to me because of all the things I told you."

Benjamin was appreciative of the information Lizzie had shared, but he would rather not have a conversation about it with Lizzie. Without Rose, he'd slipped back to a more emotionally isolated place. "I'm sure she will forgive you," he said to Lizzie.

"Are you going to talk to her?" Lizzie's pleading eyes longed for a yes.

"*Nee*, I-I don't think I should push her."

Her face clouded with uneasiness and regret, but her expression quickly shifted into a hostile glare. "You *have* to talk to her, to help her get through this. And I can't stand her being mad at me."

Benjamin hung his head and avoided her scorching stare. He just wanted to go home, away from this crowd and away from Lizzie.

She stomped a foot before she stormed off, and Benjamin breathed a sigh of relief. Until Esther met up with him.

"Lizzie and I aren't going to stay for the meal. We want to get home before it gets too hot." Esther handed him a glass of tea. "The men are getting seated, and the food is on the table. I just wanted to let you know that Rose will find her way. I know you must be disappointed that she chose not to be here today."

"Is she really sick?" A hard knot formed in the pit of his stomach.

"I doubt it," Esther said before she put a hand on Benjamin's arm. "Maybe just give her some time."

"*Ya*, okay."

His thoughts were scurrying all over the place. Lizzie rushing him to talk to Rose, and Esther saying he should give her some time.

Benjamin thanked Esther for her advice, then went to join the men for the meal. But his appetite wasn't what it usually was.

On the ride home, Esther began to doubt what she'd told Benjamin, about giving Rose time. Gus and Lizzie were both against that, and maybe they were right. Perhaps time was the enemy in this case. But all things happened on God's time frame, and Esther wasn't sure anyone should push Rose. It was all very confusing, but Lizzie was so quiet that Esther wanted to distract her sister from her worries.

"Rose said something interesting related to the mysterious flowers I received." Esther glanced at Lizzie, who perked up right away.

"Does she know who sent them?" Her face brightened, which was nice to see since Lizzie had held a pout throughout the worship service.

"*Nee*, but she said you would probably call our driver, Henry, suspect number three." Esther laughed. "It's not Henry, but I thought it was funny that she would mention him."

Lizzie held the reins in one hand as she rubbed her chin with the other and shifted her dentures around. "Why didn't I think of him?"

"Because he is younger than me, I don't know him well, and he wouldn't have sent me flowers. With everything going on, I haven't given much thought to that delivery."

Lizzie sighed. "I guess I need to beg for Rose's forgiveness. Again."

Esther had managed to distract her sister but not for long. "She'll come around."

When Lizzie turned into the driveway, Rose was standing on the front porch. Lizzie bolted from the buggy and ran across the yard without even tethering the horse. Esther scurried to secure the animal, then hobbled toward them.

"I'm sorry!" Lizzie flung her arms around Rose, who was

fully dressed now. "I'm sorry. Don't stay mad at me. I'll never meddle in your business again."

When Rose wrapped her arms around Lizzie, Esther's heart warmed. Every family had issues, and hers was no exception. But she was absolutely certain that Lizzie would meddle in Rose's business again.

There was still a hint of anger in Rose's expression when she eased out of the embrace. "I forgive you, Lizzie. But do you understand that you took away *mei* right to tell Benjamin about *mei* past in *mei* own way? I know your intentions were *gut*, and I know how you like to play matchmaker, but this was one time when you should not have interfered."

Lizzie hung her head. "I know."

After she saw that Rose and Lizzie were making amends, Esther turned back and went to the barn to check for messages. There weren't any.

By the time she returned from the barn, Lizzie and Rose had gone inside. Esther sat in one of the rocking chairs and gazed at the cottage. What would it be like without Gus's grumbling and stomping across the yard to complain about something? No sparring with Lizzie either. She closed her eyes. *Please* Gott, *heal Gus. I'm not ready for him to go.*

Chapter 22

Friday was Esther and Lizzie's day to go see Gus, and Esther used the ride to think back on the week. Lizzie was scheduled to give more blood today. Naomi and Amos had visited Gus on Monday and had even taken the babies. Rose and Evelyn had gone on Tuesday, and Jayce had been by Wednesday and Thursday. The schedule would vary from week to week, but everyone agreed that Gus shouldn't be alone and without visitors.

Rose hadn't heard from Benjamin, and she definitely wasn't herself, but at least she and Lizzie were getting along. Lizzie must have apologized a dozen more times.

Esther's sister eyed Henry from the back seat of the van almost the entire ride to the hospital. After they exited the vehicle and told Henry they'd only be staying long enough for Lizzie to give blood, Esther cut her eyes at Lizzie.

"Don't look at me like that." Lizzie held her chin high.

Esther fought to keep up with her and eventually tugged on

her apron from behind. "Slow down." When she did, Esther said, "It's not Henry. I saw you eyeballing him the entire ride. We're going to forget about this topic again. I shouldn't have brought it up."

"It was Henry." Lizzie's black purse swung at her side as she picked up the pace again.

By the time they caught the elevator and made it to Gus's room, Esther was winded and stopped in the hallway to catch her breath.

"I'm off to the lab. I'll meet you back here," Lizzie said as she took off to her right.

"Lizzie."

Her sister slowly turned around.

"You need to come say hello to Gus."

Lizzie groaned as she took heavy steps back to Esther. "Isn't giving the man my blood enough?"

"Just a brief hello would be fine, and you need to be nice." Esther warned her with her eyes before turning toward the room.

Esther knocked on the door and pushed it barely ajar. "Gus, it's Esther and Lizzie."

"Come in," he responded, not much more than a whisper.

Esther tried not to look surprised when she laid eyes on him. Someone should have warned her. She'd never seen so many tubes before, and there were several monitors beeping instead of just one. Gus looked like he had lost twenty pounds in a week, which didn't seem possible, and his face had a yellowish tint where it was visible. His beard was a matted mess.

"*Wie bischt*, Gus," Lizzie said, her eyes round with surprise.

She hadn't been in to see Gus, so she had nothing to compare this to, but she was clearly shaken. Lizzie didn't move from her spot. She only took one step inside the room.

Esther swallowed hard and walked to the bed. She laid a hand on his arm, studied him for a moment, then glanced around the room and smiled. "I see Naomi brought you a painting. And it's of your cottage." Esther brought her free hand to her chest. "Aw, that's you on the front porch holding Whiskers." She eyed the flowers she'd sent with Naomi and Amos. "It's much brighter and more colorful in here." It wasn't true, but she couldn't tell Gus that his appearance took away from the efforts to make the place more cheerful.

She startled when Gus jerked his arm away from her touch. He glared at Lizzie. "Can you get out of here so I can talk to Esther?"

"I see that *mei* blood hasn't made you any nicer. I'm off to go give more." She held her arms up for him to see. They were bright purple in several places. "I look like a druggie." Clearly, another English word Lizzie had picked up from one of her novels. She stomped out of the room.

"Esther, where have you been?" Gus's voice was hoarse and not nearly as loud as usual.

"I told you I wouldn't be here every day. And I heard you've had people visit daily, except for Sunday." She tried to touch his arm again, but he pulled away.

"I don't need you sending substitutes. If you can't come, then don't send anyone." He turned away from her. "Except Jayce. Those others are doing it because you asked them to."

"Gus, that's not true. Everyone wanted to see you, so we

thought it best to come up with a schedule so we didn't all show up on the same day. And didn't you enjoy seeing the twins? Regina and Eve always brighten *mei* days."

"They screamed the entire time." Gus slowly held up both his arms. "Can you blame them for being scared? Look at me. I'm hooked up to so many gadgets, I look like some sort of alien life form." His voice was hoarse and low, but his spirit was intact.

He attempted to roll onto his side, but moaned and gave up. "Open that drawer under the nightstand. There's a small black bag in there. I need that." He glanced at her when she didn't move. "Please. Can you *please* hand me that bag?"

She reached over, pulled the drawer open, and retrieved the bag. After she handed it to him, he attempted to pull back the zipper several times.

Esther finally eased it from his hands and unzipped the bag. "Here."

"Thank you."

She smiled. "You're welcome."

He reached inside, fumbled around, and took out a rolled-up wad of money and handed it to her. "This is to pay for your driver when you come see me."

Esther shook her head and didn't take it. "I don't need money, Gus. We're fine financially."

"I had Jayce sell my truck. I can't believe they gave him two grand for it." He pulled her hand to his and placed the money in her palm." Grinning, he said, "Now you gotta come see me."

Esther chuckled. "*Nee*, I don't. I come because I choose to, but I can't come every day, and I'm not taking this money."

He sighed. "I ain't got nothing else to do with it." He moaned again as he shifted his weight and tried to get his pillow behind his head.

Esther set the money on his chest, then leaned around him and cupped the back of his neck. "Lift up, I'll get your pillow right."

"Thank you."

"You're welcome." She gently patted his arm. "See how easy that is? Manners?"

Gus nodded at the money on his chest. "I don't think any of my other family—as you call them—need money." He offered it to her again. "Maybe put it in a trust or account for the screaming twins."

Esther picked up the roll of money. "I think that is a lovely idea." Before she arrived, she might have chosen not to accept the money on the twins' behalf. She would have held out for Gus to receive his miracle. But seeing him like this led her to believe a miracle wasn't in his future.

Lizzie burst in the door like a whirlwind tornado. Strands of gray hair had blown loose from beneath her prayer covering, and she curled her fists into balls at her side, her black purse swinging from her wrist. "We have a problem."

Esther grimaced as a sense of dread filled her. *What now?*

"Gus, can you order anything you want from room service?" Lizzie struggled to catch her breath.

"I ain't hungry." Gus scowled. "What's wrong with you anyway? You look like you've been in a cat fight."

"I ran all the way back here," Lizzie said, still breathless.

Gus rolled his eyes. "I bet that was a sight."

"Lizzie can you please tell us the problem?" Esther sat down in the chair by the bed.

"They won't let me give blood." She glanced at Esther. "I told you how easily I lose weight." She thrust her hands to her hips and flashed her pearly whites. "You need *mei* blood. Today. So you best call room service." She tapped her finger to her chin. "Do you have a menu?"

Gus stared at her for a long while. "First of all, they ain't got room service here. They bring you three meals a day, and not very good ones, I might add." He glared at Esther. "I'd be hard up for good food if I had an appetite. Apparently dying robs you of that too."

"How many pounds are you short?" Esther's head felt like it might explode. Her throbbing temples were probably visible.

"Just two." Lizzie shuffled her teeth. "There's a cafeteria downstairs, *ya*?"

"*Ya*, I saw the sign when we came in." Esther stood up. "Gus, I'm hungry so I'll go with Lizzie, then I'll come back after we load her up on food and I'll get a bite to eat too."

They were almost out the door when Gus said, "Lizzie?"

Esther flinched and waited for whatever insult Gus had in store for her sister.

But all he said was, "Thank you."

Lizzie stretched her arm as far as it would go and wagged a finger at him. "I knew it. *Mei* blood is working on you already! A few more rounds and you might even be a pleasant human being."

Gus actually grinned.

Esther walked back to Gus, leaned down, and kissed him on the forehead. His eyes watered. "One nice gesture deserves another. I'll see you soon."

Perhaps Gus was going to get his miracle, just not the way Esther had imagined it.

After they stuffed Lizzie with as much food as she could possibly eat, she headed to the lab. Esther said a quick prayer that she'd make the weight.

When she got to Gus's room, he was sleeping. She watched him for a while as she yawned, wishing she could lie down somewhere and take a nap. When she covered her mouth and coughed, he opened his eyes.

"Sorry, I had a tickle in *mei* throat."

They were both quiet for a few minutes.

"Esther, I've been thinking." He scratched his beard. "I was upset that you went so long without seeing me. But . . . I'm thinking it would be selfish of me to expect you to come here every day. It would wear you out."

She stared at him and smiled. The Holy Spirit was hard at work. "I'll come as often as I am able."

"Well, okay." He lowered his hand. "I'm thinking maybe I should speak to some of that clergy you mentioned. I mean, let's face it"—he frowned, his jowls looking lower since he'd lost so much weight in his face—"you ain't really qualified to teach me about God. And I don't mean that in a bad way. Like I said, you're the holiest person I know. But I don't think I better take any chances. You know what I mean? Those clergy people have training for this sort of thing. So, no offense or anything."

Esther bit her bottom lip and tried not to smile. "None taken. What religion do you prefer? Someone from the Baptist church? Methodist, Lutheran, Catholic... or another faith? I'm sure they have someone representing all of those."

He frowned. "Does it matter? Don't they all have the same boss?" He pointed upward.

"I suppose they do." She stood up. "I'll go find out who is available."

As she made her way to the nurses' station, her heart was lighter. Gus might pass on, but he'd go with love—and the Lord—in his heart. *Thank you*, Gott.

Rose stared at the box wrapped in duct tape. She didn't know where she'd dump it, but she didn't want it in her possession anymore. She didn't expect an apology from her mother. But that didn't mean Rose still couldn't forgive her—and her father—and rid herself of the bad feelings she'd clung to. Forgiving her parents was the only thing that would set her free.

She took her pen and paper from the nightstand drawer.

Dear *Mamm* (and *Daed*),
   I forgive you.

Lieb, Rose

As soon as she wrote the words, a burden began to lift as if the weight of her suffering was slowly shedding. Her pain wouldn't go away overnight, and it might be a slow process, but forgiveness was love. She addressed the envelope to her mother and put a stamp on it, with plans to drop it in the mailbox. She would count on God to guide her to a place where she could get rid of the memories, unwilling to keep them under her bed where she might be tempted to read through her mother's letters again.

Please, dear Lord, please guide me to the perfect place, somewhere I can find freedom. Please show me the way to happiness without the demons of hate and bad will in my heart. I know Your will is to be done, but please point me in the right direction, not only by symbolically ridding myself of this box but also by discovering the direction I need to go in my life. Amen.

She picked up the wooden box and the letter, raced down the stairs, then gasped.

"Benjamin." She froze. "What are you doing here?"

"I was heading home from work, and"—he rubbed his chin—"I asked *Gott* how to fill the void in *mei* heart. And before I knew it, I was headed to The Peony Inn."

Rose couldn't keep her eyes locked with his. She reminded herself that shame was the work of the devil, but she still felt draped in a black veil of indignity.

"Did I catch you heading out somewhere?" He glanced at the box she held to her chest, along with a white envelope.

"Uh . . . *ya*." Rose began to tremble when he edged closer to her.

"Is there anywhere I can take you? I'd like to talk to you." Benjamin's sober expression made Rose suspect he wanted to talk about the things Lizzie told him.

"Benjamin, I'm sorry for the way I have behaved. And I'm humiliated that Lizzie talked to you. I just can't face that conversation right now. I hope you understand." She eased the box away from her chest. "I need to get rid of this box, and all I can say is that it is a part of *mei* own attempt to rid myself of the things that are causing me heartache."

"My heartache stems from not seeing the beautiful, lively Rose who I've grown to care about very much. I'm not here to talk about anything Lizzie said. I don't care about anything that happened before we met, except that whatever it is, it's hurting you. In that regard, I want to help."

She glared at the box. "I wish I could send this box to the bottom of the river."

Benjamin smiled. "I might be able to help you with that."

Rose tipped her head to one side. "What?"

"If you'll trust me and wait here, I need to make a phone call. This is one way I can help you, and we don't have to talk about anything if you don't want to."

The black veil was slipping off, and the peacefulness she felt in Benjamin's presence was returning.

After she nodded, Benjamin went outside and kept going until he was far enough away that Rose couldn't hear.

"Captain Hanners, I know this is short notice, but I need a favor." He explained about Rose and the box.

"I'm an old man with nothing on my agenda. I'll meet you

down by the boat dock—the private one by my cabin." He gave Benjamin directions to his place in Shoals, and after Benjamin thanked the man, he went back inside.

Rose stood in the middle of the living room, her lips slightly parted, looking wary. "Where are we going?"

"To dump that box in the deepest part of the river."

Her expression didn't change. "I can't just toss it from the bank. It will eventually float ashore."

"Not where we're going." He held out his hand to her. "Trust me."

Hesitantly, she took hold of his hand, the box back against her chest, along with the white envelope.

"We can't get there by buggy. We need a driver."

"Henry is usually available. We can check with him." Her hand tightened around his. "Are you sure about this? Do you have time?"

"I have all the time in the world. The question is"—he nodded to the taped-up container pressed against her chest—"are *you* sure about this?"

"Very," she said as she squeezed his hand.

Henry arrived a few minutes later.

They'd barely gotten into the van when Benjamin put an arm around her. She tensed at first, but relaxed into the nook of his shoulder and rested her head there. He kissed her on the forehead, and she snuggled closer to him, trembling. "Everything will be okay," he whispered.

After they turned down a steep road and passed a small cabin on the left, another road twisted downward toward the boat ramp.

Captain Hanners was there in a long, narrow boat. It was red and white and had *Sharon* printed in big letters across the side.

"You ready?" Benjamin winked at her.

For the first time since he'd arrived at her house, her face came alive.

The van door slid open. Benjamin stepped out first, then offered her his hand.

Her eyebrows shot up in surprise as she put her fingers to her lips and stared at the boat. "We're going out on that?"

"*Ya*, we are. To the deepest part of the river, as fast as you want to go." A warm glow flowed through Benjamin when she bounced up on her toes. She tossed the letter onto the back seat of the van but still clung to the box. Her eyes slowly took on the twinkle he remembered. They would be combining the good with the bad today, but hopefully it would create balance for a new beginning.

He struggled to keep up with her as they moved toward the boat ramp.

"That's a big boat. Does it go fast? I bet it does. It's so long and narrow. That man is waving." Rose waved back, as did Benjamin. "Is that the owner?" She glanced at Benjamin, smiling. "It *does* go fast, doesn't it?"

He grinned as he raised an eyebrow. "That's what I've been told."

She gazed into his eyes as they neared the boat, which was edging up to the bank. "*Danki* for this, for taking what could have been a very bad day for me and turning it into something special."

Benjamin wasn't sure what was in the box, but if getting rid of it gave Rose a new lease on life, he was all for sinking it to the bottom of the river.

"Hello, hello!" Captain Hanners threw Benjamin a line, and he gently pulled the boat close enough for them to get in. "Climb aboard."

Benjamin had only met the man once at a fishing tournament. Benjamin's people didn't believe in competition, so he hadn't entered. But he'd watched the men pulling fish up to fifty pounds out of their boats. Captain Hanners had come in second place with a forty-seven-pound channel catfish. But it was the man's exuberance and friendly smile that made him perfect for this outing.

"I can't believe you did this," Rose said as Benjamin helped her into the boat. She gasped. "What's down there?" She pointed to a small door in the middle of the boat.

"That's where I sleep when I stay overnight." Captain Hanners was probably in his sixties. He was a small man with a large personality, and he sported a baseball cap atop his salt-and-pepper hair that had *Good Things Come to Those Who Bait* etched across it. "Pretty lady, I'm told you want to take a fast ride."

Rose's face lit up. "*Ya, ya*, I do."

"I can take this baby from zero to sixty in about fifteen seconds and hit eighty miles per hour on a day without much wind." The captain lifted up one of the long seats that faced forward. "First things first." He handed each of them a life vest to slip on, and he buckled himself into one also. "So, how fast do you want to go?"

"As fast as you can!" Rose had never looked more beautiful in her bright-red life vest, dark-green dress, and brown eyes twinkling with specks of gold every time a sunray caught her face just right.

Captain Hanners nodded to the box Rose still had clung to her chest. "I'm told you have some other business to tend to. Would you like to do that first?"

Rose's expression fell as she sighed. "*Ya*, I think I would, if you don't mind."

"All righty. We'll take her at a nice steady pace to a spot plenty deep." He took off his cap and scratched his head. "It's so deep that even I don't know how deep it is." His shoulders went up and down as he laughed. Benjamin thought again how Captain Hanners was the perfect choice for this excursion.

"Sit anywhere you please." He waved an arm around. There was a long seat in the back, two others on either side of the narrow boat, and a passenger seat next to where the captain would sit. "But I can tell you, the best ride is up here next to me, if you ain't afraid of the wind in your face."

Benjamin smiled. "Well?"

She set the box on the floor near one of the side seats, so Benjamin followed her. Rose put a hand on his chest. "Are you kidding? We're not sitting back here." She tied the strings of her prayer covering under her chin. Benjamin had always wondered about the purpose of the strings since none of the women ever tied them.

"Now I know what those strings are for." Benjamin chuckled. "Fast boat rides."

Rose laughed as she made her way to the passenger seat.

"Best place for you is right behind her." Captain Hanners patted the dash. "And both of you hold on right here."

Benjamin aligned himself like Captain Hanners instructed, and the feel of Rose's back against his chest, along with the smell of her lavender shampoo, was intoxicating. After they took care of this important task, he hoped they would find their way back to each other.

Rose breathed in the musty smell of the river on a hot day as a few beads of sweat trailed down her face. But when the boat picked up speed, the wind became a fan, cooling her off as they set out across the large body of water. She could feel Benjamin's breath against her neck as he pressed up against her, his muscular arms enclosing her in a safe haven in front of the passenger seat. It touched her, more than she knew how to say, that he had arranged this.

When the boat began to slow down, Captain Hanners cut the engine and tossed an anchor over the side. Then there was a hum that sounded like a generator coming from below.

"I'll be down in my cubbyhole enjoying a little AC while you two take care of business. The Lord's blessings be with you."

After the small door had closed behind Captain Hanners, Rose stared at the box on the floor. "He probably thinks I'm out here scattering the ashes of someone deceased." She lifted the box to her chest. "Maybe in some ways I am." She paused, glancing at Benjamin. "They are letters from *mei mudder*." Maybe she would explain later, but for now, that felt like enough. Benjamin just nodded.

Rose carried her box of memories, the reminders her mother had drummed into her head about never finding a husband, talking too much, being a bad girl when she was a child, and so much more. As she held the box over the side of the boat, she prayed silently.

Dear God, with this symbolic act, I pray that these memories will not prevent me from having a good life that You will choose for me. I pray that the bad thoughts and pain in my heart will be forever gone, replaced with love and forgiveness. In Your name, Jesus, I pray.

She let go of the box and watched the river take it away, then slowly, water found its way around the duct tape and seeped in beneath the loosely fitting lid as her memories began to sink. Then they were gone.

She locked eyes with Benjamin. "I owe you so many explanations—about everything. About *mei* past, *mei* fears, the way I treated you . . ."

He tenderly put a finger to her lips. "*Nee*, you don't owe me explanations about any of that. You can tell me at some point—or not. It's up to you. But you *do* owe me something else."

She couldn't read his expression as her heart pounded against her chest. "What?" she said in a whisper.

"You owe me an opportunity to love you." He cupped her face as he pulled her close to him. She quivered at the sweet tenderness of his kiss, but all the passion of their earliest kisses was there, even more so. "Can you give me that?" he asked in a whisper, his breath warm against her neck as he kissed her there.

"*Ya*, but"—she felt him stiffen—"only if I'm given the opportunity to love you back."

Smiling, he said, "I think I can agree to that."

After they made up for lost time, he asked, "Are you ready to go from zero to sixty in fifteen seconds?"

She laughed. "I'm ready."

They summoned their captain, and he started the boat and told them to hold on tight.

"You ready?" Benjamin asked again as he stepped behind her and enclosed her within his arms.

She pressed her cheek to his as adrenaline and joy met up to form an emotion she hadn't experienced in a long time. *Peace.* "I'm ready."

Chapter 23

Esther pressed a cold rag to Gus's forehead. Over the past two weeks, he had been running a low intermittent fever, and twice Esther thought he was leaving this world. But Gus always came back, fighting to stay alive, and sometimes he was in tremendous pain.

"He doesn't even look like himself," Lizzie said in a whisper from where she stood on one side of the bed. "He's lost so much weight, and he's all yellowy looking."

Esther sat down in the chair she'd been camped out in for the past ten days. The others came and went, but Esther and Lizzie had sought the bishop's approval to stay in a hotel within walking distance of the hospital. Lizzie gave blood for the last time a few days ago, but she'd chosen to stay on for the duration. The doctors said all they could do was to keep Gus comfortable. A member of clergy from a nondenominational church came to see him daily. Esther always left when he arrived, but she often heard the pastor and Gus praying together on her way in or out of the room.

Lizzie came to the room for a short while each day, but Esther sat with Gus for hours. When the time came, she didn't want him to be alone. It was quite possible he would pass away in the middle of the night, but she wanted to give him as much of her time as she could. Most days, he was coherent, but he slept a lot. Each day, when the doctor made his rounds, he seemed surprised that Gus was still with them. "He's a fighter," Dr. Gilmore would say. Esther worried that Gus was fighting because he was afraid. She wondered if she would be scared when her time came. Would a strong faith be enough to avoid fear? She didn't want the voice of God blocked due to that unwanted emotion.

"I have got to take a break." Esther lifted herself from the small chair and stretched her arms.

"We can go to the cafeteria," Lizzie said as she shuffled toward the door.

"*Nee.* You stay here with Gus." Esther's sister never stayed in the room alone.

Lizzie's jaw dropped. "What if he croaks while you're gone? Or what if he wakes up and finds just me here?" She pointed to the machines next to Gus's bed. "All those machines are sure to start beeping like crazy if he sees only me in here."

"Boo!"

Lizzie practically jumped into Esther's arms, and even Esther had a blast of adrenaline shoot through her veins.

"Gus, don't do that." Esther scowled at him. "We about jumped out of our skins."

He took in a long, deep breath. "I didn't mean to scare you. Just her." He nodded at Lizzie. His words were soft and so different from the bellowing voice they were used to. But he grinned at Lizzie.

"I need to stretch *mei* legs. Lizzie is going to stay here with you. Try to be civil to each other. I won't be gone long." Esther trudged out the door. Every step felt heavier than the last. As she got on the elevator to go down to the cafeteria, she recalled when Joe was sick, not long before he died. Gus was getting close, but she didn't think he was quite there yet. Esther figured they had days, not weeks. She thought again about Gus dying alone, but Esther couldn't sleep in his room. Even if they brought in a cot, her back couldn't take that. She was having enough trouble staying strong enough to sit with him for hours every day. But the timing was in God's hands. Esther had repeatedly asked Gus if she could inform his daughter about his condition. His answer was an adamant no each time. Finally, he admitted to Esther that he went to visit his daughter not long after he'd given her the money from his small part in the movie. "She didn't want anything to do with me," he told her. When Esther had argued that his daughter—Heather—should at least be notified of his condition, Gus made her promise not to contact her. Esther was glad Gus had made an attempt to see Heather, but sad that Heather hadn't given him an opportunity to be in her life.

After she had coffee and a cinnamon roll, she shuffled across the cafeteria, but paused in front of the display of pies. A few weeks ago, she would have bought a piece of chocolate pie for Gus. He wasn't eating much at all now, another sign that it wouldn't be long.

When she got back to Gus's room, she lingered outside the door when she heard Gus thanking Lizzie for something.

"How did you know I sent those loaves of bread to your cottage that day?" Lizzie's voice was calm, but inquiring.

"If you ever tell Esther this, I'll come back to haunt you." Gus sounded stronger. But that had become the pattern. Stronger one moment, weaker the next.

Esther kept her ear peeled from outside the room.

"You've always made better bread than her. In every other way imaginable, Esther does everything better than you. But your bread is the best I've ever had." He paused and there was a light chuckle. "There. I threw you a bone from my deathbed."

Esther put a hand over her mouth to keep from laughing, then she composed herself and eased the door open.

"Are you two behaving yourselves?" Esther was surprised to see Lizzie sitting in the chair next to the bed. Her sister usually kept her distance. She wondered what they had talked about prior to the bread conversation. Lizzie had always baked better bread than Esther, so there was no surprise there.

Lizzie stood up and took a few steps away, making room for Esther to reclaim her spot, which she did. Her knees screamed for the chair.

"*Ya.*" Lizzie flashed her dentures. "Gus was just telling me how much better *mei* bread is than yours."

Esther pressed her lips together to keep from smiling. She glanced at Gus, who rolled his tired eyes.

"You're a wicked woman," he said, starting to sound breathless. "I'll haunt you every chance I get."

"Nah." Lizzie waved him off. "I look forward to seeing you in the next life. I figure we'll keep on sparring, just like we always have." She turned to Esther. "I'm going back to the hotel to enjoy the AC and television. Did you know there is a Hallmark Channel dedicated to nothing but sweet love stories?"

"I knew you were watching TV when I'm not there." Esther shook her head. "Shame on you."

Lizzie raised her chin. "I only watch good clean shows."

The door swung open, almost knocking into Lizzie. Amos and Naomi rushed into the room, closing the door securely behind them. Amos stood against it as if they were being chased.

"What is wrong with you two?" Esther put a hand on her heart, hoping to calm the sudden palpitations. Naomi was carrying a small piece of black luggage, like a carpet bag with holes in it.

"What's that noise?" Lizzie asked suspiciously as her eyes widened.

"We called the hospital to see if Gus could come outside in a wheelchair, but they said he wasn't strong enough for that, so . . ." She reached into the bag and pulled out one of Gus's black cats. Lizzie backed up until she slammed into the wall. "I couldn't find Midnight," Naomi said to Gus. "You know how she roams. But I know how attached you are to Whiskers." She carefully placed the cat on the bed with Gus. Amos held his position by the door. Lizzie covered her eyes and moaned.

Gus's breathing was more labored, but his expression was the brightest Esther had seen in a while. They might all get thrown out of the hospital if they were caught, but it was worth it for Gus to be able to say goodbye to his beloved cat.

"She don't like that dry food you leave out sometimes." Gus scratched behind the cat's ears. "She only eats it because she's hungry. She likes the canned kind, the small cans with the cat's picture on it."

"*Ya*, and I've been feeding her and Midnight that kind since you told me before." Naomi put a hand on the cat when it glanced around the room like it might be getting ready to sprint from the bed. The cat slept with Gus when he'd been at home, but this was unfamiliar territory.

"I have a mind to scream for help"—Lizzie still had her hands over her eyes—"before that varmint sprints over here and claws *mei* eyes out."

"Don't you dare," Naomi said in a firm voice as she cut her eyes at Lizzie, who didn't see the fierce look. "You have no idea how hard it was to get Whiskers in here without getting caught. One lady in the elevator looked alarmed when Whiskers meowed, but luckily she got off on another floor. Amos and I talked loudly all the way down the corridor in case Whiskers meowed, hoping no one would hear her."

Gus started coughing a lot.

"His blood pressure is going up. That's going to send a nurse in here soon." Esther eyed the door, then looked back at Naomi, who nodded.

She eased the cat back into the bag, then she leaned over and kissed Gus on the cheek, pushing back strands of sweaty gray hair. Gus went from cold to hot, on and off, when his fever spiked, then broke.

Naomi was about to walk off when Gus touched her arm. "Thank you, Naomi."

She smiled. "You are very welcome."

Amos waved from the door. "Take care, Gus."

No one said a word. Not even the cat made any noise. Gus's eyes were moist, as were Naomi's. It was goodbye for them, and they both knew it.

After they rushed out of the room, Lizzie uncovered her eyes, spat her teeth in her hand, and said, "I'm leaving. This place isn't safe. If you need me, Esther, I'll be back in the hotel room."

"Rule breaker." Gus coughed but grinned.

Lizzie stared at Gus for a long while until her eyes began to water. "Bye."

Then she bolted out the door.

"What was that about?" Gus grimaced as he shifted his weight.

"Lizzie doesn't like people to see her cry."

"Cry? Why would she be crying?" He moaned as he finally seemed to find a comfortable position, or as comfortable as he could get.

Esther touched Gus's arm. "Because, believe it or not, Lizzie will miss you." She held up a finger. "Think before you speak because I know you will miss her too."

He blinked his eyes a few times. "Yeah . . . I will."

By the time Esther got back to the hotel room, which was a two-block trek, she longed for a hot bath and a bed. But she skipped the bath for now and lowered herself onto one of the queen beds in the room. Lizzie was on the other bed with several pillows propped up behind her. Her eyes were fixed on the television.

"Hello? I'm back." Esther yawned.

"Watch. That man is about to tell her how much he loves her." Lizzie didn't take her eyes from the scene unfolding.

Esther sighed. "Have you talked to Rose today?"

Lizzie grumbled and pushed a knob on the remote control. She'd obviously learned to pause a show.

"*Ya*, still no reservations for the rest of this month, but three ladies from Oklahoma booked rooms for four nights in September." Esther wondered if she and Lizzie would be home by then. These things had a timeline of their own—God's timeline.

She pushed a button and the show resumed.

"Lizzie, I hope you're praying each night and asking forgiveness for giving in to worldly sins." Esther sat up. She needed to go take a bath before she fell asleep in her clothes.

"I've led a *gut* life. I think *Gott* will overlook this indulgence." She paused the show again, glowered at Esther, then ran her hand in a circle above her head. "Should we talk about this air-conditioning that we're enjoying? How do you put one worldly sin over the other one?"

Esther yawned as she stood up. "Point taken. I will miss sleeping in a cool room when we get home."

As she began to fill the tub with water, she let the water run while she cried so Lizzie wouldn't hear. She wasn't sure how much of it was pure exhaustion or the thought of losing Gus. Both, she decided.

∞

Esther was later than usual getting to the hospital. Lizzie had chosen to give blood that morning. Even though Gus didn't require it anymore, she planned to continue giving for as long as she could to help others with her and Gus's rare blood type.

Evelyn and Jayce were in Gus's room when Esther entered. She leaned down and hugged Evelyn, who was sitting next to Gus, then she moved across the room to Jayce. "Aw, hon," she said, wrapping her arms around the boy as he sniffled.

When he eased out of the hug, he wiped his eyes. "*Wie bischt*, Esther." The poor lad's voice cracked. "We've been here a while, so I guess we'll go."

Evelyn stood up and put a hand on Gus's arm. Out of their little family, Evelyn probably knew Gus least of all. "Blessings to you."

Jayce hugged the man, and Gus lifted one arm and patted him on the back. They hadn't been to see Gus in a week, and he had certainly declined a lot in those seven days. Esther was sure it was a shock for Evelyn, and especially Jayce, to see him this morning.

They were almost out the door, but Jayce turned around, tears streaming down his face. "I love you, Gus."

A knot rose up in Esther's throat, and it only worsened when Gus's lips trembled. "I love you too, son."

Jayce rushed back to Gus for a final hug, then hurried out the door with Evelyn.

Esther sat in her chair and reached for a tissue on Gus's bedside table.

"Don't you go getting all emotional on me too." Gus frowned. "Guess Rose Petal and her new beau will come say bye too." He sighed. "I dislike all of this, Esther."

She smiled as she thought about Rose and Benjamin. They spent most evenings together, and Rose had never seemed happier when she called at night.

"I'll bet you didn't know how many people cared about you, did you?"

He coughed, then there was the hint of a grin. "What can I say? I'm a likable guy."

"You're also a sweaty mess." Esther stood, wet a rag, and gently wiped his face. "This seems to happen when your fever breaks."

He didn't try to object. The cold water had to feel good.

After she sat back down, Gus coughed again, a raspy sound that sounded like it came from deep within his lungs. "I need to ask you something," he said.

Before he could get his question out, sure enough, Rose and Benjamin walked in. Esther didn't think she'd ever seen a prettier couple. They glowed with the newness of true love, and it warmed her heart to see the couple so happy.

After a quick hug from each of them, Esther excused herself. Visitors were an opportunity to stretch her legs, and Gus had been correct. Everyone was coming to say their goodbyes. Esther didn't think she could take another one without breaking down.

She went and sat in the hospital courtyard, then returned

about fifteen minutes later. Sure enough, Rose was holding Gus's hand and crying. Benjamin was by her side with his arm around her.

"I said I wouldn't cry, Gus. I'm sorry. I've been praying for healing for you. And don't worry about Whiskers and Midnight. I'll help Naomi take care of your kitties. I've cleaned your cottage." She put a hand to her forehead. "I don't know why I said that. But you have Naomi's painting in here. That was so nice of her to bring it to the hospital. I wish you all of *Gott*'s blessings, and—"

"Got it," Gus said as he held up a hand. He glanced at Esther and sighed before he turned back to Rose. "Thank you for coming. Have a good life."

It shouldn't have been funny, but Esther held a hand over her grin. That was their Gus, blunt and to the point.

After they'd said goodbye, Rose whispered to Esther and asked her to follow them out of the room.

"I'll be right back, Gus."

After they left and were a few steps down the corridor, Rose said, "When I was cleaning Gus's cottage, I found something I think you should see. I've been wanting to tell you, but I wasn't sure when it was the right time. You've been so tired, and I didn't want you to fret over anything else." Rose shrugged. "But I think you should see this and decide how you want to handle it, or if you want to say anything." She slipped a piece of folded paper into Esther's hand. "I think it's self-explanatory."

Rose and Benjamin left. Esther stood in the corridor staring at the note. Her first instinct was to tell Lizzie, but then she thought better of it. She needed time for the realization to soak in before she decided how to handle this new information.

She went back to Gus's room. He'd dozed off so she sat down and watched him sleeping. His breaths were long, and with each one it seemed more of an effort. When he began to sweat again, she rewet a cold rag and blotted his forehead, which woke him up.

"Before Rose and Benjamin left, you said you wanted to ask me something." Esther wondered if it had anything to do with the note Rose had given her, which was now in her pocket.

He took a few long breaths. "Can you shave my beard? The nurse offered to do it since I'm sweating so much. I don't need strangers touching me any more than they already do." He closed his eyes, his breathing growing heavy again. The cancer had taken over all of his organs, the doctor said.

"*Ya*, I will shave your beard if you'd like. I'm sure you'd be more comfortable. But . . . you do know, our men don't shave their beards, so I have never done it before."

"You women shave your legs, don't you? How different can it be?"

Esther wasn't about to tell Gus that she couldn't remember the last time she'd shaved her legs. "I'll go to the gift shop downstairs. I've wandered in there before, and they have various toiletries."

She left, and when she returned, Gus was asleep, so she took the piece of paper from her pocket and stared at it. As Rose had said, it was self-explanatory, and Esther needed to acknowledge it.

"You get the stuff?" Gus asked in a whisper.

Esther quickly stuffed the paper back in her pocket, then lifted the small bag she'd set on the bedside table. "*Ya*, I did. I'm assuming shaving cream and a razor should do it." She turned the can of cream over until she found the instructions.

"Esther." Gus spoke softly, but it didn't stop him from rolling his eyes. "Are you really reading the directions? I'm on borrowed time. Just lather up my beard and get this thing off of me."

She took a deep breath and got to work as best she could.

"Try not to cut me. I'll bleed out for sure," he said in a low voice.

"Be still and don't talk." She carefully ran the razor the length of his face, each swipe revealing more of the man she'd never seen without a beard. When she was done, she smiled. "There you are. A handsome man who has been hidden behind that beard all this time."

His pale face actually took on a pink tint. "Whatever." Then he stared into her eyes. "Thank you."

"You're welcome."

There was something else on his mind. She wondered if it was the same thing on her mind as she fumbled with the note in her pocket.

"I feel different, Esther. Pastor Paul seems to think I'm going to make my way to heaven. I've been talking to God through His Son, and I've never felt that kind of peace. What do you think?"

It wasn't the conversation she thought they were going to have, but this topic was certainly important. "Save me a seat," she said softly as tears built in the corners of her eyes. "This makes me very happy."

"I'm thinking I might not be on the front row, but . . . I think I'm ready when the time comes."

Esther smiled, although she still felt Gus had a little more time. But in case he didn't, she pulled the paper from her pocket and handed it to him. "Rose found this when she was cleaning your cottage." She blinked her eyes. "Why didn't you tell me? For goodness' sake, you made me think I had a stalker."

Gus stared at the paper. In his handwriting, he'd written dozens of different variations, changed the wording up, but he had apparently landed on what relayed his feelings the best.

> My Dearest Esther, these flowers can't compare to your beauty, but they are an offering of my love.

At first, he wouldn't look at her, he just tucked his chin. Without his beard, she could see his lips trembling. "I should have signed the card, and I should have told you I sent the flowers when you asked. I chickened out both times." He finally lifted his eyes to hers. "I already knew I was sick, and I wanted you to know how I feel, but I just—" He paused, barely shrugging. "And the reason I was on your porch is because I couldn't find Whiskers so I'd gone for a walk. I got winded and needed to sit for a while. I wasn't ready for you to know I was sick, and I panicked when you and Lizzie came out on the porch. So I went with Lizzie's stalker idea, which I shouldn't have done because I never meant to scare you." His watery eyes lifted to hers. "I've always loved you, Esther. I just didn't know how to tell you. I knew you couldn't love a man like me." He lowered his chin again, his lips still trembling.

Esther found his hand and squeezed. There were many

different kinds of love. And while Esther's love for Gus wasn't romantic love, she didn't feel that needed to be mentioned. "I do love you, Gus." Then she wept openly as she kept his hand in hers and laid her head on the edge of his bed.

"There, there," he said, in not much more than a whisper and in perhaps the kindest voice she'd ever heard him use. "Love knows no limit to its endurance, no end to its trust, no fading of its hope . . ." His endurance was slipping away as he spoke the words slowly. "It can outlast anything. It is, in fact, the one thing that still stands when all else has fallen."

"Corinthians," she whispered as she clung to his hand and cried.

"Don't be sad, Esther," he said in a shaky voice. "I saw Momma and Dad in a dream. I'm going to be okay."

She lifted her eyes to his as tears trailed down her cheeks. "I'm not sad, Gus. I will miss you." With quivering lips, she said, "But now I know that I will see you again. And that makes me happy."

"Do I get a dying wish?" He winked at her.

"That depends," she said as she swiped at her eyes with a tissue. "What is it?"

He gazed into her eyes. "Will you kiss me? And I don't mean on the cheek or forehead."

Esther's pulse picked up. How do you deny a man his dying wish? She could feel her face flushing.

"It's okay . . . I shouldn't have asked, and—"

Esther cupped his clean-shaven cheeks in her hands, and she kissed him on the mouth, lingering long enough that Gus would know she truly did love him.

"Wow." He raised an eyebrow before he smiled and drifted off to sleep again.

Esther reached for his hand and held it in hers, then she laid her head back on the bed. His breathing was becoming more labored. She thought of Joe's last breaths.

It wouldn't be long now.

Rest in peace, Gus.

Epilogue

They buried Gus next to his parents in the Amish cemetery after seeking the bishop's approval. Lizzie cried for two solid days, and the void in their lives was enormous.

It had only been a week, and in Esther's mind, she knew how grief worked. Time healed. But it was midmorning when she looked out the window and saw Evelyn and Jayce pulling up to Gus's cottage in their buggy. Gus never locked the door, so the couple walked in. Esther was torn about whether to give them time alone in the cottage or to join them. She finally decided to go see them.

She was about halfway between the inn and the cottage when she heard the screen door close behind her. Lizzie and Rose were heading down the steps. Shortly thereafter, Amos and Naomi emerged from their house.

Silently, they all made their way up the porch steps, then into the house.

Gus's family stood in the middle of what had been his home going on fifteen years. No one said anything at first. Then Jayce wiped at his eyes and chuckled.

"Remember the first time I met Gus? I thought we were going to get in a fistfight?"

Esther's mind traveled back in time. "*Ya*, I remember. We were in the dining room. Gus was mad about the noise the motor homes' generators were making."

"The first time I spent any real time with Gus was when the kittens were born," Rose said. "Prior to that, the man scared me. But he was so kind and protective of those kittens and constantly worrying they weren't getting enough to eat. I knew right then that anyone who cared for animals that much wasn't a bad person, no matter how much they tried to hide their goodness." She smiled. "And I liked the way he called me Rose Petal."

Naomi laughed. "I'll miss Lizzie threatening Gus with her baseball bat."

They spent the next couple of hours sharing stories about the complicated man they'd all known, but who had touched each of them in some way.

Lizzie cried softly almost the entire time, which seemed to shock everyone but Esther. They all took turns hugging her.

"Gus would have loved this, us gathering at his place to reflect on his life," Esther said as she glanced around at their family.

"He would have rolled his eyes and made a sarcastic comment," Jayce said. "But he would have loved it."

Esther thought about all the trips she'd made to the cottage over the years. How many times had she taken Gus leftovers?

How many times had she brought him slices of pie? The times she'd instructed him about his manners were endless.

She reached up, touched her lips, and recalled kissing him at the hospital. Her heart fluttered. Maybe there was a smidgeon of romantic love after all.

Acknowledgments

Like Esther and Lizzie, my sister and I are opposites in many ways, but the love we share for each other is real and treasured. Laurie, it is an honor to dedicate this book to you, and I'm blessed to have you as my sister. We always rock on through the good times and the bad! I know you have my back, and I always have yours.

To my agent, Natasha Kern, this past year has presented so many challenges for everyone. But seeing you with those little twin grandbabies was surely a highlight. The role fits you perfectly. So happy to have you on my team personally and professionally. Such a blessing. ☺

Janet Murphy, as of this writing, we have worked together for eleven years. Can you believe it? I'm not sure where the time has gone, but I know we have lots of memories to make ahead of us. I love and appreciate you!

ACKNOWLEDGMENTS

To the entire team at HarperCollins, my sincerest thanks for allowing me to continue to write stories that I hope entertain and glorify God. Special thanks to my editor, Kimberly Carlton, who is patient and kind with her editorial advice, which is almost always spot-on. I love working with you, Kim.

I'm blessed to have a fabulous street team in my corner—my beloved Wiseman's Warriors. Thank you SO much for all you do to promote my books. I hope we are all on this amazing ride for a long time to come.

To my husband, Patrick, and to my family and friends—another HUGE thank you for supporting me in my dreams to write.

God, I know You aren't done with me. There are too many stories floating around in my mind. I pray that I will continue to do good work for You. I love You.

Discussion Questions

1. When Rose and Benjamin go on their first date, Rose forces herself to be quiet in an effort for Benjamin to like her. After this backfires Rose shows her true personality in the upstairs bathroom when she doesn't know Benjamin is standing in the hallway. What do you think would have happened if Benjamin hadn't overheard Rose and gotten a glimpse of her true self?
2. Throughout the story, Esther—along with Lizzie and Rose—wonders who delivered the flowers to Esther. Who did you think sent the flowers? Did you ever suspect the bouquet was delivered by a stalker, or did you think Gus sent the flowers all along?
3. Lizzie and Gus have sparred for as long as they can remember. However, there are several instances when

DICUSSION QUESTIONS

we see that Lizzie and Gus care for each other more than either of them will let on. Can you name some of these instances?

4. Rose's childhood catches up with her when she starts to care for Benjamin. She begins to think that she won't be a good mother based on her upbringing. What are some of Rose's other fears that bubble to the surface when she and Benjamin grow close? Why do you think Rose feels she must confront these memories before she can heal and move forward?

5. Gus is unpleasant most of the time, but it's obvious that he loves his cats. What do you think it says about a person who can't necessarily relate to people in a positive way, but who showers an abundance of love toward animals?

6. It's clear that Esther and Jayce care a great deal for Gus, but so do the other characters in the story, despite Gus's obnoxious behavior at times. Aside from Esther and Jayce, who do you think cared the most for Gus and why?

7. Esther and Lizzie are as opposite as can be, but they love each other very much, and we see that play out repeatedly. Name some of the scenes when we see just how much the sisters care for each other.

8. How did you feel at the end of the story when Gus died? Had you grown to care for him? Did you root for him along the way? Have you ever known anyone like Gus?

9. At the end of the book, Rose gets rid of her trinket box filled with letters from her mother. Even though it

was a symbolic gesture, it is also Rose's way of ridding herself of the painful childhood memories she's carried into adulthood. Did you agree with Rose's decision to forgive her parents? Is there truly freedom and peace in the ability to forgive? Were you disappointed that Rose's mother never wrote her back? Did you think her mother would ask for forgiveness?

10. There are several tender moments in the story—between Rose and Benjamin, Lizzie and Esther, Gus and Jayce, and Gus and Esther. If you could be in a room witnessing one of those touching moments, which scene would you choose and why? Would you alter the outcome or sit quietly and watch?
11. The book also includes several humorous scenes. What did you think was the funniest interaction between characters and/or their reaction to certain situation?
12. When did you begin to suspect that Gus would not get his miracle? Or did he, just not the way we might have thought?
13. If there was anything in the story that you could change, what would it be and why?

About the Author

BESTSELLING AND AWARD-WINNING AUTHOR BETH WISEMAN has sold over two million books. She is the recipient of the coveted Holt Medallion, is a two-time Carol Award winner, and has won the Inspirational Reader's Choice Award three times. Her books have been on various bestseller lists, including CBD, CBA, ECPA, and *Publishers Weekly*. Beth and her husband are empty nesters enjoying country life in south-central Texas.

Visit her online at BethWiseman.com
Facebook: @AuthorBethWiseman
Twitter: @BethWiseman
Instagram: @bethwisemanauthor